Rachel Gibson's first two romance novels – *Simply Irresistible* and *Truly Madly Yours* – were named among the Top Ten Favourite Books of the Year by the membership of the Romance Writers of America. She is married and lives with her husband and children in Boise, Idaho.

Daisy's Back in Town

Rachel Gibson

little
black
dress

First published in the USA in 2004
by AVON BOOKS
An imprint of HARPERCOLLINS PUBLISHERS

This edition published in Great Britain in paperback in 2006
by LITTLE BLACK DRESS
an imprint of HEADLINE BOOK PUBLISHING

A LITTLE BLACK DRESS paperback

7

978 0 7553 3403 2 (ISBN-13)

Typeset in Transit511BT by Avon DataSet Ltd,
Bidford-on-Avon, Warwickshire

Printed and bound in Great Britain by Clays Ltd, St Ives plc

Headline's policy is to use papers that are natural, renewable and
recyclable products and made from wood grown in sustainable
forests. The logging and manufacturing processes are expected to
conform to the environmental regulations of the country of origin.

HEADLINE BOOK PUBLISHING
A division of Hodder Headline
338 Euston Road
London NW1 3BH

www.reviewbooks.co.uk
www.hodderheadline.com

This book is dedicated to the original tyrannosaurus Tex, Mary Reed, who is my inspiration for all things Texas

Acknowledgements

I would like to express my appreciation and gratitude to those who helped in the writing of this book. Craig Clark of C. C. Photography and Graphic Design, for sharing with me his experience and knowledge of photography and for making me look good. Jamie G, for his engine expertise, for drawing diagrams and patiently explaining the difference between a V8 and a straight 6, a camshaft and an intake valve. Fellow author Rachelle Morgan and her husband, Deputy David Nelson of the Morris County Sheriff's Dept., Morris County, Texas. Your time was invaluable.

Heat waves drifted across the concrete as the '63 Thunderbird slid from the shadow of the garage. Her big V8 and Holley two-barrels purred like a satisfied woman, all warm and sexy and throaty. The hot Texas sun made a hundred little bursts of light within her wire wheels, slid along the chrome fins, and poured over the glistening black paint. The owner watched as she rolled toward him, and he smiled in appreciation. Several months ago, the Sports Roadster had been little more than a home for mice. Now fully restored to her former glory, she was dazzling – a reminder of a time when Detroit had been more interested in cracking sixty in eight seconds than miles per gallon, safety features, or where to put the cup holder.

Jackson Lamott Parrish sat within the red leather interior of the big T-Bird, one wrist hanging over the red steering wheel. The light caught in his thick brown hair, and fine lines creased the corners of his green eyes as he lowered his lids against the blinding sun. He revved the big engine one last time, took his hand from the steering wheel, and shoved her into park. He swung the door open, and the sole of his cowboy boot hit the pavement. In one smooth motion, he stood and the owner of the restored Roadster stepped forward and handed him a check. Jack glanced at it, noted that all the zeros were in the right places, then folded it in half. He slipped it into the breast pocket of his white dress shirt.

'Enjoy,' he said, then turned and walked into the shop. He moved past a nineteen-seventy 'Cuda 440–6, its huge Hemi engine suspended from a cherry picker. Over the sounds of air compressors and power tools, Jack's younger brother, Billy, called out to a mechanic beneath a '59 Dodge Custom Royal Lancer.

The space just vacated by the T-Bird would be filled the next day with a nineteen-fifty-four Corvette. The sports classic had been found in a dilapidated garage in Southern California, and Jack had flown out three days ago to take a look at it. When he discovered it had only forty thousand original miles and all the numbers matched, he bought it for eight grand on the spot. Once fully restored, the 'Vette would bring ten times that. When it came to restoring vintage cars, Parrish American Classics was the best. Everyone knew it.

Ground-pounding, ear-assaulting muscle cars were in the Parrish boys' blood. Since they'd taken their first steps, Jack and Billy had worked in their daddy's garage. They'd yanked their first engine before either of them had grown their short-and-curlies. They could tell a 260 V8 from a 289 with their eyes closed and could rebuild fuel injectors in their sleep. Proud native sons of Lovett,

Texas, population nineteen thousand three, the Parrish boys had grown up loving football, cold beer, and tearing up asphalt on the flat open roads – usually while some big-haired, loose-moraled female repaired her lipstick in the rearview mirror.

The boys had been raised in a small three-bedroom house behind the garage. The original shop was gone now. Torn down and replaced by a bigger, more modern space with eight bays. The yard behind the garage had been cleaned up. The old cars and junked parts had been towed away long ago.

The house was the same, though. Same roses their mama had planted, same patches of dirt and grass beneath the towering elm. Same concrete porch and the same screen door that needed a good dose of WD40. The house had just been given a fresh coat of paint, inside and out. The same white color as before. The only real difference was that Jack now lived there alone.

Seven years ago, Billy had married Rhonda Valencia and had happily given up his wild ways for domestic bliss. As far as anyone in town could recall, Jack had never been tempted to give up his wild ways. As far as they knew, he'd never met a woman who'd made him want a one-on-one. A forever.

But they didn't know everything.

Jack made his way to his office at the rear of the garage and closed the door. He stuck the check in a desk drawer and pulled out his chair. Before he'd purchased the '54 Corvette, he'd searched out her history then flown to California to inspect her to make sure there wasn't any serious damage to the structural integrity of the car. Searching the history of a vehicle, finding replacement parts, and restoring it, compelled him and kept at him until the vehicle was once again perfect. Fixed. Better. Whole.

Penny Kribs, Jack's secretary, walked into his office and handed him the day's mail. 'I'm leaving to get my hair done,' she reminded him.

Jack looked up at the wispy black pile on top of Penny's head. He'd gone through all twelve years of school with Penny, and he'd played on the football team with her husband, Leon.

He rose and set the mail on his desk. 'You goin' to get yourself beautiful for me?'

She had rings on just about every finger and long pink nails that curled like claws. He'd often wondered how she typed without hitting extra keys or managed to put on all that mascara without poking out an eye. He didn't even want to think about her wrapping her hand around Leon's johnson. The thought sent a shiver down his backside.

'Of course,' she said through a smile. 'You know you've always been my first love.'

Yeah, he knew. In the third grade, Penny'd told him she loved him then she'd kicked him in the shin with her black patent leather shoes. He'd always figured he didn't need that kind of loving. 'Don't tell Leon.'

'Oh, he knows.' She waved a hand and moved to the door, leaving a trail of perfume in her wake. 'He also knows that I would never get involved with you.'

Jack folded his arms across his chest and leaned his butt against the edge of his desk. 'Why's that?'

'Because you treat women like an anorexic treats a Whitman Sampler. You nibble here and nibble there. Maybe you take a few bites, but you never eat one whole.'

Jack laughed. 'I think there are a few women who could set you straight on that.'

Penny wasn't amused. 'You know what I mean,' she said over her shoulder as she walked out the door.

Yeah, he knew what she meant. Like most women, Penny thought he should be married, raising children, and driving an SUV. But as far as Jack was concerned, he figured his younger brother had taken care of that task for both of them. Billy had three daughters ranging in age from six months to five years. They lived on a quiet cul-de-sac with a swing set in the backyard, and Rhonda drove a Tahoe, the alternative choice of soccer moms everywhere. With all those nieces, Jack felt no pressure to bring another Parrish into the world. He was 'Uncle Jack,' and that suited him just fine.

He returned to his chair and unbuttoned his cuffs. He rolled his sleeves up his forearms, and got back to it. It was Friday and he had a mountain of work to clear off his desk before he could start his weekend. At five, Billy opened the door to tell him he was leaving. Jack glanced at the Buick Riviera clock sitting next to his computer monitor. He'd been at it for three hours and fifteen minutes.

'I'm headed for Amy Lynn's T-ball game,' Billy said, referring to his five-year-old daughter. 'You gonna make it by the park?'

Amy Lynn was Billy's oldest and Jack tried to make it to her games when he could. 'Not tonight,' he answered and tossed his pen on the desk. 'Jimmy Calhoun's bachelor party is tonight over at The Road Kill,' he said. Until recently, Jimmy had been a real carouser. Now he was giving up his freedom for a pair of matching gold rings. 'I told him I'd stop by for a few.'

Billy smiled. 'Is there gonna be strippers?'

'I imagine.'

'Don't tell me you'd rather watch naked women than a game of T-ball?'

Jack's grin matched his brother's. 'Yeah, it was a tough choice to make. Watch women take their clothes off or five-year-olds run around bases with their helmets on backward.'

Billy laughed, in that special way he always had of tipping his head back and letting loose with a few heh-heh-hehs. It sounded so much like their father, Ray, Jack figured it had to be genetic. 'Lucky bastard,' Billy said, but without much heart. They both knew that Billy would rather watch Amy Lynn run around with her helmet on backward. 'If you need someone to drive you home from The Road Kill,' Billy added on his way to the door, 'call me.'

'Of course.' A drunk driver had taken their parents' lives when Jack had been all of eighteen. The brothers made it a point to never drive drunk.

Jack worked for another hour before he turned off his computer and headed out of the garage through the bays. Everyone else had already left for the day, and his bootheels echoed in the silence. He locked the door and set the alarm, then he jumped into his Shelby Mustang. It started to rain as he drove toward the outskirts of Lovett. A light sprinkle of drops mixed with the dust and wind, and turned the car's shiny black paint a dull gray.

The Road Kill was a lot like other bars strewn throughout the Texas panhandle. Country music poured from the juke while the patrons drained the beer spigots of Lone Star. A big red-white-and-blue DON'T MESS WITH

TEXAS sign hung on the mirror behind the bar, while old road signs, stuffed armadillos and rattlers decorated the walls. The owner of the bar was also a taxidermist, and if a patron was so inclined, or was drunk enough, he or she could purchase a rattler belt or an ultra-attractive armadillo handbag at cut-rate prices.

When Jack walked into the bar, he pushed up the brim of his Stetson and paused in the doorway long enough to allow his eyes to adjust before he made his way to the bar. He exchanged a few heys with some of the regulars. Over Clint Black on the jukebox, he could hear the sound of Jimmy's bachelor party going full tilt in the back room.

'Bottle of Lone Star,' he ordered. A bottle appeared on the bar and he handed over a five. He felt a soft hand on his arm and looked across his shoulder into the face of Gina Brown.

'Hey there, Jack.'

'Hey, Gina.' Gina was the same age as Jack and twice divorced. She was a tall, lean cowgirl who liked riding the mechanical bull at Slim Clem's over off Highway Seventy. She wore her Wranglers tight, her Justins stacked, and her hair dyed red. Jack knew she dyed her hair because she liked riding him too. But lately she'd hinted that she had him in mind for husband number three. He'd had to cool things down so she would get that idea right out of her head.

'You here for the bachelor party in the back?' She gazed up at him out of the corners of her blue eyes. He would have to be blind to miss the invitation curving her lips.

'Yep.' Jack raised the bottle to his mouth and took a long drink. He had no interest in heating things back up. He liked Gina, but he wasn't husband material. He grabbed his change from the bar and shoved it in the front pocket of his jeans. 'See ya around,' he said and turned to walk away.

Gina's next question stopped him in his tracks. 'Have you seen Daisy Lee yet?'

Jack lowered the bottle and suddenly had trouble swallowing the beer in his mouth. He turned back to face Gina.

'I saw her this morning at the Texaco. Pumping gas into her momma's Cadillac.' Gina shook her head. 'I think it's been what, about ten or twelve years since she was last in town?'

It had been fifteen.

'I recognized her right away. Daisy Lee Brooks hasn't changed that much.'

Except that Daisy Brooks was now Daisy Monroe and had been for the past fifteen years. And that had changed everything.

Gina took a step closer and played with a button on the front of his shirt. 'I was sorry to hear about Steven. I know he was your friend.'

He and Steven Monroe had been almost inseparable since the age of five when they'd sat next to each other at the Lovett Baptist Church, belting out 'Yes, Jesus Loves Me.' But that had changed too. The last time he'd seen Steven was the night the two of them had beat each other bloody, while Daisy looked on horrified. It was the last time he'd seen Daisy too.

As if she didn't notice that Jack wasn't keeping up his end of the conversation, Gina rattled on, 'I can't imagine dying at our age. It's just horrible.'

'Excuse me, Gina,' he said and walked away. An old anger, one he'd thought he'd buried, threatened to pull him into the past. He pushed against it, tapped it down tight, and shut it out.

Then he felt nothing at all.

With his beer in his hand, he wove his way through the rapidly filling bar and moved to the crowded room in the back. He leaned a shoulder into the doorframe and turned his full attention to Jimmy Calhoun. The man of honor sat in a chair in the middle of the room, surrounded by a dozen or so men, all watching two women dressed like rodeo queens bumping and grinding against each other while the Dixie Chicks sang about a sin wagon. Already stripped down to sparkly G-strings on the bottom, the girls popped the snaps to their silky blouses. In unison their shirts slid down their toned shoulders and perfect bodies, exposing big breasts crammed into tiny sequined bikini tops. Jack lowered his gaze from their full breasts to their G-strings tied at their hips.

Marvin Ferrell paused in the doorway beside him to watch the show. 'Do you think those breasts are real?' he asked.

Jack shrugged a shoulder and raised the beer to his mouth. Obviously Marvin had been married too long because he was starting to sound like a woman. 'Who cares?'

'True.' Marvin laughed. 'Did you hear Daisy Brooks is back?'

He looked down the bottle at Marvin then lowered it. 'Yeah, I heard.' Again he felt the old anger, and again he tapped it down until he felt nothing. He returned his attention to the strippers and watched them sandwich Jimmy between their half-naked bodies while they kissed each other above his head. The wet, open-mouthed tongue-thrusting kisses had the guys hollering for more.

Jack tipped his head to one side and smiled. This was getting good.

'I saw Daisy at the Minute Mart,' Marvin continued. 'Damn, she's still hot as she was in high school.'

Jack's smile flat-lined as an unbidden memory of big brown eyes and soft pink lips threatened to drag him into the black hole of his past.

'Remember what she looked like in that little cheerleader outfit of hers?'

Jack pushed away from the door and moved farther into the room, but he couldn't escape. It seemed everyone wanted a trip down memory lane. Everyone but him.

While the strippers took off each other's tiny bikini tops, the topic of conversation was Daisy. Between whistles and catcalls, Cal Turner, Lester Crandall and Eddy Dean Jones all asked if he'd seen her yet.

Disgusted, Jack left the room and made his way back to the bar. It was a hell of a deal when a man wasn't allowed to enjoy two mostly naked women making out with each other six feet in front of him. He didn't know how long Daisy would be in town, but he hoped like hell it was a short trip. Then maybe people would have something better to talk about. Mostly he hoped she had the good sense to stay the hell out of his way.

He set his bottle on the bar and made his way back out of The Road Kill, leaving behind talk and speculation of Daisy Monroe. Rain pelted the top of his hat and wet his shoulders as he made his way across the parking lot. But with each step he took, the memories followed close behind. Memories of looking into a pair of beautiful brown eyes as he kissed soft lips. His hand sliding up the back of her smooth thigh, slipping beneath her blue and gold cheerleader skirt. Of Daisy Lee wearing a pair of red cowboy boots with white hearts on the sides, and nothing else.

'Leaving the party so soon?' Gina asked as she walked toward him.

He looked over at her. 'Boring party.'

'We could make a party of our own.' Typical of Gina, she didn't wait for him to make the first move. Usually that bothered him. Not tonight. She raised her mouth to his, and she tasted of warm beer and need. Jack kissed her back. With her firm breasts crushed against his chest, the first tug of desire stirred low in his gut. He pulled Gina into him and heated things up until all he felt was lust and the rain soaking his skin through his shirt. He replaced all thoughts of brown eyes and cheerleader skirts with the woman pressing herself against his button fly.

Daisy Monroe raised her hand to the screen door then lowered it again. Her heart pounded in her chest and her stomach twisted into one big knot. Rain beat against the porch all around her, and water ran from the downspout and into the flower beds. The garage behind her was lit up, illuminating every nook and cranny surrounding Parrish American Classics. But where she stood was pitch black, as if the light didn't dare creep any farther into the yard.

The garage was new, rebuilt since she'd seen it before. The yard surrounding the garage had been cleaned up. The old cars towed away. From what she could see the house was exactly the same, though, bringing a memory of a nice summer breeze lifting her hair and carrying the scent of roses. Of the many nights she'd sat on the porch where she now stood, wedged between Steven and Jack, laughing at their stupid jokes.

Thunder and lightning boomed and lit up the night sky, shattering the memory. An omen that she should leave and come back again some other time.

She wasn't good at confrontation. She wasn't one of those people who liked to face problems head on. She was better at it than she used to be, but . . . maybe she should have called first. It wasn't polite to just show up on someone's doorstep at ten o'clock at night, and she probably looked like a drowned cat.

Before she'd left her mother's house, she'd made sure her hair was brushed smooth and flipped under just below her shoulders. Her makeup looked perfect and her white blouse and khaki pants pressed. Now she was sure her hair had frizzed, mascara had run, and her pants were splattered with mud from the puddle she'd accidentally dashed through. She turned to go, then forced herself to turn back. Her appearance wasn't really important, and there was never going to be a good time for what she had to do. She'd been in town three days already. She had to talk to Jack. Tonight. She'd put it off long enough. She had to tell him what she'd been keeping from him for fifteen years.

She raised her hand once more and nearly jumped out of her skin when the wooden door swung open before she could knock. Through the screen and dark interior, she could make out the outline of a man. His shirt was missing, and a light from deep within the house cast a warm golden glow from behind, pouring over his arms and shoulders and halfway down his naked chest. She definitely should have called first.

'Hello,' she began before she could give into her trepidation. 'I'm looking for Jackson Parrish.'

'My-my,' his voice drawled in the darkness, 'if it isn't Daisy Lee Brooks.'

It had been fifteen years and his voice had changed. It was deeper than the boy she'd known, but she would have recognized that nasty tone anywhere. No one could pack as much derision into his voice as Jack. She'd understood it once. Known what lay behind it. She didn't kid herself that she knew him anymore.

'Hello, Jack.'

'What do you want, Daisy?'

She stared at him through the screen and shadows, at the outline of the man she'd once known so well. The knot in her stomach pulled tighter. 'I wanted to . . . I need to talk to you. And I-I thought . . .' She took a deep breath and forced herself to stop stammering. She was thirty-three. So was he. 'I wanted to tell you that I was in town before you heard it from someone else.'

'Too late.' The rain pounded the rooftop and the silence stretched between them. She could feel his gaze on her. It touched her face and the front of her yellow rain slicker; and just when she thought he wasn't going to speak again, he said, 'If that's what you came to tell me, you can go now.'

There was more. A lot more. She'd promised Steven that she'd give Jack a letter he'd written a few months before his death. The letter was in her coat pocket, now she had to tell Jack the truth about what had happened fifteen years ago, then hand over the letter. 'It's important that I talk to you. Please.'

He looked at her for several long moments, then he turned and disappeared into the depths of his house. He didn't open the screen for her, but he hadn't slammed the wood door in her face either. He'd made it clear that he was going to be as difficult as possible. But then, when had he ever made things easy?

Just as it always had, the screen door squeaked when she opened it. She followed him through the living room toward the kitchen. His tall outline disappeared around the corner, but she knew the way.

The inside of the house smelled of new paint. She got an impression of dark furniture and a big-screen television, saw the outline of Mrs Parrish's piano pushed against one wall – and she wondered briefly how much had changed since she'd last walked through the house. The light flipped on as she moved into the kitchen, and it was like stepping into a time warp. She half expected to see Mrs Parrish standing in front by the almond-colored stove, baking bread or Daisy's favorite snicker-doodle cookies. The green linoleum had the same worn patch in front of the sink and the counter tops were the same speckled blue and turquoise.

Jack was in front of the refrigerator, the top half of him hidden behind the open door. His tan fingers were curled around the chrome handle, and all she could really see of him was the curve of his behind and his long legs. One pocket of his snug Levi's had a three-corner tear, and the seams looked like they were just about worn through.

Adrenaline rushed through her veins, and she balled her hands into fists to keep them from shaking. Then he rose to his full height, and everything seemed to slow, like someone flipped a switch on a movie projector. He turned as he shut the refrigerator door, and he held a quart of milk in his hand by his thigh. Her attention got momentarily stuck on the thin line of dark hair rising from the waistband of his Levi's and circling his navel. She lifted her gaze up past the hair on his flat belly and the defined muscles of his chest. If she'd had any lingering doubts, seeing him like this removed them. This was not the boy she'd once known. This was definitely a man.

She forced herself to look up at his strong chin, the etched bow of his tan lips, and into his eyes. She felt the back of her throat go dry. Jack Parrish had always been a good-looking boy, now he was lethal. One lock of his thick hair hung over his forehead and touched his brow. Those light green eyes that she remembered, that had once looked at her so full of passion and possession, glanced back at her as if he were no more interested in seeing her than a stray dog.

'Did you come here to stare?'

She moved farther into the kitchen and shoved her hands into the pockets of her raincoat 'No, I came to tell you that I'm in town visiting my mother and sister.'

He raised the milk and drank from the carton, waiting for her to elaborate.

'I thought you should know.'

His gaze met hers over the carton, then he lowered it. Some things hadn't changed after all. Jack Parrish, bad boy and all around hell-raiser, had always been a milk drinker. 'What makes you think I give a shit?' he asked and wiped the back of his hand across his mouth.

'I didn't know if you would. I mean, I did wonder what you'd think, but I wasn't sure.' This was so much harder than she'd envisioned. And what she'd envisioned had been pretty dang hard.

'Now you don't have to wonder.' He pointed with his milk carton toward the other room. 'If that's all, there's the door.'

'No, that's not all.' She looked down at the toes of her boots, the black leather spotted by the rain. 'Steven wanted me to tell you something. He wanted me to tell you that he's sorry about . . . everything.' She shook her head and corrected herself. 'No . . . was sorry, I mean. He's been gone seven months and it's still hard for me to remember him in the past tense. It seems wrong somehow. Like if I do, he never existed.' She looked back at Jack. His expression hadn't changed. 'The flowers you sent were really nice.'

He shrugged and set the milk on the counter. 'Penny sent them.'

'Penny?'

'Penny Colten. Married Leon Kribs. She works for me now.'

'Thank Penny for me.' But Penny hadn't sent them and signed *his* name without *his* knowledge.

'Don't make it a big deal.'

She knew how much Steven had once meant to him. 'Don't pretend you don't care that he's gone.'

He raised a dark brow. 'You forget I tried to kill him.'

'You wouldn't have killed him, Jack.'

'No, you're right. I guess you just weren't worth it.'

The conversation was headed in the wrong direction and she had to turn it around. 'Don't be ugly.'

'You call this ugly?' He laughed, but not with pleasure. 'This is nothing, buttercup. Stick around and I'll show you how ugly I can get.'

She already knew how ugly Jack could get but while

she might be a coward, she was also as stubborn as ragweed. Just as Jack was not the same boy she'd once known, she was not the same girl he'd once known either. She'd come to tell him the truth. Finally. Before she could get on with the rest of her life, she had to tell him about Nathan. It had taken her fifteen years to get to this point, and he could get ugly all he wanted, but he was going to listen to her.

A flash of white caught the corner of Daisy's eye a second before a woman entered the kitchen wearing a man's white dress shirt.

'Hey, y'all,' the woman said as she moved to stand by Jack.

He looked down at her. 'I told you to stay in bed.'

'I got bored without you.'

Heat crept up Daisy's neck to her cheeks, but she seemed to be the only embarrassed person in the room. Jack had a girlfriend. Of course he did. He'd always had a girlfriend or two. There had been a time when that would have hurt.

'Hello, Daisy. I don't know if you remember me. I'm Gina Brown.'

It didn't hurt any longer, and Daisy was a bit ashamed to admit to herself that what she mostly felt was an over-whelming relief. She'd come all the way from Seattle to tell him about Nathan, and now all she felt was relief. Like an axe had been lifted from her throat. She guessed she was more of a coward than she thought. Daisy smiled and moved across the kitchen to offer Gina her hand. 'Of course I remember you. We were in American Government together our senior year.'

'Mr Simmons.'

'That's right.'

'Remember when he tripped over an eraser on the floor?' Gina asked as if she weren't standing there wearing Jack's shirt and, Daisy would bet, nothing else.

'That was so funny. I just about—'

'What the hell is this?' Jack interrupted. 'A damn high school reunion?'

Both women looked up at him and Gina said, 'I was just being polite to your guest.'

'She isn't my guest and she's leaving.' He pinned his gaze on Daisy, just as cold and unyielding as when she'd first walked in the door.

'It was nice to see you, Gina,' she said.

'Same.'

'Good night, Jack.'

He shoved his hip into the counter and crossed his arms over his chest.

'See you two around.' She walked back through the dark house and out the door. The rain had stopped and she dodged puddles on her way to her mother's Caddie, parked on the side of the garage. Next time, she would definitely call first.

Just as she reached for the car door, she felt a hand on her arm whipping her around. She looked up into Jack's face. Security lights shined down on him and shadowed the angry set of his jaw. His eyes stared into hers – no longer cold, they were filled with a burning rage.

'I don't know what you came here looking for, absolution or forgiveness,' he said, his drawl more pronounced than before. 'But you won't find it.' He dropped her arm as if he couldn't stand the touch of her.

'Yes, I know.'

'Good. You stay away from me, Daisy Lee,' he said, drawing out the vowels in her name. 'You stay away or I'll make your life a misery.'

She looked up into his dark face, at the passion and anger that had not abated in fifteen years.

'Just stay away,' he said one last time before he turned on his bare heels and disappeared into the shadows.

She knew she would be wise to heed his warning. Too bad she didn't have that option.

Although he didn't know it yet, neither did he.

2

Daisy blew into the mug of hot coffee as she raised it to her lips. The sun had yet to rise, and her mother was still asleep in her bedroom down the hall. Besides updated appliances, little had changed in her mother's kitchen. The counter tops and floor tiles were the same matching blue, and the same Texas bluebells were painted on the white cabinets.

As quiet as possible Daisy slipped into her raincoat, hung by the back door the night before. She threaded one arm then the other through the slicker until it covered her short pajamas. She crammed her feet into her mother's garden clogs, then she slipped outside into the deep shadows of early morning. Cool air touched her face and bare legs, and a slight breeze pulled several strands of hair from the claw at the back of her head. The Texas air filled her lungs and brought a smile to her lips. She didn't know why, or how to explain it, but the air was different here. It just seemed to settle in her chest and radiate outward. It whispered across her skin and answered a hidden longing she hadn't even known rested deep in her soul.

She was home. If only for a short time.

For fifteen years she'd lived in the Seattle, Washington, area. She'd grown to love it there. She loved the rich green landscape, the mountains, the bay. Snow skiing. Water skiing. The Mariners. So many things.

But Daisy Lee was a Texan. In her heart and in her blood. In her DNA, like her blond hair. Like her birthmark in the shape of a little love bite on the top of her left breast. And like her love bite, Lovett hadn't changed in the past fifteen years. The population had grown by several hundred; there were a few new businesses and one new grade school. The town had recently added an eighteen-hole golf course and a country club to its landscape, but unlike the rest of the country, and more urban Texas, Lovett still moved at its own laid-back pace.

Daisy gazed into the shadows of her mother's backyard. The outline of the five-foot windmill, an Annie Oakley statue, and a dozen or so flamingos were etched in black. Growing up, her mother's taste in exterior decor had been a constant source of embarrassment for her and her younger sister, Lily. Now the parade of flamingos brought a smile to her lips.

She took a drink of coffee, then she sat on the top concrete step next to a stone armadillo with several babies stacked on its back. Daisy hadn't slept well the night before. Her eyes felt puffy and her mind sluggish. She shivered and set the mug on her knee. Before she'd seen Jack last night, her plan had been so clear. She'd come to Lovett, intending to visit with her mother and sister for a few days, then talk to Jack and tell him about Nathan. All within twelve days. Which, until last night, she'd figured would be plenty of time.

She'd known it would be difficult, but clear-cut. She and Steven had talked about it before he'd passed. In her pocket, she still had the letter Steven had written before he'd lost the ability to read and write. When he'd accepted that he would die, that there would be no cure for him, no more experimental drugs to take, no more radical surgeries to try, he'd wanted to make things right with the people he'd felt he'd wronged in his life. One of those people was Jack. At first he'd thought to send the letter, but the more the two of them talked about it, the more they'd concluded that it should be delivered in person. By her. Because ultimately, she was the one who had to deal with Jack Parrish, and she was the one who'd wronged him most.

They'd never really meant to keep Nathan a secret from him. Her mother knew. So did her sister. Nathan knew too. He'd always known that he had a biological father named Jackson who lived in Lovett, Texas. They'd told him as soon as he'd been capable of understanding, but he'd never expressed any interest in meeting Jack. Steven had always been enough father for him.

It was time. Perhaps past time that she told Jack he had a son. A moan escaped her lips and she took a sip of coffee. A fifteen-year-old son with a pickle green Mohawk, a pierced lip, and so many dog chains hanging off him he looked liked he'd broken into the animal shelter.

Nathan had had such a hard time these past two and a half years. When Steven was diagnosed, he'd been given five months to live. He'd lasted almost two years, but it hadn't been an easy two years. Watching Steven fight to live had been hard on her, but it had been hell on Nathan.

And she hated to admit it, but there had been times when she hadn't been at all attentive to her son. Some nights, she hadn't even known he was gone until he'd returned. He'd walk in the door and she'd scold him for not telling her where he'd gone. He'd look at her through those clear blue eyes of his and say, 'I told you I was going to Pete's. You said I could.' And she'd have to admit to herself that it was entirely possible that he'd told her, but she'd been focused on Steven's medication or his next surgery – or perhaps that had been the day when Steven lost his ability to use a calculator, drive a car, or tie his shoes. Watching her husband struggle to maintain his dignity while trying to recall a simple task he'd been performing since he was four or five had been heartbreaking. There were times when she'd simply forgotten whole blocks of conversations with Nathan.

The day Nathan had walked in the house with that Mohawk had been a real wake-up call for her. Suddenly, he was no longer the little boy who played soccer, loved football, and watched 'Nickelodeon' curled up on the couch with his special blanket. It hadn't been the color of his hair that had alarmed her most. It had been the lost look in his eyes. His empty, lost gaze had shocked her out of the depression and grief she hadn't even known she'd fallen into for almost seven months following Steven's passing.

Steven was gone. She and Nathan would always feel his loss, like a missing part of their souls. He'd been her best friend and a good man. He'd been a buffer, a comfort, someone who made her life better. Easier. He'd been a loving husband and father.

She and Nathan would never forget him, but she could

not continue to live in the past. She had to live in the present and begin to look toward the future. For Nathan, and for herself. But in order for her to move forward, she had to take care of her past. She had to quit hiding from it.

Fingers of morning sun crept into the backyard and sparkled in the dew-covered lawn. The early sun cast long patterns in the wet grass, crept up the windmill, and shot sparks off the tip of Annie Oakley's silver rifle. Daisy wished she had her Nikon and wide-angle lens on her. It was up in her room, and she knew if she ran up to get it, she'd miss the shot and the rising sun. Within seconds, dawn broke over Daisy's feet, legs and face; she closed her eyes and soaked it all in.

Living in the Northwest, Daisy had lost most of her accent, but she'd never lost her love of wide-open spaces and the huge blue sky stretching across the horizon in unbroken lines. She opened her eyes and wished Steven were here to see it. He would have loved it as much as she did.

Daisy looked down at the rubber garden clogs on her feet. She wished for a lot of things. Like more time before she had to confront Jack again. She was in no hurry to see the anger in his face. She'd known that he would not welcome her back with open arms, but she was surprised that after all of these years, he clearly hated her as much as he had the last time she'd seen him.

You call this ugly? he'd said. *This is nothing, buttercup. Stick around and I'll show you how ugly I can get.*

She wondered if Jack had realized he'd called her buttercup. His old name for her. The name he'd first called her on her first day at Lovett Elementary.

She remembered being nervous and scared on that day,

so long ago. She'd been afraid no one would like her, and she'd suspected that the big red bow clipped to the top of her head looked stupid. Her mother had pulled it off the handle of a Welcome Wagon basket filled with coupons, a recipe book, and Wick Fowler's chili kit. Daisy hadn't wanted to wear the bow, but her mother had insisted that it looked good and matched her dress.

All that first morning, no one had spoken to her. By lunch, she'd become so upset, she was unable to eat her cheese yum-yum sandwich. Finally, during recess, Steven and Jack walked up to where she stood with her back against the chain link fence.

'What's your name?' Jack had asked.

She'd looked into those green eyes of his, surrounded by long black lashes, and she'd smiled. Finally someone was talking to her, and her little heart leapt with joy. 'Daisy Lee Brooks.'

He'd rocked back on the heels of his boots as he looked her up and down. 'Well, buttercup, that's the stupidest hair bow I ever did see,' he'd drawled, then he and Steven howled with laughter.

Hearing that the bow was stupid confirmed her worst fears, and the backs of her eyes started to sting. 'Yeah, well y'all are so stupid you have to take off your shoes to count,' she'd responded, proud that she stood up for herself. Then she'd ruined everything by bursting into tears.

The memory of that day brought a sad smile to her face. She'd vowed to hate those two boys as long as she lived. It lasted until Jack had asked her to play on their softball team, three weeks later. It was Steven who showed her how to play second base without getting hit in the face with the ball.

At first, Jack had called her buttercup to tease her, but years later, he'd whispered it as he kissed the side of her throat. His voice would go all dark while he discovered whole new ways to tease her. There had been a time when just the memory of his kiss had sent a warm shudder through her chest, but she hadn't felt anything warm and tingly for him in years.

She thought of how he'd looked last night, half naked and fully ticked off. His lids lowered over his sexy green eyes, and that sardonic curl of his lips. He'd grown even more handsome than the last time she'd seen him, but Daisy was older and wiser and no longer tempted by good looks and bad attitudes.

Nathan didn't resemble Jack much. Except maybe the attitude part. He was staying with Steven's sister in Seattle while Daisy was in Lovett, but he knew the reason behind her trip. She'd learned her lesson about lies, no matter how well intentioned, and she never lied to Nathan. But she had purposely chosen his last week of ninth grade to make the trip so he couldn't come along. She didn't know what Jack's reaction would be once she told him about Nathan. She didn't think he would be cruel, not to Nathan anyway, but she wasn't certain. She didn't want Nathan here if Jack got truly ugly. Nathan had had enough pain in his life.

From inside the house, she heard her mother moving around. She stood and walked back inside.

'Good morning,' she said as she hung up her coat. The warm scent of her mother's kitchen filled her nose. The smell of baked bread and home-cooked comfort food surrounded her like a familiar blanket. 'I watched the sun come up, and it was absolutely gorgeous.' She kicked off the garden clogs and looked over at her mother, who was stirring cream into her coffee. Louella Brooks wore a blue nylon nightgown, and her blond hair was piled on top of her head like cotton candy.

'How was your party last night?' Daisy asked. Every second Friday, the Lovett single's club held a dance, and Louella Brooks hadn't missed one since she'd joined in nineteen ninety-two. She paid fifty dollars a year to belong to the club, and she believed in getting her money's worth.

'Verna Pearse was there, and I swear she looks a good ten years older than her real age.' Louella placed her spoon in the sink and raised her mug to her lips. Her brown eyes looked back at Daisy over her coffee. 'She was surely saggin', baggin' and draggin'.'

Daisy smiled and filled her own mug. Verna had once worked at the Wild Coyote Diner with Louella. The two had been friends at one time. During Daisy's junior and senior years of high school, she'd worked at the diner too, but she couldn't recall what had happened to break up the friendship. 'What happened between you and Verna?' she asked.

Louella put her mug on the counter and grabbed a loaf of bread from the pantry. 'Verna Pearse is as loose as a slipknot,' she said. 'For a year she told me she got paid ten cents more an hour than me because she was a better waitress. She bragged and held it over my head, but come to find out, she was earning it in other ways.'

'How?'

'With Big Bob Jenkins.'

Daisy remembered the owner of the diner, and he hadn't been called Big Bob for nothing. 'She was having sex with Big Bob?'

Louella shook her head and pursed her lips. 'Oral gratification in the storeroom.'

'Really? That's criminal.'

'Yes. It's a form of prostitution.'

'I was thinking it was more like slave labor. Verna blew Big Bob for what turns out to be like – eighty cents a day? That's not right.'

'Daisy,' her mother scolded as she got out the toaster. 'Don't talk filth.'

'You brought it up!' She'd never understand her mother. 'Oral gratification' was okay, but somehow 'blew' wasn't.

'You've been in the North too long.'

Maybe she had, because she just didn't get the difference. Although there had been a time when she never would have uttered the word in that context.

Louella opened the loaf of bread. 'Do you want toast?'

'I don't eat in the morning.' She took a drink of coffee and moved to the corner breakfast nook. The bright morning sun poured in through the sheers and lit up the yellow table.

'Did you go out last night?' her mother asked as she toasted one slice of bread.

Meaning, did she work up her nerve to drive to Jack's. 'Yes. I went to his house last night.'

'Did you tell him?'

Daisy sat on one of the bench seats and looked down at her hands wrapped around her mug. She had a chip in her red fingernail polish. 'No. He wasn't alone. His girlfriend was there, so it wasn't a good time.'

'Maybe that was a sign you should leave it alone.'

Growing up, her mother had always liked Steven more

than Jack. Although, Louella liked Jack too. When the three of them got into trouble, Jack was often blamed. And while it was true that he'd usually come up with the offense that landed them in hot water, Daisy and Steven would gladly go along with him. 'I can't do that,' Daisy said, 'I have to tell him.'

'I still don't understand why.' Louella's toast popped up and she set it on a little plate.

'I told you why.' Daisy didn't feel like discussing her reasons again. She opened the bottle of fingernail polish she'd left on the table yesterday and set about repairing the chip.

'Well, if you're determined to do this, you shouldn't go over there at night.' Louella lifted the lid off the butter dish and buttered her toast. 'People talk about widows. They say you're desperate.'

Daisy's father had died when she was five, but she'd never heard any gossip about her mother being desperate. 'I don't care.' She covered her index fingernail with red polish, then screwed the lid back on the bottle.

'You should.' Louella grabbed her plate and coffee and sat across the table from Daisy. 'You don't want people to think you're going over there for relations.'

Daisy blew on her wet fingernail to keep from laughing. It had been over two years since she'd had *relations*, and she wasn't sure she knew how to do it anymore. After Steven's diagnosis and first surgery, they'd tried to have a normal, healthy married life, but after a few months, it just got too difficult. At first she'd really missed sex with her husband. Then the more she'd gone without, the less she'd missed it. Now, she really didn't think about it all that much.

'Tell me about all those flamingos in your backyard,' Daisy said to change the subject.

'I think they're pretty,' her mother said. Growing up, her mother had been into Disney. Their yard had been overrun with Snow White, the Seven Dwarfs, and several characters from *Alice in Wonderland*. 'I got the big flamingo with the little pocket book in its beak from Kitty Fae Young. Her granddaughter Amanda makes 'em up special order. You remember Amanda, don't you?'

Just like she was a kid again, Daisy felt her eyes glaze over. Her mother had always had a tendency to ramble on forever about people Daisy didn't know, had never met, and didn't give a rat's about. Growing up, she and Lily had been involuntary victims, trapped into listening to the hottest gossip going around the diner, which usually wasn't all that hot. It didn't matter how often they hinted that they didn't care about so-and-so's new Buick, arthritis or yummy homemade cookies, Louella was like a needle stuck in a record groove and absolutely couldn't stop until she came to the end.

She shook her head and said a weak, 'No.'

'Sure you do,' her mother said. 'She had those really bad buck teeth. Looked just like a little beaver.'

'Oh yeah,' she said although she didn't have the foggiest. There were quite a few kids in west Texas with buck teeth.

Daisy slid from behind the table and stood. While her mother talked about Amanda and her yard art, Daisy walked to the sink and rinsed her mug. She glanced up at the purple and green stained-glass frame making patterns on the sill. She'd taken the photo in the picture frame. It was Steven and Nathan on Nathan's fourth birthday, and she'd used a wide-angle lens to distort the closeup shot. Both wore party hats and were grinning like lunatics fresh from the asylum, their eyes huge. She'd taken it when she first started photography classes and was experimenting. They'd all been so happy then.

A frown creased her brow and she looked away. She didn't want to think about the past today. She didn't want to get sucked into the emotional morass of it. She put the mug in the dishwasher and her gaze fell on a grocery list clipped in a clothespin recipe holder.

'. . . but of course you didn't live here then,' her mother was saying. 'That was the year a twister took out Red Cooley's trailer.'

'Are you going to the store?' she interrupted.

'I need a few things,' her mother answered as she rose from the table and put the bread away. 'After church tomorrow, Lily Belle and Pippen are coming over for Sunday dinner, and I thought we'd have a nice ham.'

Lily was three years younger than Daisy, and Pippen was her two-year-old son. Lily's husband had run off with a cowgirl, and they were in the process of a messy divorce. She was having a difficult time, and as a result, men in general were on Lily's hit list. 'I'll go to Albertsons for you,' she offered. That way she could choose something beside ham. She'd never been a big pork fan, and after Steven's funeral, a lot of well-meaning people had dropped off baked hams. Some of them were still in her freezer in Seattle.

She took a shower then dressed in a pair of jeans and a blue T-shirt. She dried her hair and put on a little makeup. With the list in her back pocket, she jumped in her mother's Cadillac. The car had several dents up and down each side due to her mother being nearsighted. A flamingo air freshener hung from the rearview mirror, and the Caddie whined when she turned corners.

Inside Albertsons, the Muzak of choice was Barry Manilow's 'Mandy,' an abomination in any state, but especially Texas. She tossed a box of tea bags and a can of coffee into her cart, then she headed for the meat section. She was in the mood for steak and grabbed a package of three rib-eyes.

'Well hey, Daisy. I heard you were back in town.'

Daisy glanced up from her steaks. The woman in front of her looked slightly familiar. Her hair was pinned up in big pink rollers, and she held a large can of Super Hold Aqua Net in one hand and a pack of bobby pins in the other.

It took Daisy a few seconds to place a name with the face. 'You're Shay Brewton, Sylvia's little sister.' Daisy and Sylvia had been on the same cheerleader squad at Lovett High. They'd been good friends but had lost touch when Daisy and Steven had moved away. 'How's Sylvia?'

'She's good. She lives in Houston now with her husband and kids.'

'Houston?' She set the steaks back in the case and placed her foot on the bottom rung of the cart. 'Shoot. I'm sorry she moved away. I'd hoped to look her up before I left.'

'She's in town this weekend for my wedding.'

Daisy smiled. 'You're getting married? When? To whom?'

'I'm marrying Jimmy Calhoun over at Whiley Baptist Church. Tonight at six.'

'Jimmy Calhoun?' She'd gone all through school with Jimmy. He'd had flaming red hair and a silver tooth. There were six Calhoun boys; all of them trouble. If she'd had to lay odds, she would have bet the lot of them were living in Huntsville with prison tattoos by now.

Shay laughed. 'Don't look at me like I've come off my spool.'

Daisy hadn't realized her mouth was hanging open and she snapped it shut. 'Congratulations, I'm sure you'll be very happy,' she said.

'Come to my reception afterwards over at the country club. It starts at eight.'

'Crash your wedding?'

'It's going to be a big party. Lots of food and liquor, and we hired Jed and the Rippers to play music for us. Sylvia will be there, and I know she'd just love to see you. Mom and Daddy, too.'

Mrs Brewton had been an adviser for the squad. Mr Brewton had made his own liquor in the back shed. Daisy knew from experience that it could eat a hole in your esophagus. 'Maybe I will.'

Shay nodded. 'Good, I'll tell her I ran into you and that you're coming to the reception. She'll be tickled.'

Daisy hadn't brought anything to wear to a wedding reception. The only dress she'd brought was a white tank, and it really wasn't appropriate. Maybe she'd just send a gift. 'Are you registered anywhere?'

'Oh, don't worry about that.' She smiled. 'But yes, I am. Donna's Gifts on Fifth.'

Of course. Everyone registered at Donna's.

'See ya tonight,' Shay said as she moved away.

Daisy watched her disappear around a corner and she smiled again. Little Shay Brewton was marrying wild Jimmy Calhoun. Growing up, there really hadn't been any boys more insane than Jimmy and his brothers.

Except maybe Jack.

Jack had always been wrapped crazy. It had never been enough for him to race his bike as fast as it would go; he had to lift his hands from the handle bars, or stand on the seat. It wasn't enough to chase dust devils; he had to play outside when the weather service predicted an F1 tornado. He thought he was invincible, like Superman.

Steven had been more daredevil than Daisy, but even he hadn't attempted half the stuff Jack had. He'd never jumped from his roof into a pile of leaves and broken his leg. Or put a motorcycle engine on a homemade go-cart and driven around town as if he were at Talladega.

Jack had done that. He'd done it even though he knew his dad would whoop his butt. And Ray Parrish had, but it'd been worth it to Jack.

Steven Monroe had always been the safe one – dependable – while Jack had raced through life full throttle as if his hair was on fire.

Hanging around with the craziest boy in school had been a lot of fun. Getting romantically involved with him had been a huge mistake.

One in which she and Steven and Jack had all paid a high price.

T he Lovett Country Club sat on the edge of an
eighteen-hole golf course. Elm trees lined the drive
from the gates to the entrance of the building. Visitors had
to walk across a bridge to get to the front doors. A stream
ran beneath the bridge and emptied into a pond filled with
koi, their red and white bodies swaying in the slow
current.

At half past eight, Daisy pulled into a parking spot next
to a Mercedes. This was the first time she'd gone out by
herself since Steven's passing, and it did feel strange. Like
she'd forgotten something at home. The sort of panicky
feeling she'd usually get when she was in line at the airport
before a trip, like she'd left the tickets on the dining room
table even though she knew they were in her purse. She
wondered how much longer until the panicky feeling went
away? Until she was used to going out alone.

And dating. Forget it. She didn't think she'd ever be
ready for that.

Daisy entered the glass double doors and caught a glimpse of her smeared reflection in the polished brass railing as she walked past the restaurant and down a long hall toward the banquet room. She wore a red sleeveless cocktail dress she'd borrowed from Lily. Daisy was a few inches taller than her five-foot-two-inch sister, a little bigger in the chest too. Red might not be the most appropriate color to wear to a wedding reception, but it was the only dress Lily owned that wasn't too short or too tight across Daisy's breasts.

Covered silk buttons ran up the right side from the hem to her armpit, and her mother's small red purse hung from a long gold chain on her shoulder.

She set the gift she'd bought earlier on a table beside the door, and she moved just inside the banquet room. The bridal party stood before teal-and-gold swags in a traditional line while a male photographer snapped pictures with a digital camera.

About two hundred people toasted the happy couple with flutes of champagne. Teal and gold festooned everything and colored candles flickered atop round tables covered in white cloths. To Daisy's left, rows of chafing dishes served what looked like barbeque chicken, roast beef, vegetables, and chili. Most of the guests were already seated while others milled around.

The photographer wasn't using a video light to capture the glow of the room, which Daisy thought was too bad. If she'd been hired for the shoot, she would have packed a number of cameras and numerous lenses in her gearbox. In this particular room, she would have used 1600 color film with on-camera flash and a video light to enhance ambient light in the background. Every photographer worked a little differently, though. This guy's photographs would probably turn out all right.

'. . . to Jimmy and Shay Calhoun,' someone toasted. Daisy grabbed a flute of champagne and turned her attention from the photographer to the bridal party. As her gaze scanned the line, she raised the glass to her mouth, careful not to smudge her red lipstick. Behind her flute, Daisy smiled as her eyes took in her friend from high school. Sylvia was decked out in some sort of teal gauze and gold satin harem-girl outfit. She was as big as a house. Not fat. Very pregnant. She looked tired, but as cute as ever, and was as short as Daisy remembered; and she still wore the same lacquered bangs and big hair as in school.

Shay looked beautiful with her Texas-sized curls bouncing at her shoulder and soft veil floating like a cloud around her. Jimmy Calhoun was better looking than he'd been when Daisy had lived here before. Or maybe he just cleaned up nice in his tux. She wasn't sure, but his red hair was a shade or two darker and all his freckles had faded.

'Excuse me, ma'am,' a voice she instantly recognized spoke directly behind her. She scooted sideways out of the doorway and glanced over her shoulder, looking past the defined line of Jack Parrish's mouth and up into his beautiful eyes.

His gaze locked with hers as he passed, and the sleeve of his charcoal blazer brushed her bare arm. Surprise halted his footsteps for about half a heartbeat, and within that fraction of a second, something hot and alive flashed behind his eyes. Just as quickly it was gone, and Daisy wasn't sure if it had been a trick of the two chandeliers overhead or of the flickering candlelight. He moved past, and she watched his broad shoulders and the back of his head as he wove his way through the crowd toward the bride and groom. His dark hair brushed the back of his collar and looked finger-combed, as if he'd just taken off his hat, tossed it on the seat of his car, and fixed his hair. In his suit, he looked liked he'd just stepped out of a fashion magazine. And as always, he moved with an easy, laid-back stride that made it clear he was in no great hurry to get anywhere.

A little flutter that had nothing to do with his looks, and everything to do with who he was to her and her son, stirred in her stomach.

'Daisy Lee Brooks!' Sylvia hollered and Daisy turned her gaze to her friend. 'You get over here.' Sylvia's voice had always been bigger than the rest of her. It had made her an excellent cheerleader.

Daisy laughed and walked to the front. She moved to stand beside Jack, who was speaking with the groom. She hugged her friend and Mr and Mrs Brewton. Sylvia introduced her to her husband, Chris, then said, 'You remember Jimmy Calhoun.'

'Hello, Daisy.' Jimmy grinned, his silver tooth gone, replaced by porcelain. 'You look great.'

'Thank you.' She glanced up at Jack who was doing a good job of pretending she wasn't alive. Her gaze lowered to his shoulders and the blue dress shirt between the lapels of his suit jacket. He wasn't wearing a tie. She returned her attention to the groom. 'You look good yourself, Jimmy. I can't believe you married little Shay Brewton. I remember when Sylvia and I tried to teach her to ride a bike and she ran into a tree.'

Shay laughed and Jimmy said, 'I bet you thought I'd be in prison by now.'

In the seventh grade, Jimmy and his Calhoun brothers had piled into their daddy's Monte Carlo, pressed their naked behinds to the windows, and mooned the middle school. In the tenth, Jimmy had called in a bomb threat because he wanted to get out of school a few hours early. He got caught because he used the pay phone outside the principal's office. 'The thought never entered my head.'

Sylvia laughed because she knew better. Daisy felt herself relax. The flutter in her stomach calmed. Now wasn't the time nor place to tell Jack about Nathan. She didn't have to think about it. She could relax. Have fun with old friends. It had been a long time since she'd had a little fun.

'Jack, do you remember the time you and Steven and I got arrested for racing out on the old highway?' Jimmy asked.

'Sure.' He pulled back his cuff and looked at his watch. 'Were you there that night, Daisy?'

'No.' She once again glanced up at the man by her side. 'I never liked it when Steven and Jack raced cars. I was always afraid someone would get hurt.'

'I was always in control.' Jack dropped his hand to his side and his fingers brushed her dress. He lowered his gaze to her, and his eyes were without expression when he said, 'I was always safe.'

No, being with him had rarely been safe.

'I was real sorry to hear about Steven,' Jimmy said and she returned her gaze to him. 'He was a good guy.'

Daisy never knew what to say to that, so she raised her glass to her lips.

'Shay told me he died of brain cancer.'

'Yes.' It had a name, glioblastoma. And it was horrible and always fatal.

'I've been fixin' to get a hold of your momma to ask how you're doing,' Sylvia told her.

'I'm okay.' Which was the truth. She was okay. 'Goodness, when's this baby due?' she asked Sylvia, purposely changing the subject.

'Next month.' She rubbed her big belly. 'And I am more than ready. Do you have children?'

'Yes.' She was very aware of Jack, of the sleeve of his jacket so close to her arm that if she moved just a fraction, she would feel the texture of it against her bare skin. 'My son, Nathan,' she said and purposely didn't reveal his age. 'He's in Seattle with Steven's sister Junie and her husband Oliver.' She glanced up at Jack and gone was his carefully blank expression. Surprise filled his green eyes and lifted a brow. 'You remember Junie don't you?'

'Of course,' he said and looked away.

'I remember her,' Sylvia elaborated. 'She was a lot older than us. I remember Steven's parents were pretty old too.'

Steven had been a real surprise when his parents were in their mid forties. They were both sixty-three when he graduated high school. His mother was gone now, and his father lived in a retirement community in Arizona.

'Shay and I are gonna get to work on making a baby tonight.' Jimmy laughed. 'Don't want to wait too late in life to have a baby.'

Jack reached inside his jacket and pulled a cigar from the breast pocket of his dress shirt. 'Congratulations,' he said and handed it to Jimmy.

Jimmy pulled the cigar through his fingers. 'My favorite. Thanks.'

'Don't I get one?' Shay protested with a smile.

'I didn't know you smoked cigars,' Jack said as he

reached for her hand. He took it from the folds of her dress and brought it to his mouth. 'Congratulations, Shay. Jimmy is a very lucky man.' He kissed her knuckles and drawled just above a whisper, 'If he doesn't treat you right, you let me know.'

Shay smiled and touched her curls with her free hand. 'Are you going to open a can of whoop ass on my behalf?'

'For you, I'll open two.' He dropped her hand, then he excused himself.

Daisy's gaze fell to his broad shoulders as he made his way to the bar set up in one corner.

'He could always charm the pants off anyone,' Sylvia sighed. 'Even in the fifth grade.'

She turned her attention to Sylvia as the others around them talked about football. While they debated whether the Cowboys needed stronger defense or offense, Daisy leaned her head closer to Sylvia.

'What happened with you and Jack in the fifth grade?' she asked her friend.

A wistful smile curved Sylvia's lips, and the two of them turned to watch Jack order a beer at the bar.

'Come on,' Daisy wheedled.

'He talked me into showing him my bottom.'

In the fifth grade? She and Jack and Steven had been playing NASCAR in the fifth grade. Not doctor. 'How?'

'He told me he'd show me his if I showed him mine.'

'That's all it took?'

'I don't have brothers, and he doesn't have sisters. We were curious and checked out each other's bottoms. Nothing bad happened. He was real sweet about it.'

She'd never known that while he was boring her with Richard Petty stats, he was running around checking out other girl's bottoms. She wondered what else she didn't know.

'Don't tell me you were friends with Jack Parrish all those years and never showed him yours.'

'Not in the fifth grade.'

'Honey, sooner or later, everyone showed Jack their bottom.' She ran her hand over her big belly. 'It was just a matter of time.'

Daisy was seventeen and practically had to beg him to look at her bottom. If she remembered correctly, his words had been, 'Stop, Daisy. I don't mess around with virgins.' But he had, and they'd begun a wild sexual relationship that they'd kept secret from everyone. Even Steven. Especially Steven. It had been crazy and thrilling and intense. A roller coaster ride of love and jealousy and sex. And it had ended very badly.

Long forgotten memories rushed at Daisy, as if suddenly set free. One here, another there. A tangled mess of memory and chaotic emotion, as if they'd been smashed together, thrown in a box, and hurriedly taped shut. Waiting all these years for someone to rip the tape off and throw open the tabs.

She recalled her own wedding. She and Steven at the courthouse. Her mother and his parents standing with them. Steven squeezing her hand to keep it from shaking. She'd loved Steven Monroe for years before she married him. Maybe not a hot burning kind of love. Maybe she didn't crave him like a drug, but that kind of love didn't last. It burned out. The love she'd felt for Steven had always been warm and comfortable, like coming home cold and tired, curling up in front of a fire. That kind of love lasted, and it would last long after Steven's passing.

She remembered riding with Steven in his car, on their way to tell Jack about their marriage. Her pregnancy had made her sick to her stomach. What they were about to do made her chest tight. She'd started to cry even before they pulled onto Jack's street. Again, Steven had held her hand.

She and Steven had been through a lot together, and everything they'd faced had brought them closer. Their first few years of marriage while he was attending school had been rough financially. Then when Nathan turned four, Steven got a good job and they decided to add another child to their family only to find out that Steven had a low sperm count. They'd tried everything to conceive, but nothing worked. After five years, they decided to give up and were happy with their lives.

The room suddenly went dark and Daisy was jarred from the past. A spotlight shined on the center of the dance floor, and she tried to push all thoughts of the past from her head. Jed and the Rippers picked up their instruments and Jimmy and Shay danced their first dance as husband and wife.

When Daisy had decided to come home and tell Jack about Nathan, she hadn't counted on the memories. She hadn't even known they were there, locked away, waiting for her.

Daisy moved away from the dance floor and placed her empty glass on a table. She headed to the bathroom in the bar down the hall, and while she washed her hands, she looked at her reflection. She was no longer a scared, heartbroken girl. She was a lot tougher than she'd been growing up. While she wasn't here to relive memories, she wouldn't hide from them either. She was here to tell Jack about Nathan. She would tell him that she was sorry and hope he'd understand. Although she was fairly certain he wouldn't understand and would make things difficult, she still had to do the right thing. No more putting it off. No more hiding.

She reapplied her red lipstick and dropped it into her purse. Let Jack do his worst. She might even deserve some of it, but she'd survive. She'd lived with just about the worst that life could deal her, and nothing Jack could do would be as bad as that.

Daisy stopped in the bar and bought a glass of wine, then made her way back toward the banquet room.

Jack stood in the long hall with one shoulder shoved against the wall. He held a cell phone in one hand, the other was in the front pocket of his pants. He glanced up and watched her as she moved toward him.

'That'd be fine,' he said into the phone. 'I'll see y'all first thing Monday.'

Her first impulse was to hurry past, but she stopped in front of him instead. 'Hey, Jack.'

He disconnected and put the phone in his pocket. 'What do you want, Daisy?'

'Nothing. Just being friendly.'

'I don't want to be "friendly" with you.' He straightened away from the wall and took his hand from his pocket. 'I thought I made myself clear last night.'

'Oh, you did.' She took a drink of her wine, then asked, 'How's Billy?' All she remembered of Jack's brother was a pair of shiny blue eyes and sandy blond hair. Other than that, she couldn't recall much about him.

He looked over her head and said, 'Billy's good.'

She waited for him to elaborate. He didn't. 'Married? Kids?'

'Yep.'

'Where's Gina?' His gaze met hers and, in that suit, his eyes appeared more gray than green.

'At Slim Clem's, I imagine.'

'She's not here?'

'I don't see her.'

She took another sip of her wine. She was going to be pleasant if it killed her. Or him. 'You didn't bring her with you?'

'Why would I?'

'Isn't she your girlfriend?'

'Whatever gave you that idea?'

They both knew what had given her that idea. 'Oh, maybe because she was wearing your shirt last night, and nothing else.'

'You're wrong about that. She was wearin' a black lace thong.' One corner of his mouth slid up, purposely provoking her – *the jerk*. 'And a satisfied smile. You remember that smile, don't you, Daisy?'

She would *not* lose her temper and give him what he wanted. 'Don't flatter yourself, Jack Parrish. You weren't that memorable.'

'What? I was talking about Gina's smile last night.' The other corner of his mouth slid up and laugh lines appeared in the corners of his eyes. 'What were *you* talking about, buttercup?'

They both knew he hadn't been talking about *Gina's* smile. 'You haven't changed since high school.' She gave him a withering glance and walked away before she lost her temper and said something she might regret. Like that he should grow up.

Jack watched her go. His smile flat-lined, and his gaze slid from her blond hair, all slick and smooth, down the back of her red dress to her behind and the backs of her thighs. Who the hell was she to judge him? She'd screwed around with him, said she'd love him forever; then married his best friend the same week he buried both his parents. In his book, that made her a hardcore bitch.

She disappeared into the banquet room, and Jack waited a few moments before he followed. At thirty-three, Daisy was even more beautiful than she'd been at eighteen. He'd seen it last night. In his kitchen, and he saw it now. So much about her was different, yet the same. Her hair was still the same shiny blond, but it wasn't big and curly and sprayed stiff. Now it was smooth and sexy as hell. She'd grown an inch maybe two, to what he figured was about five-foot-five, but she carried herself like she was still queen of the Lovett Rose Festival. Her large eyes were still the color of rich mahogany, but they'd lost the innocence and passion that he'd once found so fascinating.

He walked down the hall and entered the dark banquet room. Marvin stopped him to talk about the '67 Ford Fairlane he'd just bought.

'It has its original 427,' he said while Jed and the Rippers sang a Tim McGraw song about a girl in a miniskirt.

Like a magnet, Jack's gaze found Daisy. She stood at the edge of the lighted floor across the room, chatting with J. P. Clark and his wife, Loretta. Daisy's red dress hugged the curves of her body without looking too tight. She clearly hadn't gone too fat. Didn't have thick ankles or a droopy butt. Which was too bad, as far as Jack was concerned.

For years he'd forgotten about her and Steven. He'd buried them in the past and got on with his life. Now here she was, dredging it all back up again.

Cal Turner approached her and she followed him to the

middle of the dance floor. Everyone knew Cal was a horny bastard and would naturally take all those buttons on the side of that dress as an invitation to let his fingers do the walking. Maybe that's what she wanted. To get something going with Cal. Didn't matter, though. It was none of Jack's business.

'The vinyl roof needs to be replaced,' Marvin said, then rambled on about the interior.

Cal wrapped an arm around Daisy's waist and she smiled up at him. Light from the crystal ball slid along her cheek and got caught in her hair. Her red lips parted and she laughed. Daisy Lee Brooks, the fantasy of every horny guy at Lovett High, was back in town, turning heads and leading guys on with a smile.

Some things never changed.

Only she wasn't Daisy Lee Brooks. She was Daisy Monroe and she had a kid. A son. A baby with Steven. He didn't know why that surprised him. It shouldn't. Of course they'd had a kid. When he thought about it, it was more surprising that they'd just had the one.

Unexpected and unwanted, the memory of her flat stomach flashed across his brain. His mouth tasting her bare skin just above her navel as he gazed up into her face. At the hot drowsy passion in her eyes as he worked his way down. Her lips moist and abraded from his kiss.

'Excuse me,' he said just as Marvin was getting all hot about the Ford's dual carbs. He walked toward the exit sign and out the doors. He moved down the hall and out the front doors of the country club. The warm June night touched his face and throat. The sound of insects was thick in the air. There was some sort of pond to Jack's right and lightning bugs blinked like white Christmas lights on the golf course beyond. A memory of catching lightning bugs with Steven and Daisy flashed across his brain. That had been back before insecticides reduced their numbers, and they were still easy to catch in Mason jars. He, Steven and Daisy would smear the bugs on their arms, making fluorescent streaks that lasted a good ten minutes.

He pulled a cigar from his breast pocket and walked to a stone bench just beyond the lights of the club. He sat and slid off the cigar band. He stuck it in the corner of his mouth and patted his pockets, searching for the box of matches he'd picked up in the tobacco store. He didn't smoke that often, but he did occasionally enjoy an expensive cigar.

His pockets came up empty and he stuck the cigar back in his breast pocket. A bank of windows from the restaurant threw watery light on the pond. He ran his fingers through his hair, leaned his head back against the building, and stared out at the night. His life was good. He had more business than he could handle and was making more money than he needed. He'd taken Parrish American Classics and made it bigger and better than his father had ever dreamed. He owned his home and his business. He drove a Mustang worth seventy grand and a new Dodge Ram truck to pull his twenty-one-foot boat.

He was content, so why did Daisy have to show up now and dredge up old memories that were better left long buried? Memories of him and her. Of him and Steven. Of the three of them.

From almost the first day in grade school, he and Steven had both been a little in love with Daisy Brooks. It'd started out innocent enough. Two boys looking across the playground and seeing a little girl with gold hair and big brown eyes. A girl who could play baseball, swing on the monkey bars, and outrun them. The attraction had been pure and naive.

In the third grade, when Daisy had worried about who she'd marry when she grew up, they'd all three decided that she would marry the both of them. They'd all live in the tree house they planned to build, and Jack would get rich and famous driving NASCAR. Steven would become a lawyer like his dad, and Daisy a beauty queen. They'd never heard of polygamy, and neither he nor Steven had thought of Daisy in a sexual way. Not that he and Steven hadn't talked about sex. They just hadn't thought about it in relation to Daisy.

But all that changed the summer going into the eighth grade. Daisy had gone away to work on her aunt's ranch in El Paso, and by the time she'd come back, she'd popped out a pair of perfect breasts. She'd left looking like the girl they'd always known, skinny and flat-chested, but she came back changed. Her legs longer. Her breasts bigger than his hands. Her hips fuller. Even her hair had seemed shinier.

Back then, his body had never needed a reason to get an erection. It was just something that happened to all pubescent boys for no reason at all and was embarrassing as hell. Sometimes it'd just happened when he was doing nothing more exciting than geometry or mowing the lawn.

But that summer, he'd taken one look at Daisy, and his body had reacted to the two very distinct reasons pressed against her T-shirt. His thoughts had dropped right to his crotch, and he'd gotten so hard he'd about passed out from lack of blood to his brain. She'd come over to tell him about her aunt's ranch, and while she was sitting there beside him on his front porch, talking and laughing and filling him in on the horses she'd ridden, he was trying not to stare at her tits. *Yee-freakin'-ha!*

That summer, he and Steven had known without exchanging words that each felt an attraction for her that was no longer innocent. It was there between them. For the first time in their friendship, they had a real big problem. One that wasn't going to be solved with an apology or an extra slug to equal things out.

Later they'd talked about it, about how they felt about Daisy. They decided that neither could have her. In order to remain friends, they promised to keep their hands to themselves. Daisy was off limits. Jack had broken that promise, but Steven had ended up with her.

The front door of the club swung open, and as if his thoughts had conjured her, Daisy stepped outside. She settled the little gold chain of her purse on her shoulder and glanced around as if she couldn't quite recall where she'd parked her car. Her gaze locked with his, and she stared at him across the distance. The light from the front of the club lit half her face and left the rest in variegated shadow.

'Shay's going to throw her bouquet in a minute,' she said as if he'd asked. 'And I don't want to pretend to catch it.'

'You don't want to get married next?'

She shook her head and her hair brushed her shoulders.

He didn't ask why. He didn't want to give a shit. His gaze moved to her full breasts pressing against the red material of her dress and down all those buttons on the side.

'This morning I was thinking about my first day at Lovett Elementary,' she said and took a step toward him. 'Do you remember that?'

He stood and looked back up into her face. 'No.'

Her red lips turned up at the corners. 'You told me my hair bow was stupid.'

And she'd burst into tears.

'My mama made me wear that dumb thing.'

He looked down into her face, with her smooth perfect skin, straight nose, and full red lips. She was as beautiful as she'd always been, maybe more so, and he was doing a really good job of feeling nothing. No anger. No desire. Nothing. 'What are you doing here?'

She took a step closer. If he reached out, he could touch her. Daisy's big eyes stared into his and she said, 'Shay invited me to her reception this morning when I saw her buying a can of Aqua Net at Albertsons.'

That wasn't want he'd meant. 'Why are you in Lovett? Dredging up the past?'

She lowered her gaze to his chest but didn't answer.

'What do you want, Daisy?'

'I want to be friends.'

'No.'

'Why, Jack?' She looked back up, her gaze searching his face. 'We were friends once.'

He laughed. 'Were we?'

She nodded. 'Yes.'

'I think we were more.'

'I know, but I mean friends like in before all that.'

'Before all that sex?'

He wasn't sure, but he thought she blushed. 'Yes.'

'And before you had sex with my best friend?' He folded his arms across his chest. Maybe he did feel something. Maybe he was a little more pissed off than he'd thought, because he said, 'Are you here to start things up again? Continue right where we left off?'

She looked away. 'No.'

'I know I'm not supposed to flatter myself, but are you sure you don't want to tear one off in the back of my car?' She shook her head, but he didn't stop. 'For old time's sake?'

Her gaze returned to his. 'Don't, Jack.' She raised her hand between them and pressed her fingers against his lips. 'Don't say any more.'

The touch of her fingers took him off guard. He caught the scent of perfume, but underneath that, he smelled her. Daisy. She might cover it with perfume and move away for fifteen years, but it hadn't changed. Even at the age of seventeen, when she'd worked at The Wild Coyote Diner; even beneath the scent of fried chicken and barbeque, she'd always smelled like a warm summer breeze.

With her fingers pressed to his mouth, he stared at her for several long heartbeats. Sometimes he'd had to search hard for the scent of her beneath the smell of all that grease, but he'd always found it. Usually in the crook of her neck. He grabbed her wrist and took a step back. 'What do you want from me?'

'I told you. I want to be friends.'

There had to be more. 'We can never be friends.'

'Why?'

He let go of her wrist. 'You married my best friend.'

'You broke up with me.'

No, he'd told her he needed time to think. 'So, to get back at me, you married Steven.' It wasn't a question. Rather a statement of fact.

She shook her head. 'You don't understand. It wasn't like that.'

It was exactly like that. 'You and I were lovers. We were doing it every which way to Sunday. Then you up and married my best friend the same week I buried my parents. What part did I get wrong?' Through the darkness he watched a crease draw her brows together.

'The timing was real bad.'

Bitter laughter clogged his chest. 'Yeah.'

'I'm sorry Jack.' She looked sorry, too.

He didn't care. 'Don't be. It all worked out for the best.'

'I came back because I have to talk to you.'

There was absolutely nothing she had to say that he wanted to hear. 'Save your breath, Daisy,' he said as he walked past her toward the bridge separating the entrance from the parking lot.

'It's the reason I'm here,' she called after him.

'Then you've wasted your time.'

'Don't make me chase you.'

That stopped him and he looked back at her. Her hands were on her hips, and although he couldn't see her features clearly, he could feel her gaze on him, staring him down. It was like looking at the old Daisy.

'I'm trying to be nice about this, but you really don't have a choice. You're going to listen to me; and if you get ugly like you said, I'll become your worst dang nightmare.'

Damn, but she was the old Daisy. All hot temper and feisty belligerence wrapped up in such a soft girly package. He almost smiled. Almost.

'Too late, buttercup,' he said as he turned to go. 'You became my worst nightmare years ago.'

D aisy hung her dress in the closet, pulled the red slip over her head, and put on her short nightgown. Then she washed her face. It was a little after ten, and her mother was already asleep.

She sat on the edge of her bed and dialed her son in Seattle. It was only eight in Washington; she was sure that Nathan was still up.

She was right. 'Hey, sugar muffin,' she said after Nathan picked up on the fourth ring.

'Mom.'

Well, it wasn't a great beginning to their conversation, but it was great to hear his voice. 'How are things?'

'Gay.'

'I miss you.'

'Then come home.'

'I will a week from Sunday.'

'Mom, I do *not* want to stay here for a week.'

She'd had this same conversation with him before she'd

even left. Junie and Oliver were not his favorite relatives. They weren't horrible, just boring. Especially to a fifteen-year-old boy. 'It can't be that bad.'

'How do you know? Have you ever lived with Aunt Junie and Uncle Know-it-Olly.'

'Nathan, they'll hear you!' Unfortunately Oliver was one of those men who liked to impress people with his limited knowledge on every subject known to man. Steven had started calling him Know-it-Olly years ago.

'No, they won't. They're not even here. They left me to baby-sit Michael Ann and Richie.'

Daisy wedged the phone between her jaw and shoulder. 'Michael Ann is only a year younger than you.'

'I know. And she's a pain in the butt. She follows me around asking me if I get food stuck in my lip ring.'

Daisy had asked him that too and thought it was a fair question. 'I think she has a crush on you.'

'Oh my *God*! That is so gross, Mom,' he said, his voice cracking with indignation. 'How can you say that? She's my cousin.'

'Haven't you ever heard of kissing cousins?' Daisy teased him.

'Yuck. She still picks her nose!'

Daisy laughed and the conversation turned to school. There was only five more days left, then he would be out for the summer. He'd just turned fifteen in December, and since about first grade, he'd been counting the days until he could take driver's education. He had one more year to go, but he already had his car picked out. For this week anyway.

'I'm gonna get a Nova Super Sport. A four-on-four, too. None of that wussy three-speed crap. Why bother if you can't burn 'em off? It'll be fat.' She didn't even pretend to know what he was talking about. He'd been born car crazy. No way around it. She figured it was in his DNA. Plus, chances were good that he'd been conceived in the back of a Chevy. Nathan had been doomed to be a gear head.

'What color?' she asked, not in the least concerned that he would ever actually drive a Nova SS and burn 'em off. Nathan didn't have a job.

'Yellow with a black top.'

'Like a bumblebee?'

There was a long pause before he said, 'White with a black top.'

They talked for a few more minutes about the weather and where he might want to go on vacation when she got back. He'd just seen a teen skin-flick and thought Fort Lauderdale would be good. Or Hawaii.

By the time she hung up the telephone, they'd pretty much decided on Disney World, although with Nathan that could change by the next time she talked to him. She squirted almond-scented lotion into her hands and rubbed it up her arms. A thin white strip of skin barely marked her left finger where her wedding ring had been for fifteen years. She'd slipped the two-carat solitaire into the inside breast pocket of Steven's burial suit. She thought it appropriate that it should rest above his heart.

As she rubbed the lotion into her hands, she glanced about the room where she was staying. It was her old bedroom, but nothing remained except the bed itself. Framed posters of windmills, the Alamo, and the River Walk in San Antonio hung on the walls, replacing her certificates from local photography contests she'd entered, her cheerleading plaques, and a poster of Rob Lowe she'd pinned up during his *St Elmo's Fire* days.

She stood and moved to the closet and opened the door. The closet was empty except for a few old prom dresses, a pair of her old red cowboy boots with white heart inserts, and a big box with her name written across it in black. She scooted the box across the floor to the bed, then sat looking at it for several long moments. She knew what she would find in there. Bits and pieces of her life, the memories she'd long ago shoved in a box and taped shut. Earlier at the reception, she'd pushed the memories from her head, now here she sat staring at them. Did she really want to look into her past?

No, not really.

She tore off the tape and opened the box.

A dried wrist corsage, her graduation tassel, and a few name tags that said HI MY NAME IS DAISY, sat on top. She couldn't recall why she'd kept the name tags, but she recognized the corsage. She touched the dry rosebuds that had once been pink and white but were now a faded yellow. She brought the dried corsage to her nose and breathed deep. It smelled of dust and of old memories. She set it next to her on her bed, then pulled out her baby blanket and christening gown. A heart-shaped box with the necklace her grandfather on her daddy's side had given her was next, followed by her school annuals. She reached for her tenth-grade yearbook and opened it. She flipped through the pages and paused on a group photograph of the teaching staff standing in front of the school. She'd taken the photo her first year of photography class, before she'd learned much about composition and lighting.

She turned to the pictures of her and Sylvia and the rest of the cheerleading squad. The picture had been taken of them in their gold-and-blue uniforms doing Herkie, toe-touch jumps, and handsprings. That was the year she'd cut her hair short like Princess Diana. While Diana had looked great, Daisy had looked like a boy in a short pleated skirt.

She flipped to her class picture and cringed. Her big smile was filled with braces, and she had raccoon eyes from all the makeup she'd spooned on her face.

She turned a few pages and her finger moved along the row of photos and stopped on Steven. She touched the smooth paper and smiled. He'd always been such a handsome all-American boy, with his wavy blond hair, smiling brown eyes, and a Texas grin as if he hadn't a care in the world. He'd played football and basketball and been involved in student government, going on to be class president his senior year.

Daisy thumbed a few more pages and looked at Jack's yearbook photo. Unlike Steven, Jack never grinned and smiled as if he didn't have a care in the world. It wasn't that he was more serious than Steven, it was just that he didn't waste energy laughing and smiling when he didn't feel like it.

During that school year, he'd turned sixteen, a year older than Nathan was now. The two had the same dark coloring in hair and skin tone, and perhaps their noses were similar. She looked for other resemblances and found none.

That was also the year Jack had quit football because his father needed him after school in the garage. Up until his sophomore year, Jack had always been the first string quarterback. When he quit, Steven took over the position. As far as she recalled, he'd never had any hard feelings toward Steven, only a sadness that he could no longer play ball.

That was also the year she'd started to fall in love with

him. Oh, she'd always loved Jack in the same way she'd loved Steven, but it seemed that one moment she'd been looking at him as she always had, and in the next everything changed.

On that particular day, he'd been waiting for Steven to finish football practice, sitting on the tailgate of his daddy's old truck. She'd stayed after school to make posters for the homecoming dance and later saw him in the parking lot, sitting and watching instead of playing.

Perhaps it had been a trick of the light, an early fall sunset casting him in gold. She didn't know, but she'd noticed more than his usual good looks. More than his lashes that were longer than hers. More than the slight stubble on his jaw. More than his arms folded across his chest and the defined balls of his biceps and the hard cord of muscle of his forearms. Jack did not lift weights. He lifted car engines.

'Hey there,' he said, and patted the tailgate next to him.

'What are you doing?' she asked as she sat. She placed her school books in her lap and looked out over the field as the Lovett Mustangs broke practice and the players jogged toward the locker room.

'Waiting for Steven.'

'Do you miss playing, Jack?'

'Nah, but I miss the pretty girls.' It was of course true that the football players did get the prettiest girls. But it wasn't true that just because he no longer played, he didn't get his share.

'Now you have to settle for the ugly ones,' she teased and looked at him out of the corner of her eye.

'Daisy, don't you know there aren't any truly ugly girls in Texas?'

He was so full of it. 'Where'd you hear that?'

He shrugged. 'It's just a fact. Like the Alamo and the Rio Grande, is all.' He took her hand and brushed his thumb over her knuckles as he studied her fingers. 'You'll still be seen with me, though, won't you?'

She turned her head and gazed more fully at him, all prepared with a flip answer, but he glanced up and something in his green eyes stopped her. For about half a second, she saw something, something in the way he looked back at her, something that made her think the answer was important to him. As if he wasn't sure. She got a surprising glimpse inside of Jack that she'd never seen before. Maybe things didn't bounce off him like he was Superman. Maybe he felt things like everybody else. Maybe more.

Then he flashed her a smile and it was gone.

'Of course, Jack,' she said. 'I'll always be seen with you.'

'I knew I could count on you, buttercup.' For the first time, his voice slid inside her chest and warmed her up with hot tingles. It was all so incredible and fantastic and left her stunned. And it absolutely could not happen. She couldn't fall in love with Jack. He was a friend, and she didn't want to lose him. But even if he wasn't her friend, she'd be an idiot to let it happen.

He squeezed her hand and stood. 'Do you need a ride home?'

She looked up at him, standing in front of her with his hands shoved in the front pockets of his Levi's, and nodded. Jack Parrish had many wonderful qualities. Being faithful to one girl wasn't one of them. He'd shatter her heart like glass. If that happened, they couldn't be friends anymore. And she'd miss him terribly.

By the time Steven walked out of the boys' locker room with his wet hair slicked back, she'd convinced herself that she wasn't falling in love with Jack. He'd made her momentarily confused. Like when they'd been kids and would ride the merry-go-round too long. Jack used to spin it so fast that for a while after she couldn't think or see straight.

But she was over it now. Thinking straight once again. Thank God. 'Are y'all going somewhere?' she asked.

'We're driving over to Chandler,' Jack answered, referring to a town the size of Lovett and about fifty miles to the west.

'Why?'

'There's a '69 Camaro Z–28 I want to look at.'

'A '69?' She'd never understood Jack's fascination with old cars. Or as he called them, 'classics.' She preferred new cars with upholstery that didn't snag her nylons. With Jack, it was more than just a case of not having money for a new car. Although he certainly didn't. In that respect, she and Jack had a lot more in common than either did with Steven. Steven's father was a lawyer and his family had money. His biggest responsibility was to maintain his grades. By contrast, her mother was a waitress who depended on survivor benefits from the government, and Jack's family had a garage that never seemed to bring in a lot of money. She and Lily were responsible for keeping the house clean and starting supper, while Jack helped out in the family business. 'Does the car run?' she asked.

'Not yet.'

Exactly.

'Hey, Daisy,' Steven said as he approached. 'What are you doing at school so late?'

'Making homecoming posters. Are you going to the homecoming dance?'

'Yeah, I'm thinking about asking Marilee Donahue. Do you think she'll go with me?' Steven smiled and there wasn't a doubt that Marilee would say yes.

She shrugged. 'Are you going, Jack?' she asked, although she was fairly sure she knew the answer.

'Nope. You know I only put on a suit when my mom forces me to for Sunday School and funerals.' He shut the tailgate and walked to the driver's side. 'And I hate to dance.'

Daisy suspected that it wasn't so much that Jack hated to dance as much as he just didn't know how to dance. And he'd always been the kind of person that if he didn't do something well, he didn't do it at all. 'You could just wear a nice shirt and tie,' she told him, but for some reason, the fact that Jack wasn't taking a girl to the school dance warmed her heart more than it should have, given that she was over her earlier confusion.

'Not a chance.' The three of them got into the old truck and Jack fired it up.

'Have you been asked yet?' Jack asked her as he drove from the parking lot with her sitting between them like always.

'Yes.' They were so weird about who she dated she didn't want to say.

'Who?' Steven asked.

She looked straight ahead at the dashboard and the road beyond.

Steven hit her with his elbow. 'Come on, Daisy Lee. Who asked you?'

'Matt Flegel.'

'You're going with Bug?'

'He doesn't like to be called that anymore.'

Jack looked at Steven over the top of her head.

'What's wrong with Bug . . . I mean Matt?' She held up a hand before either could answer. 'Forget I asked. I don't care what y'all think. I like Matt.'

'He gets around a lot.'

'He's the wrong kind of boy for you,' Jack added.

She folded her arms and was silent the rest of the way home. The pair of them were serial daters, and that was putting it nicely. She wasn't about to listen to their opinion, and if there ever was a 'wrong kind of boy' for her or any girl, it was Jack. Which made her doubly glad she wasn't really falling in love with him.

She spent the rest of her sophomore year dating boys that neither Steven nor Jack approved of, but she didn't care. Like most girls her age, she learned how to make out and drive boys crazy. And more important, she learned where to stop before things went too far. As a result, she developed a reputation for being a tease. Which she didn't think was fair at all. Boys kissed her. She kissed them back. As far as she could tell, a girl was either a prude, which meant she didn't kiss at all. A tease, meaning she kissed and perhaps a bit more, or was a slut. And everyone knew what that meant.

That summer, she'd let Erik Marks touch her breast on the outside of her T-shirt. Jack and Steven heard about it and made a special trip over to her house to talk to her. She'd gotten mad and slammed the front door in their faces.

The hypocrites.

She made varsity cheerleader her junior year. Her hair

had grown out to her shoulders and she got a spiral perm. Steven was still in football and basketball, and of course, student government. Jack was racing his Camaro on the flat Texas roads, and she was still telling herself that she wasn't attracted to him. She told herself that she loved him but she wasn't in love with him, and that her heart didn't pinch when he drove by with his arm around some girl. He was her friend, just as he'd always been. Nothing more. And she wouldn't allow herself to feel anything more either.

All that changed a few weeks before Christmas her senior year when she got asked to the Christmas prom by J. T. Sanders. J. T. was gorgeous and drove a new Jeep Wrangler. Black. Daisy worked nights at the Wild Coyote Diner, and she'd managed to save enough money to buy the perfect dress. White satin. Sleeveless with tiny rhinestones on the tight fitting bodice and tulle skirt. It was the most beautiful thing she'd ever owned. The night before the dance, she picked up J.T.'s boutonniere on her dinner break. When she got home, he called and canceled. He said his grandmother died and that he had to go to her funeral in Amarillo. Everyone knew that he'd actually started dating another girl the week before. Daisy had been dumped. Flat.

And everyone knew it.

The Saturday of the prom, Daisy worked the lunch shift at the Wild Coyote. She kept it together and acted like she wasn't humiliated. She pretended she wasn't sad or hurt. She joked with her co-workers about J. T. being a loser anyway.

No one bought it. Getting dumped the night before the prom with some lame-o excuse was the worst thing that could ever happen to any girl.

And everyone knew it.

After her shift, she went home and locked herself in her room. With her dress hanging on her closet door, she threw herself on her bed and had a nice long cry. At four, her mother stuck her head in the room and asked if she wanted some mint chocolate chip ice cream. She didn't. Lily made her a cowboy pie sandwich, but she couldn't eat it.

At five-thirty Jack knocked on her bedroom door, but she wouldn't let him in. Her face was splotchy and her eyes puffy, and she didn't want him to see her that way.

'Daisy Lee,' he called through the door. 'Come out of there.'

She sat up on her bed and pulled a Kleenex from the box. 'Go away, Jack.'

'Open up.'

'No.' She blew her nose.

'I have something for you.'

She stared at the door. 'What?'

'I can't tell you. I have to show you.'

'I look really bad.'

'I don't care.'

Well *she* did. She slipped from the bed and opened the door a crack. She stuck her hand out. 'What is it?' He didn't answer and she was forced to peer out the crack. Jack stood in the hall, the light from her sister's bedroom shining on him like a dark angel or at the very least a choirboy. He wore his navy blue Sunday suit, and a cream-colored shirt. A red tie hung loose around his neck. 'What's going on, Jack? Did you go to a funeral?'

He laughed and brought his hand out from behind his back. He laid a wrist corsage of white and pink roses in her palm. 'Will you go to the prom with me?'

'You hate school dances,' she said through the crack.

'I know.'

She brought the corsage to her nose and breathed deep. Her nose was clogged so it wasn't that deep. She bit her bottom lip to keep it from trembling. And as she looked at him, standing in the hall of her house, wearing a suit he hated and asking her to a dance he loathed, she fell helplessly in love with Jack Parrish. It expanded her heart and flooded her chest and scared her to death. All those years of fighting it faded away to nothing.

She'd fallen in love with Jack and there hadn't been anything she could do about it.

That night Jack kissed her for the first time. Or rather, she'd kissed him. During the dance, while she'd been falling in love for the first time in her life, he treated her as he always had, as a friend. While he made her whole body feel hot and alive, he'd stayed cool. It had all been wonderful and awful, and after the prom, when he walked her to her front door, she wrapped her arms around his neck and kissed him.

At first he stood with his hands to his side. Then he grasped her shoulders through her coat and pushed her away, angry.

'What are you doing?'

'Kiss me, Jack.' If he rejected her, she was sure she'd just die right there. On the porch.

His grip tightened and he brought her forward and pressed his warm lips to her forehead.

'No, don't treat me like a friend.' She swallowed hard past the ache in her chest. 'Please,' she whispered as she looked up at him. 'I want you to kiss me like you do other girls. I want you to touch me like you do other girls, too.'

He pulled back and his green gaze slid to her mouth. 'Don't tease me, Daisy. I don't like it.'

'I'm not teasing you.' She ran her hand across the shoulder of his jacket to the side of his neck. 'Please, Jack.'

Then as if he didn't want to kiss her, but he couldn't fight it any longer, he slowly lowered his mouth to hers. This time the touch of his lips stole her breath. She tilted her head back and sank into his chest. Until that moment, she'd thought she knew what it was like to kiss a boy. Jack showed her she hadn't a clue. The kiss was hot and wet and filled with so much hunger that it changed her forever.

Even now, after all these years, Daisy remembered standing on her mother's porch as Jack turned her world inside out. She'd clung to him as he'd fed her those liquid kisses that had made her breasts ache and her body tremble. His hands had never moved from her shoulders, but he'd made her crave his touch. She'd wanted him to touch her all over. Instead he'd walked away, leaving her stunned and wanting more.

5

The next day, Daisy called Jack but he didn't pick up. The longer she put off telling him about Nathan, the harder it was going to get. She knew that, having already put if off for fifteen years. But what she hadn't realized before she'd arrived was that the longer she put it off, the more memories of her life in this town would drag her back into the past. Before she'd arrived, the plan had been to tell Jack, give him Steven's letter, and deal with the fallout: if not easy, at least straightforward. Now, it didn't seem real straightforward either. But it had to be done. She was leaving in seven days.

Before noon, she tried Jack's number two more times, but he didn't answer. She figured he was probably not answering on purpose. She went to church with her mother, and afterward, they had an early dinner with Lily and Pippen. Phillip 'Pippen' Darlington was two and had a blond mullet because his mother couldn't bear to cut the curls at the nape of his neck. He had huge blue eyes like Lily, and he loved Thomas the Tank Engine. He also loved wearing his faux coonskin cap and shouting NO! loud enough to be heard into the next county He hated food with texture, spiders, and his Velcro Barney sneakers.

Daisy looked at him sitting in his high chair at her mother's dinner table and tried not to frown as he poured grape Kool-Aid from his Tommy Tippy cup into his baked potato. Daisy's mother and Lily sat across the table from her and didn't seem to mind that Pippen was making a disgusting mess.

'He's a rat bastard!' Lily was telling her, referring, of course, to her soon to be ex-husband, The Rat Bastard Ronald Darlington. 'A few months before he ran off with his jailbait girlfriend, he took all the money out of our accounts and put it somewhere.'

Louella nodded her head sadly. 'Probably in Mexico.' Growing up, if either had uttered the word 'bastard' at the dinner table, they'd have been sent from the room.

'What is your attorney doing about that?' Daisy asked

'There isn't a lot he can do. We can prove the money was in the account, but not where it went. The judge can order him to give me half, but that doesn't mean he will. And for years, Ronnie was paid under the table in order to avoid paying the IRS, so it looks like he only makes twenty thousand a year instead of seventy-five.' Lily sliced a piece of meat with a vengeance. Even though they were sisters and had grown up together, they weren't very close. Growing up, they'd mostly fought or ignored each other. Lily had been in middle school when Daisy had moved away, and they'd never really maintained a relationship after that. Losing Steven had made her realize how important her family was to her. She needed to work on her relationship with her sister.

'He said that if I tell the IRS about it,' Lily continued, 'he'll fight for custody of Pippen. What can I do?'

When both her mother and Lily stared at her, Daisy realized it wasn't a rhetorical question. There were dark circles under Lily's eyes as if she hadn't had a good night's sleep in a long time. Her blond hair was cut short and framed her pretty face with soft curls, but at the moment, she looked anything but soft. No, she looked scared as hell. 'You're asking me? How should I know?'

'Darren Monroe is a lawyer,' her mother provided.

'Steven's father is retired and living in Arizona. And besides, he was a criminal defense attorney; Steven designed computer software programs. I know nothing about the family courts.' She recognized the fear in Lily's blue eyes. It was the fear of being suddenly alone with the responsibility of raising a child. But unlike Daisy, Lily wasn't financially secure, nor did she have a career to fall back on. Not that Daisy's career had ever provided a huge income, but she was a good photographer and had connections. If she had to support herself and Nathan on her income alone, she could. Lily had been a stay-home wife and a mom, which was admirable but weren't marketable skills. She was terrified. 'I'll try to think up something,' Daisy said, although she had troubles of her own and was only here for a week now.

Lily smiled, 'Thanks, Daisy.'

'I ran into Darma Joe Henderson, the other day,' her mother said as she dug into her okra, Lily's worries apparently solved for the moment. 'You girls remember Darma Joe. She used to work at the Trusty Hardware across from the Wild Coyote. Her son Buck had that car accident a few years back, and they had to amputate his leg below the knee. Well, he has a daughter who sings with the church choir. You girls might have noticed her today.' Louella paused to take a bite before launching into, 'She kinda looks like Buck, bless her heart, but she has such a nice voice and a kind personality. She was dating the boy . . . oh, what was his name? I think it started with a G. George or Geoff or something like that. Anyway . . .'

Daisy slid her gaze from her mother to her sister. Lily's eyes were starting to glaze over and her head was drifting back. Things really hadn't changed very much since she'd been gone. She knew it would be useless to ask her mother to get to the point, because she already knew there wasn't a point and there never was going to be one.

Daisy started to laugh. Lily's eyes refocused and she looked at Daisy. She laughed too. Pippen threw his coonskin cap on the floor and broke in giggles as if he knew the joke. He was only two, but he'd been around his grandmother enough that perhaps he did.

Louella looked up from her plate. 'What are you girls laughing about?'

'That Darma Joe's granddaughter looks like Buck,' Lily lied through a grin. 'Bless her heart.'

'It's unfortunate.' Louella frowned. They continued to laugh and she shook her head. 'Well, y'all have come off your spools and taken poor Pippen with you.'

After dinner, Daisy got up her nerve for the fourth time that day and called Jack; he didn't pick up, but she left him a message this time: 'It's Daisy. I'm not going anywhere until you talk to me.'

He didn't return the call, of course, so she phoned him

the next day at work. She and Penny Kribs chatted about old times and she thanked her for sending flowers to Steven's funeral. Then she asked for Jack. 'Don't tell him it's me on the line,' she said. 'I want to surprise him.'

'He could use a good surprise,' Penny said. 'He's in a nasty mood.'

Great. Daisy was put on hold and after listening to about half of 'The Night the Lights Went Out in Georgia,' Jack came on the line.

'This is Jack Parrish,' he said.

'Hi, Jack.' He didn't respond, but he didn't slam the phone down either. 'Surprise, it's me, Daisy.'

'Don't hassle me at work, Daisy Lee,' he finally responded, dragging out those vowels for all they were worth. Yep, definitely in a nasty mood.

'Don't make me. Meet me later.'

'Can't. I'm flying out for Tallahassee this afternoon.'

'When will you be back?'

He didn't answer and she was forced to blackmail him. 'If you don't tell me, I'll just call back every day. All day.' That didn't prompt a response either. 'And night.'

'That's harassment.'

'True, but filing charges is such a pain.' She didn't believe for a minute that he'd actually have her charged for harassment. 'Let's meet the day you get back.'

'Can't. It's Lacy Dawn's birthday.'

'Lacy Dawn? Stripper or hooker?'

'Neither.'

'It sounds like a stage name.'

'Probably a girl named Daisy Brooks shouldn't cast stones.'

He had a point. 'Meet me after the party.'

'No can do. Those dancing bears take it out of me.'

'Jack—'

'Goodbye.'

The dial tone filled Daisy's ear as she thought about what to do next. *Dancing bears?* What was Jack into these days? 'Hey, Ma,' she called from the kitchen into the living room. And over the sound of sirens coming from the television she asked, 'Is there some place in town that has dancing bears?'

'Dancing bears?' The sirens quieted, then her mother stuck her head into the kitchen. 'The only place I know is Showtime.'

'Is that a strip club?'

'No, it's a pizza place, but it also does little kids' birthday parties. Lily had Pippen's party there last year. He wasn't quite old enough to understand that those big scary bears weren't going to hurt him. He screamed the paint off the walls. Juanita Sanchez was there with her grandson, Hermie. You remember Juanita, don't you? She lived down the road in that pink stucco, bless her heart. One day . . .'

Daisy didn't ask why living in a pink stucco deserved a 'bless her heart,' but she wasn't about to ask. She called information and came up with a plan. She got the number for Showtime, and dialed it. After getting transferred around by teenagers who didn't know anything, she finally got put through to the party planner. 'Hello,' Daisy began, 'I've lost my invitation to the birthday party of a little girl named Lacy Dawn. I'm not sure of her last name, but if we miss that party, my daughter will be so upset. Could you please tell me what time it starts?'

The party planner sounded older than the teens working there, and it took her about thirty seconds to get back with the answer. 'I don't have a Lacy Dawn, but I do have a Lacy Parrish.'

'That's it.'

'Her mother booked a front table from six to seven-thirty.'

'On Saturday?'

'No. Wednesday.'

'Oh my gosh. I'm so glad I called. Thank you.' So, Lacy Dawn was Lacy Parrish. Obviously Jack's niece, and he'd be back in town Wednesday.

She dialed Lily and didn't feel the least guilty for what she planned to do next. She'd warned Jack that she'd become his worst nightmare. At the time she'd been mostly bluffing. She wasn't bluffing now, and she wasn't going away. She didn't plan to tell him about Nathan at his niece's birthday party, but he needed to know that he wasn't going to get any peace until he agreed to meet with her.

When Lily picked up, she asked if she and Pippen would go with her to Showtime Wednesday night. Her sister wanted to know why, and she explained the situation.

'This will be good,' Lily said. 'Not only will Pippen be your cover, but I went to school with Billy and Rhonda. Rhonda's sister, Patty Valencia, was your age.'

'Was she a real pretty Hispanic girl with long black hair?'

'Yeah, they're both real pretty. Although, I hear Rhonda and Billy have been cranking out the kids, so she may look a little crazy these days.'

'Probably.' Daisy glanced at her mother's calendar of Texas landscapes. 'Are you sure you want to do this with me? Mom told me Pippen screamed the paint from the walls last time.'

'He doesn't do that anymore.' She turned her mouth from the phone and said, 'Pippen, you're a big boy now. Aren't you Momma's sweet baby?'

'No!'

Great. Daisy hung up and spent the rest of the afternoon helping her mother pull weeds in her flower gardens. She brought out her Nikon and knelt amid the pink flamingos, resting her elbow on her knee to steady the camera. She positioned herself toward Louella's shadow so that the sunlight hit one side of her face. She wished she'd loaded the camera with black-and-white film so that the vibrant pink of the flamingos wouldn't take on more importance than her mother. Or if she'd brought her Fuji digital, she could have loaded it on her computer once she got back home and made the image real high-impact.

She moved to her stomach and rested the weight of the camera equally on both elbows. She shot up at her mother, catching Annie Oakley in the background.

'Daisy Lee,' her mother said through a frown, 'don't take a picture up my nose.'

She sighed and sat up. It had been a while since she'd felt the urge to bring out her cameras and get back into something she used to love. She'd had to quit working for Ryan Kent, an artistic photographer in Seattle, in order to take care of Steven.

She'd gotten into photography in high school, and when Nathan had turned four, she'd signed up for classes at the University of Washington. After four years, she'd received her BA and began interning with top photographers in the area. Her photographs hung in some studios and galleries around town. And a photograph she'd taken of a man standing on top of a crushed vehicle after the earthquake in two-thousand and one, had been featured in a local magazine.

She'd thought that once things settled, she'd go back to work for Ryan, but lately she'd been thinking of opening her own studio. One of the most successful photographers she'd ever worked for had once told her that the key to success was finding a visible location and staying there for at least five years. Talent was important, but visibility was most important when starting out.

The more she thought about it, the more she thought that's exactly what she'd do. Once she put the past behind her, she'd be free to start over completely. Maybe she'd sell her house. Upon Steven's death, the home owner's insurance had paid off the mortgage. Maybe she'd sell it, and she and Nathan could move into a loft in Belltown.

She shrugged and focused her lens on an orange-and-yellow rose. 'I'm thinking of selling my house once I get back,' she told her mother as she snapped the picture.

'Don't get ahead of yourself,' her mother warned. 'Colleen Forbus sold her house soon after her husband, Wyatt, took his journey to heaven, and she's been sorry ever since.'

Maybe she could wait a few more months just to be sure. She'd find out how Nathan felt about it first, of course. But lately she'd started to feel as if too much of her past was tied to that house. She didn't have to decide today. It was something to think about. Something to put at the bottom of her mental to-do list.

She placed her elbow on her knees and adjusted the aperture to bring the roses and flamingos behind Louella's head into focus, giving the photograph a nice rich texture and depth of field. She snapped the photo and thought how nice it would be if everything in her life could be made clear by the turn of a focus ring.

6

Jack was late. He'd waited until that morning to call Rhonda and ask what to get Lacy for her birthday. Rhonda told him she wanted something called a Kitty Magic. She told him to make sure it was a *Kitty Magic* and not a Fur Real Friends. According to Rhonda the latter didn't nurse her babies. Then she wished him luck finding it.

He'd called around to the few stores in Lovett that carried toys, and ended up driving into Amarillo. He'd spent the afternoon looking for the damned thing, and finally found it in one of the last stores he'd walked into.

He'd stood in the aisle, reading the back of the box, making sure he had the right one, and feeling the back of his skull tighten. The pink Mommy Kitty had long fur and two fluffy kittens. The three of them had toys and matching bows for their heads and god-awful heart-shaped sunglasses.

He'd kept reading and uttered, 'For the love of Christ.'

According to the box the mother cat purred and said, 'I love you' and made nursing sounds when one of the kittens was stuck to her side.

What the hell was a nursing sound? he'd wondered.

Jack had the present wrapped in bright pink paper with fairies on it. A big iridescent pink bow about the size of his head was taped on top. The bow was beyond frilly, but Billy's girls loved that kind of crap.

The kind of girl stuff that had been completely foreign to him and his brother growing up. They'd played with cars and BB guns and had set their army men on fire. They'd been hell on wheels, but as soon as Billy's first girl had been born, Billy had taken to baby dolls, Barbie sneakers, and pink tutus like a duck to water. He made it all look easy and natural while Jack was left watching and wondering where Billy's paternal instincts had come from. Jack didn't have any. At least he didn't think he did. Although he was learning fast, he didn't know very much about little girls. Maybe because until Amy Lynn, he'd never been around little girls. Except Daisy, and if she'd played with dolls, and dressed up like a fairy princess as Billy's girls did, she'd done it with her friends that were girls. Not with him and Steven.

He pulled open the door to Showtime and stepped inside. He hadn't seen Daisy for four days. Hopefully she'd given up on her plan to pin him down and make him relive the past. Hopefully she'd left town.

The inside of Showtime was a collision of bright color and sound – of flashing arcade games directly at eye level, and those big plastic tubes that kids climbed through overhead. Of bells and sirens and screaming children. Jack had been here once before, on Amy Lynn's birthday, and he wondered how anyone worked here without going insane.

He moved to the dining room and discovered that it was relatively quiet – for now. He knew that would all change once the show started. He found his brother and Rhonda and the girls sitting at a round table near the stage.

And Daisy.

About ten feet from the table, he stopped in his tracks. Daisy Monroe had managed to get herself invited to his niece's party.

She'd tracked him down. She'd told him she'd become his worst nightmare. It hadn't been an idle threat. His anger rose but he pushed it back. Controlled it for now. She didn't belong here. With his family.

His gaze moved to the woman sitting next to Daisy. He recognized Lily, and he supposed the kid with the mullet belonged to one of them. The boy had some sort of pudding on his face like someone had been feeding him with a slingshot. He wondered if the kid belonged to Daisy and Steven.

'Uncle Jack!' five-year-old Amy Lynn yelled. She jumped up from her chair and ran toward him. The birthday girl, three-year-old Lacy ran toward him too. Lacy tended to watch her feet while she ran, and he picked her up with his free arm to keep her from head-butting him in the nuts. 'Hey there,' he said. 'Someone feels like she's three years old today.'

'Me,' she said and held up three fingers.

'I'm still five,' Amy Lynn told him and wrapped her arms around his leg.

As he approached the table with Amy Lynn on his leg and Lacy in one arm, Billy glanced up from the dark-haired baby on his knee and smiled. 'Hey, Jack, look who's in town.'

Daisy looked at him, her brown eyes sparkling. She'd pulled her smooth hair back in a ponytail and her full lips were a soft shiny pink. She wore a tight green tank top with the name Ralph Lauren in black across her breasts.

'You didn't tell Billy I was back in town,' she scolded, as a smile curved that mouth of hers.

Jack stood Lacy in her chair. His brother didn't know his history with Daisy. Billy'd been too young, and it wasn't something that Jack had ever wanted to talk about. Not even with his brother. Billy probably remembered her, though. Growing up, she'd been over at their house a lot. He probably thought they were still friends. Probably thought Jack'd be slaphappy to see her. 'It must have escaped my mind,' he said as Amy Lynn let go of him and took her seat.

Daisy laughed, very amused with herself, and that bumped up his anger a notch. 'You remember my sister Lily?' she asked.

'Of course. How are you?'

Lily came out from behind the table and gave him a big hug as he set the present on the table. 'I've been better.' She looked a lot like Daisy, only with blue eyes. A lot like she had growing up, only for some reason she looked terminally pissed off now.

'How're you, Jack?'

He looked over her head at Daisy. 'I've been better.'

'This is Lily's son Pippen.'

So, the kid belonged to Lily. For some reason, he was relieved that the boy with the mullet wasn't Daisy and Steven's. But he couldn't begin to understand why he should care.

Lily stepped back and shook her head. 'You look as good as you always did.'

'Thanks, Lily. You do too,' he said, and meant it. 'Hey, Rhonda' – his sister-in-law had *I haven't had sleep in five years* smudges under her dark brown eyes – 'You okay, girl? Billy tells me you had a hard night.'

'I was up most of it with Tanya. She has an earache, but we got a bottle of the pink medicine today, so she's feeling better.'

Billy pulled the baby's sock up her pudgy leg. 'We yanked the 'Vette engine while you were gone today.'

He pulled out a chair between Lacy and Rhonda and across from Daisy and Lily. 'Did you get a look at the clutch?'

'You were right,' Billy said. 'It needs to be completely replaced.'

'I found one in Reno,' he told his brother.

'How was Tallahassee?' Daisy asked him.

'When were you in Tallahassee?' Billy wanted to know.

'Last year.'

Daisy's eyes rounded and her mouth fell open. 'You lied to me.'

He smiled as he leaned forward and poured himself a Dr Pepper from a pitcher. She gave him that *grow up* glare like she had the other night, then she turned to his brother.

'Do you mind if I hold Tanya?'

'Not at all.' Billy handed her over the baby, and Daisy stood Tanya in her lap. Jack half expected the six-month-old to start screaming, instead she laughed and pinched Daisy's cheek.

'Look, Pippen,' Daisy said to the kid in the high chair beside her. 'Isn't Tanya just a sweet little love muffin?'

'No!'

'Can I open my pez-ent from Uncle Jack?' Lacy asked in her tiny three-year-old voice.

'It's okay with me if it's okay with your Uncle Jack,' Rhonda answered.

'Have at it kid,' he said, although he would have preferred that Daisy wasn't sitting across the table when that stupid cat present was opened. Why he should give a shit, though, he didn't know that either.

Lacy tore off the bow and chucked it behind her shoulder. She ripped the paper and gasped as she tossed the shredded remains on the floor. 'Kitty Magic! My fav-rut thing in the world!'

'Hey, that's what you said this morning when you got your Barbie Power Wheels,' Billy reminded her.

Lily leaned across the table, and she and Rhonda chatted about what they'd been doing since high school. While Lacy and Amy Lynn took the cat and her kittens out of the box, the two women talked about kids and their lives; and when Lily said something about 'Ronnie the Rat Bastard,' Jack took it to mean she was getting a divorce. It also explained why she looked terminally pissed.

He took a long drink of his Dr Pepper and sucked an ice cube into his mouth. He glanced across the table at Daisy and Tanya and Pippen. Tanya still stood in Daisy's lap, blowing raspberries. The little boy laughed and Daisy laughed, too. His gaze moved to her hands and her blood-red fingernails. A thin silver bracelet circled her slim wrist and a tiny heart rested against her pulse. The bracelet sparkled in the light, and as if she felt his gaze on her, she looked at him over the top of Tanya's dark head. Her smile fell and her brows drew together slightly. She stared at him through brown eyes that he used to think looked like melted chocolate. But that had been when he'd been ten years old and thought chocolate was the best thing in the world. Then he'd gotten older and discovered something better. Something darker and richer in those eyes. A knot twisted low in his belly. He wouldn't call it desire, but it wasn't disinterest either.

Billy plugged the mother cat with batteries and set it on the table. Lacy stood in her chair again, and Jack turned his attention to his niece. She stuck the kittens on the mother's side, and damn if it didn't make weird sucking sounds.

'It's a . . . well it's a nursing kitty.' Daisy looked up from the pink Persian and laughter lit up her eyes. 'Jack, why that's so sweet.'

'Are those nipples on that thing?' Billy wanted to know.

'It looks like she has hearts instead of nipples,' Jack told him.

'How come?' Amy Lynn wanted to know. They had a real mother cat at home, and she knew mommy cats didn't have hearts there.

Neither Billy nor Jack could think of an answer. Daisy looked at Amy Lynn and said, 'Because hearts are cuter than nipples.'

If they'd been alone, Jack might have told her exactly why she was wrong about that. Instead, he bit his ice cube in half and pushed it to one cheek.

'And they got some sunglasses, Lacy,' Amy Lynn pointed out.

The center curtains on the stage parted and three big mechanical bears sprung to life, dancing and pretending to play instruments. A song about a happy frog filled the dining room, and Lacy clapped her hands.

Lily's kid let out a scream at the top of his lungs. Daisy

handed Tanya back to Billy and she took the little boy from the high chair. She said something to Lily and walked from the room with the boy still screaming. Jack's gaze slid down the back of her tank top to her behind in those jean shorts.

'Did you see "Monster Garage" the other night?' Billy asked over the music.

While Jack occasionally watched the show, Billy was a fanatic. 'No, I missed that one.'

'They turned a school bus into a pontoon boat?' he said, but the noise from the stage made it impossible for him to say any more.

Jack waited about five minutes before he followed Daisy and her nephew. He found the two of them in the play area. She'd cleaned Pippen's face, and he was playing in a pit of multicolored balls surrounded by mesh that went clear to the ceiling. She stood outside the mesh watching him wade through the balls as if he were walking upstream.

'How'd you manage to get yourself invited to Lacy's birthday party?' he asked as he came to stand beside her.

She glanced up into his face. 'Lily and Pippen and I were already here when they walked in.'

'And it was a complete surprise?'

She shook her head and her ponytail brushed her bare shoulders. 'No. I knew you were going to be here, but I didn't expect Rhonda and Billy to invite us to sit with them.'

'What's it going to take for you to leave me alone?'

She turned her attention back to her nephew. He picked up a plastic ball and threw it. It missed a little girl by about a foot. 'You know what I want.'

'To talk.'

'Yes. There is something important we need to talk about.'

'What?'

Sirens from a skeet-ball machine blared in the background. 'Something too important to talk about in the middle of Showtime.'

'Then why are you here, tonight? Stalking me and my family?'

'I'm not stalking you. I just wanted to remind you that I'm here, and I'm not going anywhere until you talk to me.' She glanced down at her feet. 'I have a letter Steven wrote to you. I don't have it on me, though.'

'What does it say?'

She shook her head again, then stared straight ahead. 'I don't know. I haven't read it.'

'Send it to the shop.'

'I can't do that. He asked me to give it to you in person.'

'If it's so damn important, why didn't he give it to me himself? Instead of sending you?'

'Pippen, don't throw that,' she told her nephew before she turned to face Jack. Red and blue lights from a video game to the right flashed on her bare shoulder, the side of her neck, and the corner of her mouth. 'I think he meant to at first. For the first year of his illness, he believed he'd beat his cancer. We knew all along that no one had ever survived glioblastoma, but he was young and healthy and the early treatments seemed to be working. He fought so hard, Jack.' She turned back to Pippen and grasped the mesh with her hands. 'By the time he accepted that he was going to die, it was too late to talk to you in person.' The little heart on her bracelet dangled from her wrist. He stared at it, not wanting to feel anything for Steven or for her. Not wanting to give a shit.

But he did have one question. 'How long did he live after he accepted that he was going to die?'

'About eight or nine months.'

That's what he thought. Steven had always wanted someone to 'go first' – whether it was telling Daisy she had a big ugly hair bow, or jumping off a roof, or throwing rotten tomatoes at cars. Growing up, it had never bothered him, but that was a long time ago. 'Then there was time to come and talk to me before he died. He didn't have to send you.'

She laughed ruthlessly. 'You've obviously never seen anyone who's gone through radical cancer treatments. If you had, you wouldn't say that.' One of her hands dropped to her side, and tears shimmered along the bottoms of her eyelids as she gazed up at him. 'You wouldn't have recognized him, Jack.' One tear slid from her lashes and ran down her cheek. He clenched his hands to keep from reaching up and wiping it with his fingertips. 'Toward the end,' she continued, 'he forgot how to tie his shoes, but he insisted on getting dressed every day like it mattered. So, I tied his shoes for him . . . every day. Like it mattered. And it did because it gave him a little dignity, I think. Some feeling like he was still an adult. A man.'

A piece of his heart fell to his stomach and his breath with it. 'Stop it, Daisy.'

'Jack—'

'No.' He knew she would not stop until she carved him up. Just like before. He wasn't about to let that happen. Not again. Not for anything, 'I don't want to hear any more.' He was sorry for Steven. Sorrier than he would have thought possible two minutes ago, but he would not let her tear him to shreds.

'I didn't mean to talk about this now.' She wiped the

tear from her cheek. 'Meet with me later so you can hear me out.'

'The only thing I want to hear from you, Daisy Monroe, is the word goodbye,' he said, and then he walked away. He moved back into the dining room and told his brother and Rhonda he was leaving. For once he was grateful to the damn dancing bears and their loud annoying music that didn't allow for questions. He gave his nieces some money for game tokens and left. He didn't see Daisy when he walked back out, but he wasn't looking for her either.

He took a deep breath and kept right on moving. He didn't think he took a full breath again until he was home. Shut up in his house. Locked tight against the memory of Daisy and Steven and him. But the memories followed him inside, and he sat down hard on his mother's piano bench and put his hands on his knees.

He'd hated Steven for about as many years as he'd loved him like a brother. But even in his earliest rage, he'd never wanted Steven dead. Not really. Maybe there had been a time in the beginning when the thought of Steven wiped off the planet had held a certain appeal, but he had never wanted him to die the way Daisy had described it. Not like that. Not even back when his anger had burned the hottest.

When it came right down to it, he'd never wanted him to die at all. Because in the end, he understood Steven. He understood that he had betrayed Steven every bit as much as Steven had betrayed him.

It'd been Steven who'd told him about Daisy being stood up for that damn high school prom their senior year. It had been both their ideas that Jack take her since Steven already had a date. It had seemed so simple at the time.

Take Daisy so she wouldn't spend the night crying her eyes out. No big deal, but that night had changed all their lives.

Jack didn't really remember the actual dance, other than trying to touch as little of Daisy as possible. What he did remember, though, was standing on her front porch looking down at her, wanting her so much he ached, and telling himself to leave. To get into his car and drive away.

Then she kissed him.

Compared to kisses he'd experienced with other girls, it was nothing really. Just her closed lips pressed to his, but it had hit him square in the chest. He'd been stunned and angry and he'd pushed her away. Then she'd touched the side of his neck and looked up at him as if she wanted him every bit as much as he wanted her. As much as he'd always wanted her.

'Please, Jack,' she'd whispered, and even as he'd lowered his mouth for more, he'd told himself it was a mistake. Even as he'd stood there, kissing her and tasting her mouth, he'd told himself to stop. Even as he'd kept his grasp on her shoulders, he'd pulled her into his chest and felt the weight of her breasts against him. Even as he told himself that it could not happen again, he'd known that it would. He'd wanted her for years, and one little bite had not been enough.

Not nearly

He'd told himself to stay away, but even if he'd been able to control his eighteen-year-old lust, Daisy wouldn't let him. At Jimmy Calhoun's party the next night, she'd pulled him into a dark closet and put his hand on her breast.

'Touch me, Jack,' she'd whispered into his mouth, and he'd about gone off in his boxer shorts.

A few days later he'd told Steven he couldn't hang out

because he was grounded. Then he'd jumped in his Camaro, picked Daisy up at her house, and they'd driven out to a deserted road. He'd parked and told her about Steven, about the two of them being attracted to her, and he explained why he and Daisy had to stop.

She said she understood. She agreed, then she'd kissed his ear and told him that Steven didn't have to find out.

'I love Steven. He's my friend,' she'd said. 'But I don't think of him the same way I think of you. I'm in love with you, Jack. I want more from you. I want you to show me how to make love.'

That night he'd taken off her shirt and unhooked her bra. White with tiny blue dots on it. Her breasts were the most beautiful things he'd ever seen. Firm and white, her tight pink nipples fit perfectly into his mouth.

He hadn't made love to her that night. No, he'd tried to do the noble thing. He'd told her he didn't mess with virgins. He'd told himself it was okay as long as he didn't stick his hand in her panties and touch her there. He'd told himself to go slow with her, but that resolve quickly disappeared like a kid with candy. Then he'd had to tell himself it wasn't really wrong unless he took her hymen.

After two weeks of touching and kissing and rubbing against each other, he'd picked her up and driven with her to a hotel on the outskirts of Amarillo. They'd taken it all the way that night, and he'd learned the difference between sex and making love. He'd learned the difference between sex where just his genitals were involved, and sex that involved his soul. He'd learned that being inside of Daisy Lee burned him up and left his chest aching. And the whole time he'd known it was wrong. He'd known Steven loved her as much as he did, but he'd told himself that Daisy was right. It was okay as long as Steven didn't find out.

In public, he and Daisy behaved as they always had, as friends, but it hadn't been easy. Seeing but not touching had driven him insane. Watching her walk down the school halls or jump around in her little cheerleader skirt, had made him insanely jealous.

He hadn't been the only one driven crazy by their situation. Daisy had always wanted him just as much as he'd wanted her, and when he couldn't meet with her, which wasn't often, she'd accuse him of not loving her. Of being with other girls. She'd tell him she didn't love him anymore, then the next chance they got, they'd tear at each other's clothes and satisfy the lust that burned too hot.

Neither of them wanted to hurt Steven and they decided to wait until he left for college to be more open about their relationship. Steven had been accepted to the University of Washington, and after high school graduation, he planned to live with his sister and brother-in-law until he could afford his own apartment. Both Jack and Daisy planned to take classes at West Texas A&M, about seventy miles south. They'd planned to tell Steven that they were in love when he came home for Christmas that year.

Jack rose from the piano bench and moved into the dark kitchen. He flipped on the light and opened the refrigerator. He pushed aside a quart of milk and reached for a Lone Star instead.

Being with Daisy had been like having one long orgasm while on a roller coaster. Damn exciting, but not if you wanted some calm.

He popped the top off his beer and tossed it on the counter. Two weeks after he graduated from high school, his parents had been killed in a car wreck. They'd been out driving in their '59 Bonneville when a drunk driver hit them. That old Pontiac may have been built like a tank, but it hadn't been built with safety features. His father had been killed instantly. His mother died on the way to the hospital. And at the age of eighteen, he'd suddenly become responsible not only for himself but for Billy too.

Jack raised the bottle to his mouth and took a drink. Whenever he thought back on that time in his life, he had a hard time remembering details. He'd been torn up and confused and scared. And just plain raw. His whole life had changed in an instant, and it had seemed that the more he wanted space to think, the more clinging Daisy got. The more he pushed her away so he could breathe, the tighter she'd held on to him. He remembered the night he'd told her they needed time apart, that he needed time away from her to think. That he didn't want to see her for a while. She became hysterical Then the next time he saw her, she was Steven's wife.

He recalled exactly what she'd been wearing that night. A blue sun dress with little white flowers. She and Steven had stood in his front yard and asked him to come outside. He remembered walking toward her and her looking so good to him that he'd wanted to grab her and hold her and tell her to stay with him forever.

Instead, Steven told him that the two of them had married that afternoon. At first, he couldn't believe it. Daisy didn't love Steven. She loved him. But he'd taken one look at her guilty face and knew it was true. He grabbed her and told her she belonged to him, not Steven. He tried to kiss her and touch her and make her admit she loved him. Steven got between them, and Jack smashed his fist into Steven's face. They proceeded to beat the hell out of each other, but Steven Monroe had never been a fighter. He'd ended up taking the bad end of the beating.

Jack raised the beer to his mouth again and swallowed hard. The night he'd lost Daisy, he'd lost Steven too. He'd lost the girl he'd loved and craved and wanted to live with forever.

He'd lost his best friend. The boy who'd been by his side during every hare-brained adventure. Steven might have been a 'you go first' kind of guy, but Jack had always known that Steven was right there behind him. Backing him up. Ready to go next. Then in the course of one night, they were both gone and Jack was alone.

He'd learned a valuable lesson that night that he'd lost everything. He'd learned that no one could take from you what you didn't give them. No one could slice your insides up if you didn't hand them the knife. He didn't think that made him bitter, just a man who learned from mistakes. And it didn't make him one of those commitment-phobic guys Rhonda was always accusing him of being.

Hell, he might get married one day. Marriage wasn't something he'd ever rule out, but it wasn't something he was looking for either. If it happened, it happened. He had a family. Billy and Rhonda and the girls were enough for him, but there was room in his life for someone else. He was only thirty-three. There was time.

Except Daisy. There would never be room for Daisy Monroe. Not only had she sliced up his insides, she'd stomped them into the ground. He would never allow Daisy into his life again.

No, he'd learned his lesson the first time.

7

Daisy shoved her tortoise-shell Vuarnet sunglasses onto the bridge of her nose and looked over at Lily, who concealed her eyes behind lavender Adrienne Vittadinis.

Like a cop on a stakeout, Lily backed her Ford Taurus in between a truck and a minivan and shoved the car into park. The last strain of 'Earl Had to Die' wound to a close, and the dying notes of an electric keyboard filled the space between the two sisters. Normally, Daisy had nothing against the Dixie Chicks, in fact she had two of their CDs, but if Lily hit the back arrow on the car's stereo one more time, Daisy wasn't responsible for what she might do next.

'Do you see him anywhere?' Lily asked as she scanned the parking lot to a stucco apartment complex off Eldorado Street. Her hand lowered from the steering wheel, hovered, then she hit the back button.

'Damn it!' Daisy swore, driven to near madness. 'That's the fifth time in a row you've played that song.'

Lily looked across the seat at Daisy. Her brows lowered, and frown lines creased her forehead. 'You're counting? That's warped.'

'Me! I'm not the one wearing out 'Earl Had to Die' while parked outside my soon to be ex-husband's apartment.'

'It's not his apartment. He's renting a house over on Locust Grove near the hospital. It's *her* apartment. Kelly the skank,' Lily said and returned her attention to the complex.

The Chicks started with the first verse *again,* and Daisy leaned over and hit the off button. The car was blessedly silent. After leaving Showtime last night, Lily had taken a detour, passing Kelly's apartment. She'd driven past three times like some crazed stalker before dropping Daisy off at their mother's house.

This morning she showed up bright and early to drop Pippen off so she could 'find a job.' Daisy took one look at her sister's flat hair and wrinkled running sweats, and she knew something was up. She told Lily she was coming along. She pulled on a pair of jean shorts, a black T-shirt, and shoved her feet into flip-flops as she twisted her hair up onto the back of her head and secured it with a claw.

'How long have you been doing this?' she asked.

Lily's hands tightened on the gray steering wheel. 'Awhile.'

'Why?'

'I have to see them together.'

'Why?' she asked again. 'That's crazy.'

Lily shrugged, but didn't take her gaze from the apartment complex.

'What are you going to do if you see them together? Run them down with your car?'

'Maybe.'

She didn't think her sister would actually mow Ronnie down, but the fact that she was sitting here thinking about it was a bit worrisome. 'Lily, you can't kill them.'

'Maybe I'll just clip them with the bumper. Or ram Ronnie's balls so he'll be useless to his girlfriend.'

'You can't ram Ronnie Darlington's balls. You'll go to jail.'

'Maybe I won't get caught.'

'You'll get caught. The ex-wife always gets caught.' She reached over and rubbed Lily's shoulder through her red jogging suit. 'You have to stop doing this.'

Lily shook her head as a tear slipped beneath her glasses and ran down her cheek. 'Why does he get to be happy? Why does he just get to move on with his girlfriend and be happy while I feel like I have acid eating a hole in my heart? He should have to feel what he's done to us, Daisy. He should suffer like Pippen and me.'

'I know.'

'No, you don't. No one has ever broken your heart. Steven died, he didn't run off with a woman and break your heart.'

Daisy dropped her hand to the seat. 'You don't think watching Steven die broke my heart?'

Lily looked over at Daisy and brushed the tears streaming down her cheeks. 'Yes, I guess. But it's different. Steven didn't leave you because he wanted to.' She sucked in a deep breath and added, 'You're lucky.'

'What? That's a horrible thing to say.'

'I don't mean that you're lucky Steven died, just that you don't have to think about Steven having sex with another woman. You don't have to wonder if he's kissing her and touching her and loving her.'

'You're right. I have to think of him dead in the ground.' She folded her arms beneath her breasts and stared at her sister. 'I'm going to let that go because you're having a bad day.' But she guessed she wasn't quite ready to let it go because she couldn't keep from adding, 'I know you don't mean to be an insensitive brat. That's just the way you are.'

'And I'm sure you don't mean to be so selfish. That's just the way *you* are.'

Daisy's mouth fell open. She was sitting in her sister's car to keep Lily from doing something stupid, and *she* was selfish. 'Yeah right, and I want to sit here watching Ronnie's apartment because I have nothing better to do.'

'Do you think I wanted to sit in Showtime last night while you stalked Jack Parrish?'

'It's not the same thing. It's important that I speak with Jack. You know that.' She turned her head and looked out the passenger-side window at an old lady in a pink house-coat walking her beagle down the sidewalk. 'And I'm not stalking him.'

'I don't think he sees it that way.'

No, he didn't. And after last night, she supposed he had reason to think that. Going to Showtime and crashing his niece's birthday party might not have been one of her brightest ideas, but she was running out of time. She only had a few more days, and if Jack hadn't lied to her about being out of town, she wouldn't have wasted four of those days already. She was under the gun and felt the pressure mounting.

'Did you see how he was with Billy's little girls?' she asked. Watching him walk toward her with those two girls clinging to him, she'd felt a surprising little pinch in her heart. 'He was really good with them, and you could see that they really love him. You can't fake something like that with kids.'

'Did it make you think you should have stuck around and not married Steven?'

Daisy sank down in her seat and looked out the front. 'No, but it made me realize that when I tell him about Nathan, he's probably going to be a lot angrier with me than I'd figured. Not that I thought he wouldn't be, but there's always been a part of me that hoped he'd understand.' She took the claw out of her hair and leaned her head back against the seat. 'Jack wasn't ready for a family. He'd just lost his mother and father, he wouldn't have been able to handle the news that I was pregnant. I did the right thing.'

'But . . . ?' Lily prompted.

'But I've never let myself wonder what kind of father he would have made.' She tossed the claw onto the center console. 'I've never let myself think about that.'

'And now you're thinking about it?'

'Yeah.' Although it was probably best not to, she couldn't help *but* think about it.

The door to an upstairs apartment opened and Ronnie stepped out with one of his arms around a dark-haired woman. Daisy had met Ronnie only twice, when he and Lily visited Seattle, but Daisy recognized him. He was good-looking with strategically disarrayed blond hair and a gee-shucks smile that fooled some women. Unlike Lily, Daisy had never been impressed, much less fooled.

'Turn off the car,' Daisy told her sister. This morning, Ronnie's Stetson shaded his face and cast a shadow on the shoulders of his red cowboy shirt. He wore a belt buckle the size of a dessert plate and his wranglers were so tight they looked painted on.

'I'm not going to run him down.'

'Turn it off Lily.' They were too far away for Daisy to get a good look at Kelly's face, but even at this distance, she could see that her hair was pulled up on top of her head in a ponytail and that she had a big behind covered in black spandex shorts.

The engine shut off and Daisy reached over and took the keys from the ignition. She grabbed Lily's arm to keep her from opening the door.

'He's not worth it, Lily.'

The two moved to a white monster truck with metallic red flames blazing down the sides. Ronnie helped 'Kelly the skank' up into the truck, then he fired up the Ford and the two of them took off. Anger for her sister burned in Daisy's stomach as she watched them drive out of the parking lot. Lily covered her mouth but a high-pitch keening leaked through her fingers. Daisy reached across the center console and pulled her sister into her arms the best that she could.

'Lily, he's not worth your tears,' she said as she smoothed her hair.

'I still love him so-ho much. Why can-can't he love me-me?' Lily cried. Daisy held her and felt her heart breaking too. What kind of worthless man abandoned his wife and child? What kind of A-moral A-hole ran around with another woman and emptied the family's bank account so he wouldn't have to pay for his child? The more Daisy thought about it, the angrier she got. Somehow, Ronnie would have to pay for hurting her sister.

'Honey, have you thought of maybe getting some counseling?' she asked her sister.

'I don't want to ta-talk about it with a stranger. It's

too-too humiliating.' After that her sentences became incoherent, and she mostly sounded like a distressed dolphin.

'Let me drive us home,' Daisy said. Lily nodded and while Daisy ran around to the other side of the car, Lily crawled to the passenger seat. 'Do you want a Dr Pepper?' Daisy asked as they drove out of the parking lot. 'It might help your raw throat.'

Lily wiped her nose on her sleeve and nodded. 'Eee-hee,' she managed.

She drove to the Minute Mart and pulled into a slot in front of the store. She pocketed the keys in case Lily got ideas, grabbed a five from her purse, and put her sun-glasses on the dashboard. 'I'll be right back,' she told Lily and opened the door. Once inside the store, she filled up a twenty-four-ounce cup with Dr Pepper, sealed the top with a lid and grabbed a straw. When Lily calmed down, she'd talk to her about her lawyer and see what he was doing to help her.

'Good morning,' the clerk said, his green uniform hung on his bony shoulders. His name tag said he was Chuck and that she should have a nice day. She doubted that was possible now.

'Morning.' As Daisy handed over the five-dollar bill, a white Ford truck with red flames down the sides pulled into a parking slot a few cars away from Lily's Taurus. She watched with a sense of impending doom as Ronnie and Kelly stepped out of the truck. 'Oh no.'

The passenger door of the Taurus flew open and Lily shot out of the car like a bullet. She confronted the two right there on the sidewalk in front of the Minute Mart. Daisy could hear Lily's hysterical screaming through the glass, and she was sure the people at the gas pumps were getting a good show.

She set the straw on the counter and held up one hand, palm out. 'I'll be right back.' As Daisy yanked open the store's door, Lily called Kelly a whore and a fat-ass, and Kelly swung and slapped Lily across the face. Lily's sunglasses sailed off, and she raised her hand to retaliate. Ronnie grabbed her arm and shoved.

Lily fell and everything within Daisy narrowed, like looking in the wrong end of a telescope. Rage flowed through her like a toxic chemical, and she ran full steam, launching herself at her soon to be ex-brother-in-law Years ago, Steven and Jack had taught her how to defend herself. She'd never used those lessons before, but she hadn't forgotten. Like riding a bike. She got a shoulder into his sternum. He grunted and grabbed her hair. He shook her but she hardly felt it as she tucked her thumb and punched him in the eye.

'Ow, you crazy bitch!'

Without thinking about it, she kneed him just below his belt buckle. She didn't think she'd hit him square between the legs like she'd been aiming, but enough that the air left his lungs in a big whoosh. His fingers loosened and she stepped back. Ronnie doubled over and several long strands of Daisy's hair got tangled in his fist.

'You ever touch my sister again,' she told him between breaths, 'and I'll kill you, Ronnie Darlington.'

He groaned and stared at her through squinty eyes. 'You can try, you stupid bitch.'

Daisy didn't mind being called a crazy bitch, because sometimes it was true. But she hated being called a stupid bitch. She launched herself forward again, but someone grabbed her around the middle and pulled her back. 'You've won, buttercup.'

She pushed at the arm around her stomach, but he pulled her onto her toes. 'Let go. I'm going to kick his butt!'

'I think it's more likely that he'd kick yours. Then I'd have to step in and knock the shit out of him for laying a hand on you. And I really don't want to do that. Buddy and I came here for a fill-up and a cup of coffee, is all. We weren't planning on a brawl.'

Daisy blinked and her peripheral vision came into focus again. She was aware of her heart pounding in her throat as she looked over her shoulder. 'Jack?'

The shadow from his beige cowboy hat cut across his face, and she watched his mouth form the words, 'Good mornin',' but he didn't sound like there was anything good about it.

She turned her attention to Lily standing with her back against the front of the store. She had a cut on the bridge of her nose and a red palm print on her cheek. A man in a blue T-shirt stood next to her, talking to her as she shook her head. Kelly sat on her butt on the ground, and her ponytail was pulled to one side of her head. Ronnie straightened with a grunt and felt his crotch as if to make sure everything was still there.

'I hope you can't use it for a month.' Daisy spat at him, and Jack pulled her tighter against the solid wall of his chest.

Then Jack spoke to Ronnie from beside Daisy's temple. 'Take your girlfriend and get out of here while the two of you can still walk.'

Ronnie opened his mouth, shut it again, then grabbed Kelly, who'd started screaming at the top of her lungs. He shoved her inside his truck, fired the engine, and the two of them took off, monster truck tires squealing out of the parking lot.

'Are you okay, Lily?' she called out to her sister.

Lily nodded and took her sunglasses from the man talking to her.

'What was that about?' Jack asked. 'The two of you out here spreadin' sunshine for the hell of it?' He didn't let go, and she looked up at him again. The breeze picked up several strands of her blond hair and carried them across the front of his dress shirt. She raised her gaze past his mouth and looked deeper into the shadow created by the brim of his hat. His light green eyes stared back at her. Waiting.

'That's Lily's husband and his girlfriend.'

He tilted his head back and the shadow slid from the middle of his nose to the deep bow of his top lip. 'Ah.'

The adrenaline in her veins made her feel suddenly shaky, and she was glad Jack held her so tight. 'He's a rat bastard.'

'So, I've heard.'

Daisy wasn't surprised that Ronnie's reputation proceeded him. Lovett was a small town. 'He emptied their bank account and won't give her any money for Pippen.'

Jack slid his palm across her stomach as he dropped his arm. He took a step back, and the solid wall of his chest was replaced with cool morning air. Her hand throbbed, her head hurt, her shoulder ached, and her knees felt wobbly. It had been a long time since she'd felt a man's strength surrounding her, supporting her, and she would have liked nothing better than to melt right back into his chest and arms again. Of course, that was impossible. 'I hurt my hand.'

'Let me see.' He turned her to face him and cradled her hand in his warm palm. The sleeves of his blue broadcloth shirt were rolled up his forearms, and over his breast pocket, was embroidered PARRISH AMERICAN CLASSICS, in black. 'Wiggle your fingers for me,' he said.

With his head bent over her hand, the brim of his hat almost touched her mouth. He smelled of soap and clean skin and his starched shirt. His thumb brushed the heel of her hand and little tingles radiated outward from her palm over her wrist and traveled up the inside of her arm. Her adrenaline was doing funny things to her. Either that or she'd pinched a nerve.

He lifted his gaze and his eyes stared into hers. For several long seconds he just looked at her. She'd forgotten that when you looked real close into Jack's eyes, you could see darker green flecks. She remembered now.

'I don't think it's broke, but you probably should get an X-ray.' He dropped her hand.

She made a slow fist and winched. 'How do you know it's not broken?'

'When I broke my hand, it swelled up almost immediately.'

'How did you break your hand?'

'Fighting.'

'With Steven?'

'No. At a roadhouse bar in Macon.'

Macon? What had he been doing in Macon? In the last fifteen years, he'd had a whole life she knew nothing about. She was curious about it, but she doubted he'd tell her much if she were to ask.

The clerk from inside the store moved toward Daisy and she turned to him as he handed her her sunglasses.

'Thanks, Chuck,' she said and slid them on her face. He gave her the change and she took the Dr Pepper with her good hand.

'Should I call the police?' he wanted to know. 'I saw them hit the other blond woman first.'

A police report might help in Lily's divorce, but Lily wasn't completely innocent. There was the little matter of Lily's stalking. She didn't know if Ronnie knew about that, but he might. 'No. That's okay.'

'If you change your mind, let me know,' Chuck offered and headed back inside.

Daisy turned her attention to Lily and the man talking to her. 'Is he with you?' she asked Jack.

'Yeah. That's Buddy Calhoun.'

'Older or younger than Jimmy?'

'A year younger.'

Daisy didn't remember much about Buddy beyond having the bad teeth and flaming red hair of all the Calhouns. She glanced around at the people in the parking lot and at the gas pumps at the far end. The ramifications of what she'd done that morning began to sink in. 'I can't believe I fought in public.' She raised the cool Dr Pepper to her cheek. 'I never even swear in public.'

'If it's any consolation, I don't think you swore.' No, it wasn't much comfort, especially when he added, 'But your sister has a mouth like a trucker. We heard her clear over at the gas pumps.'

Daisy didn't live in Lovett anymore, but her mother did. Her mother would be mortified. Daisy and Lily would probably be the latest topic at her single's dance. 'Do you think very many people noticed us?'

'Daisy, you're standing at the intersection of Canyon

and Vine. In case you've forgotten, it's about the busiest intersection in the city.'

'So people are going to know that I socked Ronnie Darlington in the eye.' She removed the cool cup from her cheek. Good lord, could things be any worse?

Evidently. 'Yep, and that you kneed his balls.'

'You saw that?'

'Yeah. Remind me not to piss you off.' He glanced over her head. 'Ready, Buddy?'

Buddy Calhoun turned and flashed Jack a straight white smile. So much for Buddy having the Calhoun bad teeth. His hair was a dark red too, not carrot like the others. He was better-looking too. 'Be right there, J. P.,' he drawled.

J.P.?

'Try to stay out of trouble,' Jack said to her as he turned to go. 'Next time someone might not be around to save you from doing something stupid, like going after a man who weighs twice what you do.'

She put her bad hand on his arm to stop him. He was right. 'Thanks, Jack. If you hadn't stepped in, something really bad could have happened.' She shook her head. Maybe he didn't hate her as much as he wanted her to think. 'When I saw him shove my sister . . . I don't even remember how it happened, but I just lost my mind and went after him.'

'Don't make too much of it, Daisy.' So much for feeling special. 'You could have been anyone.' His gaze dropped to her hand on his arm.

'Since I'm not just anyone, you should let me thank you properly,' she offered in the hopes that perhaps they could now relate to each other on friendlier terms, and she could talk to him about Nathan.

One corner of his mouth slid up as his gaze moved to her breasts, up her chin, to her mouth. He wasn't fooled by her offer and was purposely trying to annoy her. 'What did you have in mind?'

'Not what you have in mind.'

From within the shadow of his hat, he finally looked into her eyes. 'What then?'

'Lunch.'

'Not interested.'

'Dinner.'

'No, ma'am.' He stepped off the curb and said over his shoulder, 'Come on, Buddy.'

Daisy watched him move across the parking lot to a classic black Mustang parked at one of the gas pumps. Two razor-sharp creases ran down the back of his shirt and were tucked into the waistband of his Levi's. He wasn't wearing a belt, and his wallet made a bulge in his back pocket. Buddy followed and Daisy turned to her sister. The red welt on Lily's cheek had started to fade.

'Are you okay?' Daisy asked as Lily moved toward her.

'I'm okay.' She reached for the Dr Pepper and took a long drink. 'I think I'm going crazy.'

Really? 'Maybe a little.'

The two of them moved to Lily's Taurus and got inside. Lily spoke as she buckled her seat belt. 'I'm sorry about what I said about Steven. You're right. I was being an insensitive bitch.'

'I think I said you were a brat.'

'I know you did. Let's go home.'

Daisy started the car. 'How long do you think it will take for Mom to find out?'

'Not long,' Lily sighed. 'She'll probably try to ground us.'

Through the rearview mirror, she watched Jack's Mustang pull out of the parking lot.

'Daisy?'

'Yeah?'

'Thanks. You were really something going after Ronnie like that.'

'Don't thank me, just promise you'll stop stalking him and Kelly the skank.'

'Okay.' She took a drink of her cup. 'Did you see her butt, though?'

'It was huge.'

'And flabby.'

'Yeah, and you're a lot cuter and have better hair.'

Lily smiled. 'And breath.'

Daisy chuckled. 'Yeah.'

When they got back to their mother's house, Lily grabbed Pippen and lay down on the couch with him. She turned on a Blue's Clues video and nestled her nose in his little mullet. 'Love you, Pippy,' she said. Without taking his eyes from the television, he raised his face and kissed his mother's chin.

'Did you get the job?' Louella asked from the kitchen, where she was baking cookies and filling the house with the smell of peanut butter.

'They said they'd call,' Lily answered, hiding her smile behind her son's head.

'Chicken,' Daisy whispered.

Lily was a mess, no doubt about it. Daisy had three days before she needed to return to her life in Seattle. Nathan's last day of school was today, and she needed to call him and ask how it went.

She had a lot to do. She had three days to help

straighten out her sister's life, give Steven's letter to Jack and tell him he had a son. Then she could return home and get on with *her* life. She and Nathan could lie around on a beach somewhere, soaking up rays. She'd drink piña coladas while he watched girls in bikinis. Heaven for both of them.

But right now, all she wanted was to take a shower, put ice on her hand, and take a nap. Her adrenaline spent, she was tired and achy, but if not for Jack, she was positive she would be feeling a lot more achy right about now. Going after Ronnie like that hadn't been real smart, but she hadn't thought at all. She'd just reacted to him pushing Lily to the ground.

I think it's more likely that he'd kick yours. Then I'd have to step in and knock the shit out of him for laying a hand on you, Jack had said. He'd also said he would have come to the rescue of any woman. He'd told her not to make too much out of it.

But now as she thought back with a clearer head, she doubted he would have held just any woman a little bit longer than was absolutely necessary. Not like he'd held her, tight against his hard chest. And she really doubted he would have brushed just any woman's hand with his thumb. She also doubted he'd even known he was doing it.

She'd been so focused on everything else around her, she hadn't realized that Jack's touch had been a little more personal, lingered a second longer than just a Good Samaritan helping out any ol' woman.

She realized it now, and just the memory of his touch made her catch her breath. Her mother called out to her as she moved up the stairs to her bedroom. 'Okay,' she called back, then shut the door behind her. She leaned against it as a hot little tug pulled at her abdomen and between her thighs. The warmth of it spread across her flesh and her breasts grew heavy with it. She hadn't felt anything like this in a long time, but she knew what it was. Lust. Pent up sexual desire. Years of it pulling at her.

She closed her eyes. Maybe she'd imagined Jack's touch. Maybe it was all in her head, but she hadn't imagined how good it was to feel a solid healthy man again. So good to feel protected. So good to feel his chest against her back and his arm around her waist. God help her, she missed that feeling. Missed it so much that she'd wanted to melt into Jack. She wondered what he'd have done if she'd turned and kissed the side of his neck. Run her tongue up his throat and her hands all over the muscles of his chest. Naked, like he'd been in his kitchen that first night. Half naked with his jeans hanging low on his hips so she could slide her palms over his flat abdomen and sink to her knees as she pressed her face into his button fly.

Daisy's lids flew open. Jack was the last man on the planet she should be fantasizing about licking and touching. The last man on the planet who should make her think of sex.

It's been a long time, is all, she told herself as she pushed away from the door. She opened a drawer and pulled out a pair of bikini panties and her bra. She was thirty-three, and before Steven's illness, they'd had a very active sex life. Daisy liked sex and she missed it. She supposed it had only been a matter of time before her desire for intimacy returned. It was just too bad it had returned right now. Today. And it was really too bad Jack had been the trigger. For so many obvious reasons, sex between her and Jack was out of the question.

Daisy walked from her room to the bathroom down the hall. But sex between her and someone other than Jack might be a possibility. She'd only been with two different men her whole life, maybe it was time to experiment. She had two and a half days now before she returned to Seattle. Maybe it was time to live it up before she returned home and was a mom again. Maybe she should add 'get laid' to her to-do list.

A little stab of guilt poked her conscience. Steven was dead, so why did it feel like she was contemplating cheating on her husband? She didn't know, but there it was. Right in front of her, and she knew that her guilt would probably keep her from actually doing it with anyone.

Too bad, because she probably would have liked some no-strings-attached sex. The kind where you just grab someone, do it, and never see them again.

She turned on the bathtub and held her hand under the running water. But maybe if she just did it, she wouldn't feel guilty anymore. Maybe it was like losing her virginity all over again. The first time was the most difficult. After that, it got a whole lot easier. A whole lot funner, too.

Of course she didn't have a candidate. Maybe she should pick up some guy at a bar. Someone who looked like Hugh Jackman or that one guy in the Diet Coke commercial. No, those men reminded her too much of Jack. She should pick someone totally different. Someone like Viggo Mortensen or Brad Pitt. No, Matthew McConaughey.

Oh yeah.

But it would never be Jack. Never. That would be really really bad.

Or, a little voice inside her head whispered, *it would be really, really good.* As she dropped her shorts and pulled her T-shirt over her head, she was afraid that if she wasn't careful, the little voice in her head was going to get her into big, big trouble.

M ost weekend nights, Slim Clem's packed 'em in from as far away as Amarillo and Dalhart. The live band played country, loud country, with an occasional southern-rock oldy thrown in. The big dance floors were always crowded, and the mechanical bulls were always running, taking on all comers with a pocket full of cash. Three different bars poured a continuous stream of icy beer, straight shots, or fruity drinks with paper umbrellas.

All manner of stuffed mammals and reptiles peered through glass eyes from built-in platforms high on the walls. If the Road Kill Bar was a taxidermist's dream, Slim Clem's was his wet dream. Although why anyone would proudly display a hog-nosed skunk was anyone's guess.

Within the dim bar, Wranglers, Rockies and Lees ruled. Worn tight and in every imaginable color by women stuffed into fringed cowgirl blouses with horses appliquéd on the back. T-shirts with conches and feathers, the bottoms shredded to look like fringe, were also a big favorite as well as prairie skirts with big ruffles or jacard dresses with sweetheart collars. Hair ranged from Texas big, teased and sprayed within an inch of its life – hat head – or hair so long and straight it hung to the waist or the backs of the knees.

The men preferred Wranglers or Levi's in blue or black, some so tight a person had to wonder where they'd packed their goods. While there were men who wore starched cowboy shirts with racing flames or American flags on them, T-shirts were the hands-down favorite. Most advertised beer and John Deere tractors, while others had a different message. The ubiquitous 'Don't mess with Texas' was out in full force, while 'Yeah, I'm drunk, but you're still ugly,' competed with the ever hopeful 'Let's get Nekid.'

Cowboy boots kept time with the band, and belt buckles big enough to be considered lethal weapons flashed beneath the dance floor's multicolored lights.

Daisy had never been inside Slim Clem's. When she'd lived in Lovett before, she'd been too young. But she'd heard about it. Everybody had heard about it, and she figured it was about time she experienced it for herself.

That Friday afternoon, Lily got a job at the deli counter in Albertsons, and the two of them decided to celebrate at Slim's. Daisy hadn't really brought anything to wear to a honky-tonk, but in the back of her closet, she dug out her old cowboy boots. She shoved her feet into them, and while a little tight, they still fit. Her junior year in high school, she'd saved for several months to buy the red boots with the white heart inserts. Lucky for her, cowboy boots were never out of style in Texas.

In the box with her yearbooks, she pulled out her

daddy's belt with the big silver buckle he'd won at the Top 'O Texas rodeo a few short months before a bull had stomped and killed him.

She put on her white cotton tank dress that closed down her breasts with eight little snaps, and she wrapped her daddy's rodeo belt around her hips. The name *Rowdy* was tooled into the brown leather in back. The buckle was heavy and hung down a little, but she thought she looked ready for a cowboy bar.

She rolled her hair on big curlers and stuck big hoops in her ears. She outlined her eyes with black liner, put on her shiniest red lipstick, and decided that she looked cowgirl chic.

Lily dressed for the bar in tight jeans and a pink blouse she tied just below her breasts so that her navel ring showed. Her makeup was heavier than Daisy's; and when she kissed Pippen goodbye on her mother's porch, she left big pink lip prints on his cheek.

On the way to Slim Clem's, Lily laughed and joked and seemed ready to get on with her life. Daisy was ready too. Tomorrow she was going to tell Jack about Nathan, and this time nothing would stop her. Not her own fear, not a kid's birthday party, and not even a half-naked woman in his house. She was leaving Sunday afternoon, and she had to tell him tomorrow. There was no other choice.

It was after nine when they walked into the bar. The band was singing Brooks and Dunn's 'My Maria' as they paid their five-dollar cover charge. While the band hit the high notes of the song, Daisy and Lily made their way through the crowd to the closest bar and ordered two Lone Stars from the tap. Daisy paid for the first round, and the two of them lucked out and found a table near the dance floor. They sat in chairs next to each other and their conversation turned to a critique of the people around them.

'Get a load of that guy over there in the beige cowboy shirt and hat,' Lily said next to Daisy's ear. Since that described quite a few of the men in the bar, she had to point with her glass. 'He's got on jeans so tight, he must have been poured in 'em wet.'

The cowboy in question was tall and lean and looked tough and hard enough to wrestle steers. '"Wrangler butts drive us nuts,"' Daisy recited through a smile and raised her beer to her lips.

'Yes, they do,' Lily agreed. Daisy couldn't recall the last time she'd been out with the girls; she'd forgotten how much she missed it. How much she needed to relax and laugh. Most of all, she was pleasantly surprised at how much she enjoyed being with her sister. The two of them laughed and scored the parade of male butts two-stepping and boot-scooting across the floor in front of them. Lily pointed to a guy in a pair of Roper's, and Daisy bent her head to one side. She had to admit, it took a very nice butt to look good in Roper's. Daisy gave him an eight, Lily a ten, they compromised on a nine.

'Did you see Ralph Fiennes's naked ass in *Red Dragon*?' Lily asked.

Daisy shook her head. 'I don't really like to watch scary movies now that I live alone.'

'Well, fast forward over the scary parts. You have to rent the video just to see Ralph's ass. He is definitely *fine*.'

Daisy took a drink from her beer. 'I saw him in *Maid in Manhattan*. The movie sucked, but he looked good.'

'There's a minus six,' Lily said as she pointed her glass

at a man in a pair of denim bib overalls and a tank top. 'The movie sucked because of J.Lo. They should have cast someone else.' Lily smiled. 'Like me.'

Daisy felt a hand on her shoulder and turned to look up past a T-shirt that said HOLD MY BEER WHILE I KISS YOUR GIRLFRIEND and into the face of Tucker Gooch. She'd graduated high school with Tucker. His mother, Luda Mae, had taught Home Ec at Lovett High. Tucker had often been sent to her room to sit out his punishment for some misdeed, like getting caught making out in the girls' bathroom.

Daisy stood, and from what she could see of him now, his dark hair was quite thin on top, but his eyes still shined with mischief and his mouth was curved into an irresistible smile.

'Hello, Tucker. How are you?'

He gave her a big hug. 'I'm good.' He held her a little tight, but his hands didn't roam down her back to her behind like they used to. 'Come dance with me,' he said.

She looked at Lily. 'Do you mind?'

Lily shook her head, and Daisy followed Tucker out onto the dance floor. The band struck up Toby Keith's, 'Who's Your Daddy?' and Tucker lead her in the two-step. Before his illness, she and Steven had danced in a few clubs around Seattle. For several beats of the drum and slides of the steel guitar, she was afraid she'd forgotten how to dance. But dancing to country was in her blood, and she took to it again quicker than a chicken on a Cheeto. As Tucker spun her and moved with her across the floor, she felt another part of herself slide into place. The part of her that could relax and laugh and have fun.

At least for tonight.

*

Jack grabbed his beer from the bar, then raised the bottle of Pearl to his lips. Over the bottom of the bottle, his gaze came to rest on the dance floor across the bar and the flash of white. He'd noticed Daisy the second she and Lily walked in the door. Not that he'd been looking, but those two women were hard to miss. They didn't quite fit in at Slim Clem's. Like two eclairs in a meat-and-potatoes crowd, and Jack was certain there were more than a few men in the bar thinking about eating dessert before dinner.

He lowered the bottle and shoved his free hand up to his knuckles in the front pocket of his Levi's. He returned his gaze to Gina Brown, who stood in front of him talking about the mechanical bulls in back. Apparently, since she was here so much, Slim's had offered her a job giving riding lessons on the weekends.

'The gal I taught this afternoon was about sixty-five,' she said. 'I put her up on Thunder and . . .'

Jack didn't give a rat's about Thunder. What he wanted to know was if his 'worst nightmare' had known he would be here. He wouldn't put it past her, but if she thought he was going to get all chatty with her, she was doomed to disappointment. Usually, Jack preferred bars that were a little less crowded than Slim's, but it was Buddy Calhoun's last night in town, and Buddy had talked him into coming to the bar. At the moment Buddy was taking his chances with one of the bulls in the back room. Personally, Jack didn't understand the appeal of getting thrown from a machine into a bunch of thick pads on the floor. He'd always figured that if you wanted to ride a bull, you should climb up onto a real one and take your chances.

'. . . I swear, I about died. You would have laughed your behind off, if you'd been there,' Gina said.

Jack, having missed the joke, smiled. 'You're probably right.'

'What's Buddy doing in town?' Gina asked.

'He's here on business.' He settled his weight on one foot, one hip slightly higher than the other, and his gaze returned to Daisy and Tucker Gooch on the dance floor. The smooth glide of their steps kept perfect time to Toby's song about a sugar daddy and his young thing. Jack had always disliked Tucker. Tucker was the kind of guy who bragged about how often he had sex and who he was getting it from. As far as Jack was concerned, a guy who was getting plenty didn't have to talk about it.

'Working for you?'

'Yep.' From Jack's position across the bar, all he could really see of Daisy was a flash of her shiny hair and a glimpse of that white dress of hers. He didn't need to have a front-row seat to know what she was wearing, the picture of her walking through the door of Slim's in that dress was imbedded in his brain.

A cowboy in a ten-gallon hat moved in his line of vision, and he couldn't see anything at all.

'Damn,' Buddy said as he came to stand beside Jack, 'I almost lasted two minutes that last time, but I came down on my left nut and couldn't get upright for a few.'

'Were you up on Twister?' Gina wanted to know. 'Twister set on high is a real wild ride.'

'It was the one closest to the door.' Buddy took a drink of his beer then said, 'You should give it a go, Jack.'

Buddy was a real nice guy, but sometimes Jack wondered if he wasn't a couple sandwiches shy of a picnic. 'As a general rule, I avoid anything that's gonna smash my left nut.'

'Yeah.' He shook his head and looked out over the crowd.

Gina laughed. 'I'm going in the back. Are you going to be here for a while?' she asked Jack.

'I'm not sure.'

She placed a hand on the front of his denim shirt and raised up onto her toes. 'Well, don't leave without saying goodbye,' she said against his mouth. She kissed him, her lips lingering just long enough to let him know she was interested in leaving with him. 'Don't forget.'

'Are you and Gina seeing each other?' Buddy asked as she walked away.

'Sometimes.' Jack didn't know if he was all that interested in having her leave with him. Two weekends in a row tended to give her ideas.

'Look who's sitting at that table over there all by her lonesome, Lily Brooks. I thought about giving her a call yesterday, but I don't know her married name.'

Jack glanced at Daisy's sister sitting by herself. 'Why would you give Lily a call?'

'To see how she was doing, after that fight at the Minute Mart, and all. I figure, since she's going through a divorce, she might need someone to talk to.'

Jack raised the Pearl to his lips, 'You want to talk to Lily Brooks about her divorce?' *Right*.

Buddy grinned. 'Those Brooks girls are nice-looking and built too.'

Jack took a long drink then sucked a drop of beer from his top lip. Buddy would get no argument from him. If he hadn't already seen for himself that Daisy was as hot as ever, that outfit she was wearing tonight would have settled the issue. Even from across the bar, he could see that her dress was so tight, it looked like she'd taken a spray gun and painted herself.

Buddy set his beer on the bar. 'I'm going to ask Lily to dance before someone beats me to it.'

Jack watched him weave his way through the crowd and wondered if life wouldn't be easier if he could be more like Buddy Calhoun. Nothing seemed to bother him much, not even racking himself on a mechanical bull. Maybe there'd been a time when Jack had been like that, more laid-back, but it had been so long ago, he'd forgotten.

He took his hand from his pocket, and his gaze slid to the dance floor and the flash of white. A smile lifted the corners of his mouth, and he wondered how Lily and Daisy felt today about their public brawl in front of the Minute Mart. Jack had seen women fight each other, but he'd never seen a woman take on a man. Especially a man that had to outweight her by a good hundred or so pounds.

Jack turned and placed his forearms on the bar. The morning of the fight, he'd just been standing there at the Minute Mart, minding his own business, leaning against his Mustang while it filled with fuel, when he heard yelling. He'd glanced across the parking lot and recognized Lily. She was swearing like a truck driver, and when the man she was yelling at shoved her, Jack headed in her direction. About halfway there, the store's door flew open and Daisy charged Ronnie like a defensive linebacker, ramming him with her shoulder. She was a streak of black T-shirt and blond hair, and as Jack picked up his pace toward her, she curled up her fist, socked Ronnie in the eye, then kneed him.

Jack grabbed her from behind to keep her from getting hurt, but he hadn't expected the confusing mix of anger and protectiveness that had slammed into his chest. Growing up, Daisy had been a walking contradiction, both afraid and fierce at the same time. And just as he had while growing up, he'd wanted to shake her and hold her, to yell at her even as he wanted to smooth her hair.

But he *had* held her, he reminded himself. He'd held her with her back pressed to him, her butt smashed against the front of his fly. He'd touched her and he'd smelled her hair and the scent of her skin.

He raised his gaze past the beer spigots to the animated Budweiser sign. Red neon tubes outlined Dale Earnhardt Jr.'s NASCAR. The tires spun on the legendary number eight, as if Junior was doing one-eighty on the straightaways at the Texas Motor Speedway.

Daisy had been gone fifteen years, but one thing had not changed over all that time. No matter how much he hated to admit it, he wanted her. Still. Now. After all this time. After everything she'd done.

It didn't make sense, but he couldn't deny the proof. Just a glimpse of her in that dress tightened his scrotum and gave him a semi, right there in Slim Clem's. He wanted her with the same mindless craving he'd had when he'd been eighteen. A hot ache that remembered the taste of her mouth and wanted to get reacquainted with the soft curves of her body. But he was no longer eighteen. He had more control, and getting hard didn't mean he had to do a damn thing about it.

Nope, he was going to stand right there and watch the Bud sign behind the bar. That was all. He was going to finish his beer then go home. If Buddy didn't want to leave, he could catch a ride with someone else.

As the band struck up Kenny Chesney's 'No Problem,'

Buddy and Lily joined Jack at the bar. Just as he turned to tell Buddy he was leaving in a few, his gaze landed on Daisy and Tucker walking toward him. The closer she got, the more he wished she'd just stayed the hell across the room. She wore some sort of dark smudged stuff around her eyes, her lips were a dark red, and her hair was big and curled and wild, like she'd just got laid. She looked a little smutty, which normally was his favorite, but not tonight. Not on her.

'Hey there, Jack.' Tucker offered his hand. 'How's it goin'?'

Jack shook it, then raised his beer to his mouth. 'I can't really complain,' he said just before he took a drink. 'How's your hand?' he asked Daisy.

She made a slow fist. 'It's better than it was yesterday,' she said.

'I heard about you and Lily getting into a fight with Ronnie Darlington and Kelly Newman,' Tucker told her.

'Ronnie's a rat bastard and Kelly's a skank,' Lily said.

'Where did you hear about it?' Daisy wanted to know.

'Fuzzy Wallace was driving by on Vine and saw you two.'

Daisy closed her eyes and swore.

Jack's gaze slid from her face, and he got a good look at that white dress. He could see the outline of her bra, and she must have been tan all over, because he could see the straps and the smooth edges cupping her breasts and pushing them up. His gaze slid over the little row of snaps closing the dress over her breasts, down her flat abdomen to the belt around her waist and that big silver buckle suspended right above her goodie box. The bottom of her dress hit her just about mid thighs, and when he glanced at her feet, he about choked. She was wearing red boots with white hearts. He remembered those boots. She used to wear them all the time. There'd been several times when he'd made love to her while she'd been wearing those boots. Usually when she wore a skirt, or a dress like she was wearing tonight, he'd just slip her panties off and not bother with the boots.

'If you have any more trouble, give me a call,' Tucker offered, and Jack looked up as Tucker slipped his arm around her shoulders.

'Okay, I'll remember that,' she said. She stepped forward and grabbed Jack's hand. 'Jack promised he'd dance with me.' She looked up at him with pleading eyes. 'Didn't you?'

'Did I?'

'Yes.'

He figured he had two options. He could leave her to Tucker or dance with her. He set his beer on the bar and slid his hand up her wrist to her elbow. 'I guess I have a bad memory,' he said. He took her arm and led her across the room.

The band broke into a slow smoky rendition of the Georgia Satellite's 'Keep Your Hands to Yourself.' Jack stopped in the middle of the dance floor and placed Daisy's palm against his. He placed his other hand on her waist and moved with her to the beat of the music. Through her thin dress, he felt the warmth of her skin. 'You going home with Gooch?'

'He asked me.' She set her hand lightly on his shoulder. 'But no.'

Her answer pleased him more than it should have, and he didn't like that one bit.

'I don't know where he got the idea that I'd actually consider it.'

They moved past the stage and pink light shined in her hair, slid over her smooth forehead and cheeks, and dipped between her softly parted lips. 'Maybe because your dress is so tight.'

'It's not that tight.'

He spun her then pulled her closer without missing a step. An inch of empty space separated her breasts from his chest, and he told himself that he held her there so he could hear her better. He brushed his thumb across the soft material of her dress and said just above her ear, 'It's so tight, I can see the outline of your bra.'

'Why are you staring at my bra, Jack?'

'Bored I guess.'

'Uh-huh.' She pulled far enough back to look up into his face. 'You're trying to imagine what I look like naked.'

He smiled as the band sang true love and sin. 'Buttercup, I know what you look like naked.'

Within the dark shadows of the dance floor, she blushed. A pink flush that rose up her throat to her cheeks. 'Funny, I don't remember what you look like naked.' Her eyes stared into his for less than a second before her gaze slid away and she focused on something beyond his shoulder.

She'd always been a bad liar. He didn't remember it ever bothering him before. For some reason, it did now. 'Did you know I was going to be here?' he asked her.

She returned her gaze to his. 'No,' she answered and he didn't know if he believed her. 'Are you going to be home tomorrow?'

'Why?'

'Because I'm coming over.'

He stared down into her face, with her sexy-as-hell eye

makeup and full lips. 'I don't remember inviting you.'

'You just said you have a bad memory.'

'Perhaps for some things. Other things I'm real clear about. Like I remember those boots.'

She smiled and her hand slid to the back of his shoulder. 'I know,' she said, 'I can't believe they still fit. Remember when I used to wear them with my purple Wranglers?'

Purple Wranglers? He spun her a few times and hoped she got dizzy. While he'd been thinking about her bra and couldn't get rid of the memory of those boots up around his ears, all she could think about was shit he didn't care about and didn't want to discuss.

He brought her back close to his chest and she said, 'And remember the hot-pink prairie skirt? Lord what a fashion nightmare.'

Prairie Skirt? What the hell? Just for that, he should spin her until she puked. She was talking about stupid shit on purpose, just to make him insane. As if she wasn't thinking of hot sweaty sex, too. As if the sexual desire between them was all in his own head, when he knew, he just knew she had to feel it too. 'Ah yes, the hot-pink prairie skirt,' he said even though he wasn't even sure what a prairie skirt was. He brought her so close, her breasts brushed his chest, then he said, 'I remember how it looked shoved up around your waist.'

Her steps faltered as she pulled back and looked up at him. She licked the corners of her mouth. 'I don't want to talk about sex.'

Usually, he didn't either. Usually he was more of a doer than a talker. 'Too bad.' He slid his hand from her waist to the small of her back. 'You want to talk to me, I get to pick the subject.'

'There are more important things in life than sex.'

He supposed that was true, but at the moment he couldn't think of anything. 'Name one.'

'Friendship.'

'Right,' he scoffed. 'Spoken just like a girl.'

'No, spoken like an adult.'

Now she was really pissing him off. Until she'd blown back into town, he'd moved on with his life. He'd taken on a big dose of adulthood at an early age. He'd finished raising his brother and had single-handedly rescued the business after his father's death. Now, here she was, in her red boots and white dress, digging it all up again. 'Sex was a big part of our past, Daisy, but you don't seem to want to talk about that.'

'It wasn't that big a part, Jack.'

'Bullshit.'

The song ended and she stepped back from him. 'Maybe for you. But it wasn't that big a part for me,' she said, then turned on the heels of those red boots and walked away.

Daisy tucked her chin and headed for the ladies' room. Once inside, she wet a paper towel and pressed it to her cheeks. Her heart pounded in her throat and she looked at herself in the long mirror above the sink. Her eyes shined a little too bright. Her face was a little too flushed. Her skin was ultra sensitive, every cell responding to Jack's touch. He'd pulled her hard against him, and it had felt so good to feel the wall of his chest pressed against her breasts. It was a dang good thing she was leaving soon, because Jack reminded her of things better left forgotten. Like just how long it had been since she'd been with a man, and what it was like to feel the raw ache of lust, hot and vital, tugging at her breasts and between her thighs. And it wasn't just his talking about sex, it was him. It was the touch of his hands, his thumb brushing her waist, the deep timbre of his voice in her ear, and the smell of his skin. She was afraid if the song hadn't ended when it did, she would have combusted right there in the middle of the dance floor.

A woman in a T-shirt with black fringe joined her at the sink and she scooted over to make room. 'It's really hot out there,' she said as a way to explain her flushed cheeks.

'A little.'

Daisy tossed the paper towels in the trash and opened the door.

Jack stood with one shoulder against the opposite wall, and when he saw her he straightened. 'When are you going home, Daisy?' he asked and stepped in front of her.

She looked beyond his left shoulder toward the crowded bar. 'When Lily is ready to leave.'

There was a hard edge to his voice when he clarified, 'When are you going home to Seattle?'

His lids were lowered over his green eyes as he looked down at her. She took a few steps backward so she wouldn't have to strain her neck looking up. 'Sunday.'

He followed. 'Day after tomorrow, then?'

'Yes.'

'Good.'

'That's why we have to talk tomorrow.' She took another step back.

Again he followed. 'Because you want to be friends and chat about the past.'

'Among other things.' Her shoulders hit the back door and he reached beside her right hip and turned the knob.

The door opened and he forced her outside. The warm breeze touched her face and neck and picked up the ends of her hair. He let go of the door and it slammed shut behind them.

The light above the door shined through his hair and lit up his green eyes and his knowing smile. 'You don't want to talk any more than I do.'

'Yes, I do.'

She moved away from him and somehow ended up pressed against the wood shingle siding of Slim's. They stood within the deep shadows of the building and a big blue Dumpster. Thank goodness the bar didn't serve food, and the only smell coming from the closed Dumpster was stale beer and dust.

Jack planted one hand on the building beside her head, trapping her between him and the Dumpster. 'You always were a bad liar.' He lowered his mouth to hers and said just above a whisper, 'You can deny it all night, but I know what you want, Daisy.'

She put her hands on his chest to stop him and instantly knew it was a mistake. Through the soft denim of his shirt and the hard muscles of his chest, she could feel the strong beating of his heart. It warmed her palms and spiked her blood pressure at her wrists. She turned her face to the side so she could breathe, but she couldn't quite bring herself to lower her hands. Not just yet. 'I don't think you do.'

He placed his fingers on her jaw and gently turned her face back to him. 'You want me to take you home, or take you to the backseat of my car, or take you right here against this wall.' His lips touched hers, and her breath caught in her throat. 'Just like old times.'

Her finger curled into his shirt and she held on. Oh, yes. She wanted that very much, but she wanted chocolate cake every day too. 'That would be bad, Jack.'

'No, Daisy. That would be good.'

For one brief second, it occurred to her that she'd had the same thought not long ago. Then his lips brushed hers and she shuddered. She couldn't help it. Neither could she seem to help what followed. Her palms slid up his chest, over his shoulder, then back down to his flat stomach and the waistband of his jeans. His face was so close, his nose touched hers. She couldn't see his eyes clearly, but she could feel his hot gaze on her. Then he kissed her. A gentle press of his lips that she felt in the backs of her knees and the soles of her feet. She opened her mouth beneath his and his tongue touched hers, warm and wet and that's all it took to trip her senses into overload. Heat and need and greed rushed through her, too much, too fast, and she couldn't stop it. All she could do was hold on.

His pectoral muscles bunched as she slid her hands back up his chest to his shoulders. He fed her passionate open-mouthed kisses, and she devoured them, kissing him back. Undiluted lust twisted her stomach into knots and burned her up inside, urging her to touch as much of him as possible. To eat him up and worry about it later. He tasted so good. Like a warm healthy man. The kiss turned wild as she moved her hands over his shoulders and back, ran her fingers through his cool hair, and unfastened the pearl buttons on the front of his shirt.

He pulled back and looked into her face, his breathing hard and fast as if he'd just jogged five miles. 'Daisy,' he whispered and buried his face in the side of her neck. A deep moan vibrated his chest, and he slid his open mouth to the side of her throat. His hand slipped to her waist then over her belt around her hips. His fingers pulled up the bottom of her dress. His bare hand touched the top of her thigh, and slid to her behind, cupping her through the thin layer of her silk panties.

'Someone might see us,' she warned, her voice a thin, lame protest.

He pulled her to her toes and his voice was a husky rasp when he asked, 'Would you care?'

She guessed not because she pulled the front of his shirt wide and placed her palms on his flat stomach. His skin was hot to the touch and slightly damp, a toxic sheen of desire and testosterone that seeped through her fingertips, traveled tip her arms and went straight to her head. His warm wet mouth sucked the hollow of her throat and her eyes drifted shut. It had been so long since she'd felt the push and pull of sex. The feverish rush and carnal ache. She felt it now, tugging her under until everything else was a blur.

He coaxed her leg around his waist, and the hard ridge of his erection pressed into her crotch, through the layers of his clothes and her thin panties. He grabbed her other thigh and lifted her up the wall until both her legs wrapped around his waist. Until his heated gaze met hers, then he shoved his pelvis against her.

'It's been so long,' she moaned.

With his free hand, he popped the snaps down the front of her dress. His gaze held hers as he asked, 'How long?' The backs of his fingers touched the swells of her breasts, the satin of her bra, and her cleavage. The bodice of her dress fell open and he lowered his gaze to her demi bra.

Without looking up, he asked again, 'How long has it been for you, Daisy?'

Every sensation in her body seemed to radiate outward from where their bodies touched. She ran her hands across his naked chest and combed her fingers through the short dark hair. 'What?'

'How long has it been since you've had sex?'

She hadn't meant to make that particular confession out loud. 'Awhile.'

He pushed his palm flat against her breast. 'How long's awhile?'

It was too late to take it back now. 'Two years,'

His fingers pressed into her flesh that rose above her bra. 'We can't take this any further right here.'

She moaned low in her throat and squeezed her thighs tighter. His knees buckled and he planted his hands on the side of the building by her head to keep them from falling. He moved his feet farther apart and brought his erection hard against her.

'I don't have a condom on me or in my car.' He kissed her forehead. 'Come home with me, Daisy.'

It had been so long since she'd had to worry about condoms. Not since before she and Steven had tried to have another child and discovered that he couldn't. A long time since she'd had to worry about pregnancy or anything else. Over fifteen years since she'd been with anyone but Steven. With the last rational part of her brain, she knew she couldn't do this. Not with Jack. Not here. Not at his house. Not anywhere. 'I can't do this with you,' she said before she made the second biggest mistake of her life.

He kissed the side of her neck. 'Sure you can.'

'No, Jack.' She lowered her feet to the ground and

dropped her hands to her sides. 'I'm not going to have sex with you.'

He took a step back into the gold pool of light from the building and ran his fingers through the sides of his hair. He closed his eyes and pulled air deep into his lungs. 'God damn you, Daisy,' he said, his voice a rasp of lust and anger. 'You're still as big a tease as you ever were.'

'I didn't come here to tease you or have sex with you.' His naked chest was too close, and the light from the building shined across his moist skin. She pressed her palms against the building behind her and fought the urge to reach out and touch him. To push her face to his chest and lick him like a Dreamsicle. She raised her gaze to his face. 'I told you why I'm here.'

He looked at her, his green eyes glittered with frustration. 'You still think we can talk?'

'No, not tonight.'

'That's what I thought,' he said as he wiped her red lipstick from the corner of his mouth.

'Tomorrow.'

He laughed without humor. 'Daisy, if you show up at my house tomorrow, I'm going to give you what you really want,' he said evenly as he buttoned his shirt. 'Guaran-Goddamn-teed.'

She frowned and didn't have to ask what he was talking about.

He told her anyway. 'I'm going to fuck you till you faint,' he said, then he turned and walked away.

She watched him leave, his broad shoulders disappearing as he moved down the side of the building toward the front. Within seconds, darkness swallowed him up and all she could hear was the thud of his boots and the hum of insects. She knew she should be outraged. Disgusted. Horrified. Relieved that she'd come to her senses before they'd had sex. Yes, she knew she should feel all those things, and maybe she would tomorrow. But tonight . . . tonight she felt none of those things. Beyond frustration, with lust pounding through her veins, she was more curious than anything. Was it possible to have sex until you fainted?

And if so, did Jack know from experience?

That night, Daisy dreamed she flew around Lovett in nothing but her shorty pajamas, over the tops of the trees and power poles. Mount Rainier suddenly rose up out of the flat Texas panhandle, and she flew over that too. Her toes touched the snowy peak as higher and higher she soared. Out of control like a helium balloon, up and up she went, and she was terrified because she knew there was only one outcome. She was going to fall. It was inevitable, and it was going to hurt like hell.

Then just as she was about to break through the Earth's atmosphere, gravity sucked at her feet and yanked her back down. Down past Mount Rainier and the tops of the trees, and she knew she was going to die.

Before she hit, her eyes popped open and she realized two things at once. One, she wasn't going to go smack, and two, she was holding her breath. Morning light filtered across her bed and she let out a sigh of relief. But her relief was short-lived as the events of the prior evening came back to her all at once.

Smack.

The humiliation she hadn't felt last night brought her fully awake like a bucket of cold water. Now in the light of day, she recalled every excruciating detail. Jack's slick warm mouth, the feel of his bare chest and the touch of his hands on her.

She groaned and covered her face with a pillow. The memory of her legs wrapped around his waist was especially painful. She hadn't behaved like that since . . . since . . . since she'd pulled Jack into a closet their senior year in high school. Back then she'd been young and naive. She was neither of those things now.

Now she was an idiot.

Last night she'd wanted to lick Jack. Today she had to tell him about Nathan. How could she look him in the eyes after she'd kissed him and touched him. 'Oh God,' she said as she recalled in detail her confession that she hadn't had sex in two years. How could she face him after that?

She didn't have a choice, that's how.

She tossed the pillow off her head and got out of bed. Dressed in the same shorty pajamas as in her dream, she made her way downstairs. After Jack had left her against the wall at Slim Clem's, she'd gone back into the bar, pleaded food poisoning, and made Lily take her home. She hadn't seen Jack and, for that at least, was thankful.

Her mother sat at the breakfast nook in the kitchen wearing a pink nylon nightgown. One side of her blond cotton-candy hair looked a little flat.

Last night, Pippen had been sound asleep when Lily dropped her off, so he'd spent the night. He was in his high chair next to his grandmother, eating cereal and drinking juice from his Tommy cup. He wore his coonskin cap, his Blue's Clues jammies, and a Cheerio was stuck to his cheek. 'Good morning, Mom,' she greeted as she poured herself a cup of coffee. 'How's it going, Pip?'

'Watch 'toons,' Pippen answered.

'You can watch cartoons after breakfast,' Louella told him, then she glanced over at Daisy and used the tone of voice that let Daisy know she was very disappointed. 'I heard what happened. Thelma Morgan called this morning and told me everything.'

Daisy felt her cheek catch fire. 'Thelma Morgan saw me?' Where had she been hiding? Behind the Dumpster? It was only eight in the morning, and the day was already shaping up to be pure hell.

'She pulled into the Minute Mart for a cup of coffee and a bear claw, and she saw the whole thing.'

What? 'Oh.' Daisy let out a huge sigh of relief and laughed. 'That.'

'Yes that. What where you and Lily thinking? Making a fuss in public?' Louella took a bite of her toast. 'For cryin' all night loud in a bucket.'

'We were getting a Dr Pepper at the Minute Mart,' Daisy explained and purposely left out the part about Lily's stalking her soon to be ex. She walked across the kitchen and sat at the nook with her mother. 'You-know-who,' she paused and glanced at Pippen, 'and Kelly pulled into the parking lot, and one thing led to another. Then you-know-who shoved Lily.'

Louella pursed her lips and set her toast back on her plate. 'You should have called the police.'

Probably. 'I didn't think. I just saw him push her and I

lost my mind. Without giving it a thought, I slugged him in the eye and kneed him between the legs.' She still couldn't believe she'd behaved like that.

One corner of her mother's pursed lips turned up. 'Did you damage him?'

Daisy shook her head and blew into her cup. 'I don't think so.'

'That seems a shame.' She pushed her plate aside. 'Have you seen Jack?'

Yeah, she'd seen him. His naked chest and slick abdomen. His eyes at half mast and his lips moist from kissing her, but that wasn't what her mother wanted to know. 'I haven't told him about Nathan yet,' she answered and took a drink of her coffee. 'I'm going over there this morning to talk to him.'

One brow rose up Louella's forehead. 'You've certainly put it off until the last moment.'

'I know.' She looked down at the bright yellow tabletop. 'I used to be so sure I'd done the right thing. I used to believe that not telling Jack about Nathan and moving to Washington had been best for everyone.'

'It was.'

'I'm not so sure now.' She brushed her hair behind her ears and took a deep breath. 'Before I came back to town, I was sure. I was sure moving away with Nathan was the best choice, even for Jack.' She looked back up. 'We always meant to tell him, Mom. We wanted to give Jack a few years to get his life together, and then we planned to tell him.'

Pippen dropped his empty cup on the floor and Louella bent to pick it up. 'I know you did.' She set it on the table.

'But the longer we put it off, the harder it got. Months

and years passed and there was always an excuse why we couldn't tell him right then. I was trying to get pregnant with Steven's baby or Nathan was happy and we didn't want to disrupt his life. It was always something. Always an excuse, because how do you tell a man he has a child he doesn't know about?' She leaned forward and crossed her forearms on the table. 'Now I'm not so sure I did the right thing all those years ago. I'm beginning to think I never should have left without telling him.'

'I think you're afraid and now you're questioning everything.'

'Maybe.'

'Daisy, you were young and scared and you made the right decision at the time.'

She'd always thought that too. She didn't know anymore. The only thing she knew for certain was that she'd been wrong to wait so long. How was she ever to make it right?

'Jack wasn't ready to be a father,' her mother insisted. 'Steven was.'

'You always liked Steven more than Jack.'

Her mother was quiet a moment than said, 'That's not really true. I just always thought Steven was the stabler of the two. Jack was more wild. You can't blame a person for what's in his nature, but you can't rely on him either. Your daddy was reckless like that, and look what happened to him. To us.'

'Daddy didn't die and leave us on purpose.'

'No, but he did. He left me with two children, a busted-up Winnebego and three hundred dollars.' Louella shook her head. 'When it came to taking care of you and a baby, Steven was better prepared.'

'Because his family had money'

'Money is important.' She held up her hand as if Daisy were going to argue. 'I know love is too. I loved your daddy. He loved me and he loved you girls, but love doesn't put food in your children's mouths. Love doesn't buy a winter coat or school shoes.' Her mother reached across the table and grabbed Daisy's hand. 'But even if you made the wrong decision all those years ago, it can't be changed now. Nathan has a good life. Steven was a wonderful father. You did the best thing for your child.'

Listening to her mother, made it all sound so logical. Daisy wasn't so sure anymore that the choice should have been left up to logic. Being young and scared explained why she hadn't told him fifteen years ago. It didn't explain why she hadn't told him until now.

'Look at Lily,' her mother said just above a whisper. 'Her life was chaotic long before you-know-who finally moved out. He was always running around on her. Always doing crazy things. She never should have married that wild boy, and Pippen is paying the highest price. He doesn't talk as well as he should, and he is nowhere near ready for potty training. He's actually been back sliding in his behavior.'

Daisy thought Lily could have done a lot more to protect and nurture Pippen, but she didn't say so. She hadn't been the perfect mother and wasn't about to cast aspersions on anyone else's parenting. 'I'm going to call Nathan and remind him what time I'll be home tomorrow.' She stood. 'Then I'm going to Jack's,' she said, and if she'd had any other option, she would have used it. He'd told her not to come to his house, and he'd given her that warning about fainting. Now, when she showed up, would he think she came there looking for sex?

Probably.

She took her coffee to her bedroom and called Nathan.

'I can't wait for you to get home,' he said as soon as he picked up. 'I can't wait to get away from Michael Ann.'

'Come on now, she's not that bad.'

'Mom, she still plays with Barbies. Last night, she tried to get me to be Ken.'

'Isn't she a little old for Barbies?'

'Yeah, and Ollie tried to make me play dolls with her,' he said, his voice cracking with pubescent indignation. 'I hate it here.'

'Well, this is your last night.' She set her mug on the bedside table and pulled Steven's letter from the drawer. 'Tomorrow they'll take you home, and I'll be there around three or three-thirty.'

'Thank God. And Mom?'

'Yeah, sugar lump?'

'Promise you won't ever make me stay here again.' Daisy laughed. 'I promise if you promise to get a haircut.'

There was a long pause and then he said, 'Deal.'

After she hung up the telephone, she took a shower and thought about the night before. Jack was probably over his anger by now. More than likely he'd found some willing woman to take home. While she'd been dreaming about flying, he'd probably been having wild sex and was no doubt relieved this morning that she'd stopped things between them before they'd gone too far. Now that the fever of the night before had passed, he probably wouldn't even remember that he'd threatened her.

Funny, though, the thought of him with another woman bothered her more than it should and more than she wanted to admit. The thought of him touching someone else made a lump in her stomach that hadn't been there that first night when she'd seen him and Gina together in his kitchen.

Daisy dressed in her black bra and panties and tried to understand how her feelings had changed so much in such a short time. She pulled a plain black T-shirt over her head and figured that the more she was around Jack, the more she relived the past. It was inevitable, really. She'd always loved Jack as a friend, then she'd fallen in love with him. She'd fallen so hard and so deep, and despite what she'd said the night before, sex had been a big part of their past. Being close to Jack brought up all the old feelings. All the old lust and obsession and jealousy.

She'd thought she could breeze back into town, tell Jack about Nathan and not have to deal with the rest of it. She'd thought it was buried and long gone. She'd been wrong. It hadn't gone anywhere. No, it had been waiting for her right where she'd left it.

She pulled a pair of shorts out of a drawer. If there was a consolation to this whole confusing mess, it was that once she was back home, it would all be over. No more secrets. No more confusion. No more kissing Jack Parrish.

'Daisy, if you show up at my house tomorrow, I'm going to give you what you really want,' Jack had warned. *'I'm going to fuck you till you faint.'*

His warning had intrigued her last night, this morning it gave her pause. She definitely didn't want him to think she was showing up at his house to 'faint.' No, that was the last thing she wanted him to think.

She shoved the shorts back in a drawer and walked to her mother's bedroom. She riffled through the closet until she found a sleeveless dress made of heavy denim. It was so loose it didn't have buttons or a zipper. Tigger and Winnie the Pooh were sown on the bodice and around the hem. It was the antithesis of sexy: like a kindergarten teacher, and it could in no way be confused for a dress that inspired 'fainting.'

She pulled her hair into a ponytail and wore her black flip-flops. She couldn't bring herself to go out of the house without makeup, and applied a coat of mascara, blush, and pink lip gloss. She looked herself over one last time in the mirror and determined that she looked very drab and would not inspire interest, let alone lust, in any man. Especially a man like Jack.

She shoved Steven's letter in the side pocket of the dress and grabbed her mom's car keys. All the way to Jack's, she had to fight the urge to turn around. She didn't have to guess or wonder how he would feel about Nathan now. She'd seen him with his nieces, and she knew.

She turned onto Jack's street and her fingers turned white on the steering wheel. Her mother was probably right, she'd done what she'd thought best at the time. What everyone else had thought best, too. Everyone except Jack. Jack would have a different view, and by the time she pulled her mom's Caddie behind Parrish American Classics, her stomach was in knots and she felt physically ill.

Jack's Mustang sat in front of the house, and she parked beside it. Her black flip-flops slapped her heels as she made her way across the yard and up the sidewalk. The house was still the same white color she remembered from her childhood. The same green shutters. The same yellow roses, although they weren't as well attended as they'd once been. Now they grew more wild, except for where someone had hacked at them next to the front porch.

Daisy knocked on the screen door as she had a week ago and hoped Jack was alone this time. That if he had picked up a woman, she'd left by now.

No one answered and she stuck her head inside and called out. The hum of the air-conditioner was the only sound filling the dark interior. She looked over her shoulder at Jack's Mustang and noticed that a light from inside the garage was on. Old elm trees towering overhead cast lacy shadows on the asphalt, and a slight breeze blew her ponytail as she moved to the back of the business. As quiet as possible, she opened the door and slipped inside. Sunlight from the windows high above her head threw rectangular patches of light on five classic cars in different stages of restoration. Some had their engines suspended on racks, other looked to be torn down to their frames. Along the walls, and hidden in the deeper shadows of the garage, were huge pieces of equipment, work benches, a tool chest taller than she was, and shelving that looked to hold car parts. She moved between a gutted Corvette and a shiny red-and-white land yacht that seemed to stretch out forever. The four taillights of the classic car stuck out like silver tubes of red lipstick.

She half expected to see buckets of oil and grease and metal shavings on the floor. She didn't; the garage was very clean and smelled like pine. It was a lot cleaner than it had been when Jack's father had been alive.

Despite the odds, Jack had made something of himself. Something better than what he'd been given. Certainly something more than anyone ever expected of him, and in spite of her apprehension at seeing him today, she was proud of Jack.

She looked up at the doorway to the offices and stopped

in her tracks beside the rear end of the red and white car. Jack stood with his arms folded across his chest, one shoulder shoved into the door jamb, watching her.

'Surprise,' she said, her voice a little shaky as he'd just about given her heart failure.

Fluorescent lighting shone from the room behind him and made his T-shirt appear incredibly white. A scowl turned the corners of his mouth downward and a lock of dark hair fell across his forehead. 'Not really. Those shoes you're wearing make a lot of noise.'

She looked down at her red toenails then back up at him. 'Are you hiding from me in here?'

He slowly shook his head. 'Not hardly.' He looked completely at ease, but the tension that lay between them was anything but easy. His gaze on her was hot and intense, almost tangible as it lowered from her face to the front of her dress. One corner of his mouth lifted.

'The garage sure is different,' she said into the silence. 'You should be proud of yourself, Jack.'

He looked back up into her face and his arms fell to his sides. 'You didn't come here to tell me that.'

'No.'

He pushed away from the doorframe and moved toward her, the thud of his boot heels a menacing echo as he stepped into a long patch of light. She grasped one red fin on the rear of the car to keep from backing away from him.

'I told you what would happen if you came over here today,' he said.

She didn't have to ask what he was talking about. She knew, and her failing heart pounded in her throat. 'I came here just to talk.'

'Then you shouldn't have worn that outfit.'

She looked down at her mother's dress. 'This?' She laughed despite the clog in her throat. 'Jack, it's ugly.'

'Exactly. It needs to be taken off and burned.' He stood so close that Tigger and Winnie the Pooh were almost touching the front of his T-shirt.

She looked over his shoulder at a poster of a half-naked woman sprawled out on the hood of a beefed-up Nova. 'We should talk right now.'

His fingertips touched her chin and brought her gaze back to his. 'Not now.' His thumb swept her jaw, and he lowered his face until his nose touched hers. 'Even in that stupid dress, you turn me on.' Her stomach clinched and she could hardly breathe. 'You're even more beautiful than you were growing up. And you were so beautiful back then you made me ache.' His lips brushed hers, and he kissed the corner of her mouth. 'All morning, I've been half hoping, half dreading seeing you walk through that door.' His lips touched her cheek. 'You shouldn't have come back, Daisy Lee. You should have stayed gone, but you didn't. You're here and I can't think of anything but getting inside of you. Deep inside where you're hot and wet and want me too.' The tip of his tongue touched her earlobe and her purse fell to the floor, 'The first night I saw you again, I told myself this wasn't going to happen. But it is, Daisy.'

The warmth of his breath swept the side of her neck and across her flesh. Desire tightened her nipples and pooled between her legs, and she had to stop him now, or she was a goner. 'Jack listen—'

'This was inevitable the second you stepped foot in town. I'm tired of fighting it,' he interrupted, as his hand moved to the side of her head, his thumb stroking her temple as if he were trying to soothe her. 'Tell me you feel it too. Tell me you want it as much as I do.'

'Yes, but—'

'We can talk later. After we have sex.'

She placed her palm on the front of his T-shirt. His muscles turned hard and everything in him seemed to still – except for his heart, which beat as fast as hers. Making love would make it more difficult to tell him about Nathan, but it was already going to be difficult. She didn't make a conscious decision to give in to her desire. It was just too big for her to deny any longer. It had been over two years now since she'd been with a man who desired her, and she had no willpower to resist Jack. She didn't want to resist him. He was right, this was inevitable. 'You promise we'll talk later?'

'God, yes,' he said on a rush of breath. His hands grabbed the front of her dress. 'Anything, Daisy.'

For days her body had responded to his, seeking an outlet for the passion he'd stirred back to life within her. And here it was. Here he was. Right in front of her. She pulled back and looked up into his face. 'After you left last night, were you with someone else?'

'Almost, but I wanted you.' He yanked her dress over her head and tossed it on the Corvette. She didn't even try to stop him and her T-shirt joined her dress. Within the natural light pouring in through the windows, she stood in front of him in her black bra and panties and flip-flops. He didn't give her time to think before he pulled her onto her toes and into his chest. She wrapped her arms around his neck, smashing her breasts into his chest as his mouth swooped down and covered hers in a rough kiss.

Unable to stop herself, she fell headfirst into a haze of lust and longing. And it felt good. Maybe too good. The carnal thrust of his tongue elicited an equally carnal response in her. The feel of his cotton T-shirt and Levi's against her bare skin sent a shiver down her spine. She ran her fingers through his hair as he fed her kisses from his hot, wet mouth. She moved against him, trying to get closer, trying to feel more of him. Wanting it so much her skin tingled with a powerful yearning. Wanting it all. All at once.

It had been so long. Too long to go so slow. A frustrated moan came from her throat and she dropped to her heels. She felt his long hard erection against her belly as her open mouth tasted the side of his neck. 'Jack,' she said between kisses to his throat. 'You taste good. I want to eat you up.'

'Jesus, Daisy,' he groaned as his hands roamed her bare back. He pulled the covered elastic from her ponytail and her hair came free and brushed her bare shoulders. He grabbed two fistfuls of her hair and brought her mouth back to his. She kissed him as one of his hands slid down her spine and he unhooked her bra. He pulled the bra from her and tossed it on the trunk of the red and white car. His mouth came down on hers as his hands came up to cup her breasts. Her nipples puckered in his hot palms, and she shoved her hands beneath his shirt and ran them all over him, his stomach, chest and back.

He moved his hands to her behind, and he grabbed the backs of her thighs. He lifted her onto the trunk of the car and her bare feet rested on the wide chrome bumper. The cool metal brought her out of her haze just enough that she was aware of sitting in a shaft of sunlight, naked except for her panties. She covered her breasts with her hands. 'What kind of car is this?' she asked as to cover her sudden embarrassment.

'What you have here is a Custom Lancer,' he answered as he pulled his T-shirt over his head and tossed it next to her dress. 'It seems appropriate for what I have in mind for you.'

She licked her swollen lips. 'What do you have in mind?'

'We're going to test the Level-Flight suspension.' He pushed her knees apart and stepped between her thighs. 'Drop your hands, buttercup.'

When she'd had Nathan, her breasts had grown larger and she'd never lost the weight there. 'I'm bigger than I used to be.'

'I noticed.' He grasped her wrists. 'I want to see if you still have the little mark that looks like a love bite.'

'I do.'

He didn't force her to drop her hands, just said, 'Show me.'

'I have stretch marks.' The thin pale lines were hardly visible now, but they were still there.

'I want to see all of you, Daisy.'

'I'm older, Jack.'

'So am I.'

She leaned forward and placed her open mouth on his bare shoulder. 'No, you're even better than you were.' She kissed the hollow of his throat and he took her hands from her breasts and placed them on the waistband of his jeans.

'Unzip me,' he said, his voice all smoky with passion. He reached into his back pocket, then tossed a condom on the trunk next to her.

Daisy pulled the metal top button until it came free. He

wasn't wearing underwear, and she slid the metal tab downward, exposing the line of hair that grew from his navel to his groin. He was tucked to the left and she looked up into his face as she shoved her hand into his pants. She pressed her palm against the hard length of his penis, and he gazed at her through eyes totally gone with passion.

'Take it out,' he said in a rough voice.

She pushed at the waistband of the jeans and shoved them down his thighs. His erection jutted toward her, huge and smooth like hot marble, and she took him in her hand. His hard flesh burned her palm and she stroked his long shaft. She scooted down to sit on the car's bumper and pressed a kiss on the voluptuous head. She hadn't planned to kiss him there, but it had been a long time and she wanted it all. A bead of clear moisture rested in the cleft and she licked it clean. He smelled good. Tasted better, and was bigger than she remembered too. Or perhaps she'd forgotten.

He groaned his pleasure deep, deep within his chest and pushed her hair out of her face. She looked up at him and watched his eyes as she took him more fully into her mouth. His nostrils flared slightly and he pulled in a deep breath.

'Ah, Daisy,' he whispered, then tilted his head back. Long ago, he'd taught her how to please him this way. She hadn't forgotten. She ran one hand up the back of his thigh and grasped his tight behind. In her free hand, she lightly cupped his testicles in her palm. With her tongue, she found his pulse just below the head of his penis.

It seemed she'd just started when he pushed her away. 'I don't want to get off that way,' he said and gently he lifted her onto the trunk once more. He forced her onto her back and pulled off her panties. Then he stepped between her legs. His gaze traveled from her face, down her throat to her breasts. He leaned over her and cupped between her thighs. 'You make me feel eighteen again,' he said as he rested his weight on his forearm next to her shoulder. 'Like I can't control myself.' He kissed the tip of her breast as he stroked her slick, sensitive flesh. 'Like I'm going to go off before we get to the really good stuff.'

She arched her back and moaned. 'Then get to the good stuff.'

'Daisy.'

'Mmm?'

He kissed her birthmark then brushed the seam of his lips across the tip of her breast. 'Your breasts are as beautiful as ever.'

She might have laughed or argued or something if he hadn't opened his hot mouth and sucked her nipple inside his wet mouth. Instead she ran her fingers through his hair. She shut her eyes and let the waves of sensation roll through her until she feared that *she* was going to go off before they got to the good stuff.

'Daisy open your eyes and look at me.'

She did. He gazed down at her, his own eyes intense and feverish. He grabbed the condom and tore open the package. 'I want to see your face when I'm inside of you.' He rolled the lubricated latex over the head of his penis and down the shaft to his dark pubic hair. He put his hands beneath her bare bottom and pulled her to the edge of the car's trunk, positioning her. 'I want you to see me.'

She looked into his green eyes that were so familiar to her. 'I see you,' she said as he grasped her thighs. He plunged inside of her in one smooth stroke that buried him to her cervix. His grasp tightened on her thighs and her back arched. She cried out in pain and in pleasure, she wasn't sure which was more acute.

'Damn,' he said between clenched teeth, then he cupped her face in his hands. 'Sorry, Daisy.' He placed a soft kiss on her cheek and nose and whispered against her mouth, 'I'm sorry. Sorry. I'll make it feel good now. I promise.' He withdrew, then thrust himself inside with more care, reminding her how good he was at keeping his promises. Slowly, he gave her incredible pleasure with smooth, measured strokes.

He stared into her eyes as he moved within her. 'Is that better?'

'Mmm, yes.'

'Tell me.'

'So good, Jack.' She felt weightless and she grabbed his shoulders and held on to him. 'Don't stop. Whatever you do, just don't stop.'

'Not a chance.' He tilted her pelvis up without missing a beat of his pumping hips.

Heat flushed her skin, radiating outward from where they were joined, and she dug her fingers into him. His slow pace was driving her mad. 'More. Give me more, Jack.'

He kissed her forehead and his breathing rasped against her temple. He plunged faster. Harder. In and out. Building. Thrusting her toward climax.

'Daisy Lee.' Her name on his lips sounded almost like a question, as if he pushed them both closer and closer. She was mindless to anything but the building pleasure, until she opened her mouth to scream. The sound died in her throat as wave after luscious wave rolled through her. Her muscles pulsed and contracted, gripping him hard.

On and on it went as he plunged into her. His breath hot against her temple until finally he shoved into her so hard he pushed her farther up the trunk of the car. He cursed her and God in the same incoherent sentence. He crushed her to his chest as if he wanted to absorb her and gave one final thrust. He made a sound deep in his throat, a sound somewhere between a guttural groan and a long drawn-out *ahhh*.

Daisy saw spots behind her closed eyelids, and her ears began to ring. She was going to faint. Right there on the Custom Lancer. It was going to happen. Just like he'd said she would, and she didn't care.

She didn't faint, though. Not really. She was just so light-headed she was afraid to move. She hadn't had sex in a long time, but she didn't recall it being so good. It had been. Of course it had been. But where his skin was stuck to hers, still tingled. She'd forgotten that part. Or maybe that had never happened before.

He remained embedded deep in her body, his chest smashed into hers and his forehead resting on the car next to her right ear. She could feel his heartbeat against her breast.

She opened her eyes and looked up at the ventilation overhead. Jack Parrish had just taken her some place she'd never been before. He'd just given her a devastating orgasm that had curled her toes and about made her faint. She didn't know what to think about that. In fact, she could hardly think at all. She was too stunned.

He raised onto his forearms and looked down into her face. A slow satisfied smile lifted the corners of his mouth. 'Wow. You're even better than you were at eighteen.'

Daisy looked into his sexy green eyes and felt alive

again. Like she'd been dead inside for a very long time and hadn't even realized it until that moment. Like coming into the sunlight after being trapped in the dark. Raw emotion swept through her, and she did the worst possible thing she could do.

She burst into tears.

No one had ever cried on Jack before. Not after sex, anyway. Hell, Daisy hadn't even cried the night he'd taken her virginity.

He tossed his T-shirt on the kitchen counter and glanced over at Daisy who stood across the room from him, her arms folded beneath her breasts, staring at her toes. He was reminded of the first night he'd seen her since she'd been back. She'd been wearing a yellow rain slicker then. Now she had on that stupid Winnie the Pooh dress, the one he'd helped her get back into a few moments ago.

She'd thrown him a curve that was for sure. One second she'd been having a good time, moaning and scratching, and telling him she wanted more. In the next she'd burst into tears. What the hell had happened?

He'd excused himself to get rid of the condom in the employees' bathroom, and when he'd returned she'd been fighting to get her dress over her head. He was halfway convinced that if she'd been able to get her clothes on faster, she would have been long gone by now. Which might have been for the best.

She'd been so agitated he had to help her with her dress when what he'd really wanted was to toss it in the garbage. He'd put her purse on her shoulder, and instead of sending her on her way, like he would have any other hysterical woman who'd burst into tears on him, he'd brought her into his house. Why, he did not know. Except maybe because he'd told her he'd let her talk after they'd had sex.

Yeah, that was it, but now that his head was clear, he was pretty sure he didn't want to hear anything she had to say. Unless it had something to do with her getting naked and climbing on top of him.

He'd thought once they'd had sex, his desire for her would be sated. He'd be over it. He'd been wrong, and that bothered him because he didn't want to think about what that might mean. He didn't want to feel anything for her now. Not even lust.

He reached inside the refrigerator and pulled out a carton of milk. Before his mind traveled any further in the direction of the bedroom, he stopped and reminded himself that she was upset and crying and that she was Daisy Monroe. Three very good reasons why he had to stand across the room from her and keep his hands to himself.

'Before I apologize,' he said as he shut the door with his foot, 'I need to know what I'm apologizing for.'

She looked up at him. She had black smudges beneath her red eyes and her face was all splotchy. 'You didn't do anything, Jack.'

He didn't think he had either, but with women, you just

never knew. If there wasn't a problem, they'd invent one. 'Do you want something to drink?' She shook her head and he raised the milk to his mouth and watched her over the bottom of the quart container. He lowered the milk and licked his top lip. Maybe he'd been too rough with her. He'd forgotten that she hadn't had sex in awhile. 'Did I hurt you?'

She wiped her cheeks with her fingers. 'No.'

He set the milk on the counter and opened a cabinet. He filled a glass with ice and water then moved across the kitchen and handed it to her. His fingers brushed hers and he asked, 'Why are you crying, Daisy?'

'I don't know.'

'I think you do.' She looked like crap. Kind of scary, but for some reason, the only thing that scared him was how much he still wanted her. 'Tell me, Daisy.'

She took a long drink of her water then pressed the cool glass against her cheek. 'It's embarrassing.' As if to prove her point, her face turned red and kind of connected the splotchy parts.

'Why don't you just tell me anyway?' Instead of putting distance between her body and his like he should, he leaned a hip into the counter next to her and folded his arms over his bare chest.

She glanced up at him out of the corners of her eyes then cut her gaze to the Elmo cookie jar on the counter. 'Elmo?'

'Billy's girls gave it to me last Christmas, along with a bag of Oreos. Don't change the subject.'

Her gaze remained on the bright orange cookie jar and she took a deep breath. 'I just forgot about sex for a while.' She shrugged. 'And you reminded me.'

'That's it?' There had to be more.

'Well, it was good sex.'

'Daisy, it was better than good.' They'd gone at it like two starving people at an all-you-can-eat. All hands and mouths and insatiable hunger. Racing for satisfaction. She'd come harder than anyone he'd ever been with, squeezing an orgasm from him that he felt clear to the soles of his feet.

It was a good thing she was leaving tomorrow. Because he could tell himself that he wouldn't go after her again, but he'd probably be lying about that. 'Saying it was good is like saying the Rio Grande is just a river. It's a hell of an understatement.' He put his fingers to her jaw and lightly brought her gaze back to his. Her eyelashes were stuck together over her shiny brown eyes. He brushed his fingertips across her soft skin then dropped his hand. 'Why has it been so long since you've had sex?'

If it was possible, she turned even redder. 'That's really not your business.'

'You haven't had sex in two years, but you have it with me. I think that makes it my business.'

She frowned and set her glass on the counter. Just when he thought she wasn't going to answer, she said, 'For about the last year and a half of his life, Steven couldn't.'

That surprised him. 'And you didn't go elsewhere?'

'Of course not. What a horrible question.'

He didn't think he was out of line. Fifteen years ago, she'd been having sex with him but had married Steven. 'Some women might have.'

'Not me. I was always faithful to Steven.'

'He's been gone seven months.'

'Almost eight now.'

'Eight months is a long time to go without getting laid.'

Her gaze slid from his eyes to his mouth, down his throat and stopped on his chest. 'Maybe for some people.'

'No, most people.'

She looked away. 'You know that old saying, "If you don't use it, you lose it." It's true.'

'You obviously haven't lost it.'

She grabbed her glass and he watched her move to the kitchen sink. She looked out the window into the backyard and took a long drink. She set the water back down and her hands grasped the counter. 'I did for a while. When you live with someone who is dying, sex is not a high priority. Believe me. Your life becomes consumed with doctor's appointments and trying new therapies. Figuring out the right medication to combat strokes and seizures and pain management.'

He turned to gaze at her profile. He didn't want to know any of this. He didn't want to feel sorry for Steven, but he couldn't seem to help but ask, 'Was Steven in a lot of pain?'

She shrugged. 'He never liked to admit it, but I know that he was. I'd ask him and he'd just grab my hand and tell me not to worry about him.' She laughed without humor. 'I pretended not to worry, and he pretended everything was okay. He was better at his part than I was.'

'Steven was always better at pretending than either you or me.' For years he and Steven had pretended that Daisy was just a friend. A girl who was a buddy. Steven had been so much better at it than Jack.

She nodded. 'He pretended right up until the last day. The night he died, he slipped into a coma, at home.' She looked over her shoulder and her eyes met his across the distance. 'Nathan and I watched him take his last breath. If you've ever seen something like that, it changes you. You get real clear about what's important.' She swallowed hard and added, 'About things you have to make right.'

He stood very still as his stomach twisted into a knot. Daisy's words affected him more than he would have thought. He hadn't watched either of his parents die, and for that he was grateful. He had dark enough memories.

'Did you know that coffins have springs in them?'

'Yeah.' He and Billy had had to pick out two. At that time, he hadn't had enough money to afford much of anything. His parents had been buried without springs and fancy satin pillows. 'I knew that.'

'Oh. That's right.' She looked back out the window. 'I remember your parents' funeral. You were so young to have such a horrible thing happen to you. I didn't appreciate how horrible then. Not really. I do now.'

Jack moved to stand behind her and he raised his hands to grasp her arms. But before he touched her, he thought better of it and dropped them to his sides.

She took an envelope from a pocket in her ugly dress and set it next to the sink. 'This is the letter from Steven. The one I told you about.'

He really didn't want to read it, and knew that made him all kinds of a bastard. But he really didn't want to be reminded of the black hole of his past.

'Steven and I never meant to hurt you, Jack. We were all such good friends, and it never should have ended between us the way it did. We were so young and stupid. The night we came to you was one of the worst nights of my life.' She paused a moment and said just above a whisper, 'You were wearing a white T-shirt that night too.'

Yes, they'd been standing in the moonlight. He'd been pleading with her not to leave him. He'd beaten the hell out of his best buddy, and now his best buddy was dead. Something in Jack had died that night too. For some reason, hearing about it this morning, made it more real then it had been in years. Brought it all back to life. Made the places in his soul burn. 'Stop it, Daisy.' He grabbed her arms below the sleeves of her T-shirt. 'Don't say any more.'

'I have to, Jack.' She looked up over her shoulder into his face. 'When you told me that we needed time away from each other, I was so scared. I didn't know what to do. You have to understand how scared and—' He lifted her chin as his mouth swooped down on hers, silencing her with a hard kiss. He pulled her back against his bare chest and wrapped his arm around her stomach. He did not want to hear anything; he just wanted to feel. Feel her pressed against the length of him. Naked. He wanted more mind-numbing sex again and again until he finally got her out of his system. Out of his head.

At first she stood stiff in his arms, her lips pressed together but when he softened the kiss, her lips parted. A silent invitation to take what he wanted.

The telephone rang and he let it. It rang as his tongue entered her mouth, and she tasted as she had before, on the trunk of the Custom Lancer. Warm and sweet like Daisy. She tasted of things long forgotten. Of soft skin and need and lust and a love that had ripped his heart out.

He pushed the memories from his head as he slid one hand to her right breast. The phone continued to ring as he cupped between her legs through the heavy denim. 'Daisy,' he spoke to the side of her head and breathed deep the scent of her hair. 'Come to my bed and let me remind you about sex again.'

The ringing stopped but instantly started again. Daisy slid out of his grasp and moved across the kitchen. 'That might be important,' she said.

He had a pretty good idea who it was. Buddy Calhoun was supposed to come by and pick up a Corvair Monza sitting in the shop and take it to his garage in Lubbock. Buddy was the best body man in the state, and one of the few restorers Jack trusted to take a vehicle out of his shop. But his timing sucked. Instead of pursuing Daisy, he walked to the telephone, his boot heels an angry thud against the old linoleum floor. 'This better be good,' he said into the receiver.

'Hello,' a female voice spoke, 'this is Louella Brooks. Is Daisy there?'

He glanced back at Daisy. 'Oh, hello Mrs Brooks. Yeah, she's right here.'

Daisy walked across the kitchen and took the phone from him. 'Hello?' She looked up at him and frowned. 'What? What happened? Is she okay?' Her brows lifted almost to her hairline. 'Good. Where's Pippen?' Daisy covered the side of her face with her hand. 'Thank God.' There was a pause and then she said, 'Okay. I'm on my way.' She hung up the telephone and turned to Jack.

'What's the matter?'

'My sister has officially lost her mind. That's what's the matter,' she said as she moved to the counter and picked up her purse.

He ignored the ache between his legs as he reached

for his T-shirt and pulled it over his head. 'Is Lily okay?'

'No, she's a nut. What did she and mother do before I came to visit?' she asked, distracted as she shoved her hand inside her purse and pulled out a set of keys. 'Run around acting weird and delusional? What are they going to do once I go back home?' She walked from the kitchen and through the living room. 'Good gravy, I have my act together more than either of those women. Now, how darn scary is that?'

He didn't answer because he pretty much figured it was a rhetorical question and he didn't want to upset her more.

Through the screen door, he watched her jump in her mother's car and drive away. A glimpse of the Caddy's taillights and whine of the steering linkage as she pulled around to the street, was the last he expected to see or hear of Daisy Monroe.

Jack walked back through the empty house to the kitchen. He returned the milk to the refrigerator, and his gaze fell on the white envelope she'd left behind. Steven's letter. He picked it up and turned it over in his hands. His name was written in all capital letters in blue ink on the front.

He opened a cupboard door and stuck the envelope between two coffee mugs. He'd read it someday. But not now. Not when the memory of Daisy, naked on the back of the Custom Lancer was still so fresh in his head. Not when the taste of Steven's wife was still in his mouth.

Since she'd been back, he'd wondered if being with Daisy would be as good as he remembered. The answer was that it was better. Better in some way he didn't even try to define. He just knew that being with her was different. It was more than just sex. More than the pleasure he usually found being with a woman. More than a quickie on the trunk of a car.

It wasn't love. He knew for a fact that he wasn't in love with Daisy Lee. He might talk slow, but he wasn't stupid. And loving Daisy was just plain stupid. He didn't know why being with her felt different, but he didn't want to know either. He wasn't the kind of guy who dissected his life and looked for hidden meaning. No, he was the kind of guy who pushed it down deep until it went away. All he knew for certain was that sex with her was better than any he'd had in a long time, and it was a good thing that she was leaving so he could return to his life. His life before she'd blown into town and reminded him of things that were better left forgotten.

She was gone now, and there was no reason why he should think of her again.

No reason at all.

A black-and-white tow truck pulled up to Ronnie's house as Daisy and Louella drove past on their way to the hospital. It was only a few blocks out of their way on Locust Grove, and they had to see the destruction for themselves.

Ronnie's little house was beige stucco and someone had nailed a longhorn skull over the front door. His yard consisted of stubby brown weeds, and it would have been a drab scene if not for Lily's Red Ford Taurus sticking half out the front room.

'Was Ronnie home?' Daisy asked as she floored the Caddy and sped on. She figured all the cops standing around were too busy gawking at Lily's Taurus to take notice of a speeder.

'I don't think so, but we won't know for sure until we get to the hospital.'

Daisy hated hospitals. No matter the city or state, they all smelled and felt the same. Sterile and cold. She'd spent enough time in them with Steven to know that they dispensed a lot of medication and advice, but rarely good news.

She and her mother walked through the small hospital's emergency room doors and, after a few moments, were taken to Lily. Pippen was at home with Louella's next-door neighbor, and it was a good thing he wasn't with them. The second the nurse pushed back the green-and-blue striped curtain separating the beds, Louella burst into tears.

'It's okay, Mom,' Daisy said, suddenly feeling like the only sane person in a family that had lost its collective mind. She took her mother's hand and held tight. 'Lily's going to be okay.'

But Lily didn't look okay. The left side of her face was swelling and there was a gash on her forehead. Blood caked her blond hair and the corners of her closed eyes. Some sort of bandaging immobilized her left arm, thick and very white, except where bright red blood seeped through. There was an IV in her right forearm, which wasn't bandaged, and her clothes had been cut off. A young male doctor in green scrubs lifted the sheet to listen to her heart and lungs. He looked up at them through wire-framed glasses.

Louella moved to the head of the bed and Daisy went with her. 'Lily Belle. Momma's here. Daisy too.'

Lily didn't respond and Daisy reached out to touch the side of her face that wasn't swollen. Her sister looked deadly pale, and if it weren't for the steady rise and fall of her chest, Daisy would have thought she really was dead. It was too much in an already emotionally charged day, and like the flip of a switch, Daisy's autopilot kicked in, and she felt herself go numb inside.

'What's the matter with her?' Louella asked.

'All we know so far,' the young doctor answered, 'is she has lacerations to her left arm and forehead and her ankle looks to be fractured. We won't know anything more until we get her CT scans.'

'Why isn't she awake?'

'She took a pretty nasty hit to her forehead. I don't believe her skull is fractured and her pupils are responsive. We'll know more after we get a look at her X-rays.'

'Was there anyone else hurt in the accident?' Daisy asked, praying Lily hadn't mowed down Ronnie and Kelly.

'She was the only one transported from the scene.'

Which told Daisy nothing. Ronnie and Kelly could have been treated at the scene or, God forbid, dead. She hadn't seen Ronnie, but she hadn't been looking.

They were permitted only a few moments with Lily before she was wheeled away. They were told a doctor would talk to them shortly, but Daisy knew 'shortly' could take hours.

She and her mother were shown to a small waiting room, and it looked and felt like every other waiting room she'd ever been in. She figured that all hospitals must choose colors from the same palate. Blues, greens, and a dash of maroon.

They sat together on a small blue sofa, and on the table next to Daisy sat a fake fern, a copy of *Reader's Digest*, *Newsweek*, and the Gideon Bible. She'd read a lot of

Reader's Digest over of the last two and a half years, and she didn't even have a subscription.

A man and a woman stood near the door talking in hushed tones as if they raised their voice they'd scream. Daisy knew how they felt. She'd been here before, so many times. Finding distractions so she wouldn't scream and fall apart, concentrating on nice, even breaths so she could pretend her husband hadn't been dying. And now that her sister wasn't lying on a hospital gurney with blood crusted in her beautiful blond hair.

She picked up the *Reader's Digest* and flipped to 'Humor in Uniform.'

'She looked so white,' Louella said, a tremble in her voice. 'And there was so much blood.'

'Scalps bleed a lot, Mom.' She sounded so cool. As if she wasn't trembling inside, in the place where she shoved it all away. Down deep where she could control it. She'd gotten really good at sucking up her emotions and going numb inside. Never letting things get too close to the surface, because if she let that happen, she'd lose it for sure. Like with Jack today.

'How do you know?'

'Steven,' she answered, and concentrated even harder on her magazine. She didn't want to think about Jack right now. She'd have to deal with him, and the repercussions of what she'd done, but not today. For now she pushed that problem down to the number two spot on her to-do list. Lily and the potential of murder charges moved to number one. She wondered how much a really good psychiatrist cost these days.

'Why wouldn't they tell us anything?'

'They don't know anything right now.'

A police officer walked into the room and asked if they were related to Lily. He had a crewcut and wore a blue uniform and looked as if he could bench three hundred. He identified himself as Officer Neal Flegel. 'I graduated high school with Lily and Ronnie,' he said.

'You're Matt's little brother.' Daisy shook his hand. 'I went to a high school dance with Matt our sophomore year. Does he still live in Lovett?' she asked, because after all, this was Texas and manners came before emergencies.

'He just moved back from San Antone. I'll tell him you asked about him.' He pulled out his notebook and got down to business. 'I surely hated to see Lily in that car.' He told them that the Taurus had come to a stop five feet inside Ronnie's living room. And as Daisy tried to figure out a subtle way of inquiring if Lily had killed Ronnie, Neal Flegel asked, 'Do either of you have any reason to think she might have done this on purpose?'

That had actually been Daisy's first and only thought. 'No.' She shook her head and tried to look perplexed. 'It must have been an accident.'

'Her foot must have slipped,' Louella said, and Daisy wondered if her mother actually believed it any more than she did. 'And,' Louella continued as if just struck by a thought, 'she's been getting those blinding migraines lately.'

'We spoke to Ronnie and he told us they'd been fighting a lot lately.'

'You spoke to Ronnie today?' Daisy almost laughed with relief. 'After the accident?'

'We contacted him at his girlfriend's.'

'So he wasn't even home?'

'No one was in the home at the time.'

'Thank God,' Daisy sighed. Her sister wasn't going to fry for murder. This was Texas. If you were going to commit murder, Texas wasn't a good state to do it in. On the other hand, juries filled with Texas women did tend to sympathize with the wife of a cheating dog.

'Has she been suicidal?' Neal asked.

That gave both Daisy and her mother pause. Lily was depressed and pissed off, but Daisy didn't think she wanted to kill herself. Just Ronnie.

'No,' Louella answered. 'She just got a job working at Albertsons's deli. Things are looking up for her now.'

'I was with her last night, and she was fine,' Daisy told the officer. And it was the truth. Lily had been fine the night before. Daisy had only had to listen to 'Earl Had to Die' twice. Once on the way to Slim Clem's and once on the way home.

Neal asked a few more questions and when he left, Daisy asked her mother, 'Do you think she tried to kill herself?'

'Of course not,' Louella said through a frown.

'Do you think she tried to kill Ronnie?'

'Daisy Lee, your sister's foot slipped, is all.' And that was the end of the discussion.

Except that wasn't all. Not for Daisy. With Lily in the hospital and potentially homicidal, she couldn't possibly go home tomorrow. Nathan was not going to be happy.

She excused herself and found a bank of phones next to the Coke and candy machines. She used her calling card, and when Nathan got on the phone she tried to sound cheerful. Why, she really didn't know – other than that's what she was supposed to do.

'Hey there, Nathan.'

'Hi, Mom.'

She hesitated for a heartbeat, then cut right to the chase. 'I have some news you're not going to like.'

There was a long pause. 'What?'

'Your aunt Lily was in a bad car accident this morning. She's in the hospital. I won't be coming home tomorrow.'

He didn't ask about Lily. He was fifteen and concerned with his own problems. 'You can't do this to me.'

'Nathan, Lily is really hurt.'

'I'm sorry about that, but you promised!'

'Nathan, I didn't know Lily was going to drive her car into Ronnie's living room.'

'I got my hair cut! No way. No way, Mom. I am not staying here. They tried to make me eat Swedish meatballs last night.'

They probably hadn't tried to make him do anything, but Nathan detested Swedish meatballs and chose to see it as a conspiracy. One more reason why he didn't like staying with them. Daisy sighed and wedged herself between the pay phone and the deep blue soda machine. 'I don't know what to do, Nate. I really can't leave your grandmother and Lily right now. It isn't like I'm down here partying it up while you're consigned to hell.'

'I want to come down there, then.'

'What?'

'Mom, I hate it here. I'd rather be there with you.'

She thought of Jack.

'You can't do this to me.' Over the phone line, she could hear Nathan's voice crack with emotion he tried to hold back. 'Please, Mom.'

What were the chances he'd run into Jack before she spoke to him? Next to none. He'd probably just hang out and watch TV at his grandmother's house. And even if the two did accidentally meet, so what? They didn't look anything alike. They wouldn't know who the other was. Nathan never asked about Jack, and she doubted he even remembered Jack's last name. 'If that's what you really want, I'll call around and get you a flight down here.'

His sigh of relief carried over the line. 'I love you, Mom.'

'Funny how you only remember to mention it when you're getting your way.' She smiled. 'Get your aunt Junie on the phone.'

After she hung up from talking to Steven's sister, she called around and got a flight out of Seattle for the next day. It departed at six in the morning, had a three hour and forty minute layover in Dallas, and didn't arrive in Amarillo until almost five P.M. She thought about maybe driving to Dallas and picking Nathan up there. It was a six-hour drive, one way. Maybe they could spend the night in the big D. Go to Fort Worth and Cow Town and have barbeque. The more she thought of it, the more it appealed to her. She needed a vacation from her vacation, but when she called Nathan back, he told her that he'd rather sit for three hours in the Dallas-Fort Worth airport than eat barbeque and drive for six hours the next day. So much for getting away from the chaos. But she supposed that no matter how tempting, she couldn't leave her mother and Lily right now.

She booked his ticket, and as she walked back to the waiting room, she wondered if her family had always been this insane, or if they were diving headfirst into crazy creek on her behalf.

By the time she made it back to her mother, the doctor

was sitting beside her on the short sofa. Daisy moved to stand by Louella.

'Is she awake?' her mother asked.

'She woke up about fifteen minutes ago. Her CT scans are clear. There isn't any brain trauma or injury to her internal organs. It's a good thing she was wearing her seat belt and that the car had air bags.' He glanced up at Daisy. 'Her ankle is broken and she's going to need surgery to pin the bones back together. An orthopedic surgeon is on his way from Amarillo.'

After the doctor left, Louella stayed with Lily at the hospital and Daisy left to take care of Pippen. She put him down for a nap and finally changed out of her mother's Winnie the Pooh dress. With nothing else to occupy her mind, she thought of Jack. *Even in that stupid dress, you turn me on*, he'd said, which was just absurd.

She changed into a khaki skirt and white blouse and scrounged around in the kitchen for something to eat. She made a toasted cheese sandwich, some tomato soup, and a glass of iced tea. She took it to the breakfast nook, where the sun lit up the yellow table.

Having sex with Jack on the trunk of a car had been a mistake. No, having sex with him at all had been a mistake. But at the time, she hadn't possessed the will power to do much more than put up a half-hearted objection. She'd known she would regret it, but that hadn't stopped her.

She dunked her sandwich into her soup and took a bite. She'd had sex with Jack. It had been bad. No, it had been *wrong*. The sex had been good. Fabulous. So fabulous she'd burst into tears and embarrassed herself. Her face got hot just thinking about that – about that *and* the desire in Jack's green eyes when he'd looked at her, hot and alive touching her all over. Just the thought of it warmed her up.

She blew into her soup. She hated to admit it, but if her mother hadn't called, it was likely that she would have ended up in his bed. She'd probably still be there.

She took a drink of her tea. But what now? She didn't know, and with everything else going on in her life, she didn't have to think about it until everything settled a bit.

After Pippen got up from his nap, she took photographs of him out in her mother's garden. She shot him picking forbidden flowers while standing amongst the pink flamingos. For that short time, while she gazed at the world from behind her camera, her problems receded to the background.

Later when Louella came home, she noticed her mother looked about ten years older than she had that morning. The creases around her eyes seemed deeper, her cheeks paler. Daisy made her and Pippen some soup and sandwiches then left to go visit with Lily.

Her sister was asleep when she walked into her hospital room. The cut on her forehead had been closed and bandaged. One side of her face was still swollen, her eyes were turning varying shades of black and blue, but the blood had been cleaned away.

Daisy wanted to ask her sister what had happened that morning, but Lily was heavily drugged and drifted in and out of consciousness. And each time she woke up, she started to cry and asked where she was. Daisy didn't even attempt to ask her about the accident.

She did the next day, though.

'Have the police talked to you yet?' she asked as she flipped through a *People* magazine she'd brought with her.

Lily licked her swollen lip. Her voice was a scratchy whisper when she said, 'About what?'

Daisy stood and filled a plastic glass with cool water. She held the straw to Lily's mouth and answered, 'About the car accident?'

Lily swallowed. 'No. Mom said I wrecked my Taurus.'

'You don't remember?'

She shook her head and winced. 'I hated that car anyway.'

'Did mom tell you how you wrecked it?'

'No. Did I run a stop sign?'

'Lily, you ran your Taurus through Ronnie's front room.'

She stared at Daisy and blinked her black-and-blue eyes. But she didn't look as surprised as Daisy expected. 'Seriously?'

'The police asked Mom and me if you're suicidal.'

'I would never kill myself over Ronnie Darlington,' she said without hesitation.

'Did you try to kill Ronnie?'

'No.'

'Then what were you thinking? Did something happen?'

This time she did hesitate and she looked away when she answered, 'I don't know.'

Daisy had a feeling that she did know and that her memory loss was convenient. Something had happened, but Lily didn't want to talk about it today. Fine. There was always tomorrow.

When Daisy left the hospital, she drove into town and bought a car seat for Pippen. His other seat was still in the Taurus at the wrecking yard.

As she stopped for a traffic light at the intersection of Third and Main, she heard a deep throaty rumble just before Jack's Mustang blew through the intersection. She was two cars back, and she doubted he saw her. But just the split-second sight of him caused a disturbing tumble in her stomach as if they were in high school all over again and she was waiting for him at his locker. Her feelings for him were definitely a confused jumble of old emotions and new desires and all of it was better left alone.

At three-thirty that afternoon, Daisy strapped Pippen into her mother's Cadillac and they headed for Amarillo and Nathan.

Pippen wore little jean shorts, cowboy boots, and his DON'T MESS WITH TYRANNOSAURUS TEX T-shirt. Daisy held him in her arms while they waited in the baggage claim area. The half hour they stood there seemed to take forever, but when she saw Nathan's familiar face, it was like the sun had suddenly decided to shine after a week of gloomy weather.

His green Mohawk was gone and the tips of his short dark hair had been bleached white. He looked like a tall skinny porcupine carrying a big backpack with his skateboard attached to the back. She didn't care. She was so happy to see him she forgot about the No Public Displays of Affection rule. She stood on her tip toes and wrapped her free arm around his neck. She kissed his cheek and held on tight. He must have forgotten the rule too, because he dropped his backpack and hugged her – her and Pippen, right there in the Amarillo airport.

'Man, Mom. Don't ever leave me like that again.'

She laughed and pulled back to look into his blue eyes. 'I won't leave you. I promise,' she said and turned her attention to Pippen. 'This is your cousin. Isn't he cute?'

Nathan studied him for a moment. 'Mom, the kid has a mullet.'

She pretty much figured that a guy with porcupine hair shouldn't cast stones at a guy with a mullet. 'It's not his fault,' she said and looked into Pippen's face. 'His mother won't cut off his baby curls.'

Pippen stared up at her through his big blue eyes so much like Lily's, then returned his gaze to his older cousin. Daisy didn't know if Pippen's attention was drawn to him because he was another male or if he was attracted to the lip ring and dog chains.

'Hey there, little dude. Nice hair.'

'Don't make fun,' Daisy warned.

'I'm not.' Nathan slicked his palms over the side of his hair. 'He's got business in the front, party in the back. Heh-heh-heh,' he laughed as he tipped his head back.

'Watch 'toons!' Pippen said, then started to laugh too as if he'd just cracked a joke like Nathan.

'He wants you to watch cartoons with him. His favorite is "Blue's Clues." '

' "Blue's Clues" suck.' He picked up his backpack. 'You gotta watch "Sponge Bob Square Pants," '

Nathan hadn't brought a suitcase, and as they headed for the car, it struck her that if everything had gone according to her original plan, she would have been back home now. In Seattle. Getting on with her life. Free of the past. Making a new start. Her and Nathan.

Since she'd arrived in Lovett, nothing had gone according to her plan, and she'd had to put her life on hold for just a little while longer. Her mother and sister needed her, and perhaps she could do something to help. Maybe just being here and taking care of Pippen was enough for now.

Her life hadn't completely gone to hell, she reminded herself. She'd been in hell. Lived it for over two years, and this wasn't even close. Not yet, anyway. Nathan was here and at some point, things had to get better.

11

The whine of a bench grinder filled the garage and filtered into Jack's office as he glanced over the master-parts list for the fifty-four Corvette; he simultaneously thumbed through Polaroids snapped of each part taken off the car so far. Everything from the chrome to the screws holding the taillight buckets had been cataloged and carefully stored away. The Blue Flame Six engine had been plucked from the cavity and would be torn down and steam-cleaned later. All rubber parts would have to be completely replaced as well as the leather interior. The fifty-four was supposedly a bitch to drive, but that was beside the point. The late and great Harley Earl had designed the sports car in his typical flamboyant style. The car had been designed for show rather than go.

Jack tossed the photographs aside and stood. That morning they'd removed the windshield and discovered more rust damage than he'd anticipated. The damage would have to be cut away and the brace rebuilt. He grabbed the Dodge Viper coffee mug that Lacy Dawn had given him for his birthday and walked from his office into the reception area.

Penny Kribs didn't come in until ten-thirty on Monday mornings, and a stack of mail sat on her empty desk. He refilled his coffee, and as he moved from the outer office into the garage, the noise from the bench grinder stopped. Jack blew into his mug and looked up at Billy who stood at the workbench. His safety glasses were pushed up his forehead, and he held a brake rotor in one hand. A skinny teenager stood talking to him, and they both turned as Billy pointed in Jack's direction.

Jack stopped in his tracks. The boy looked to be in his mid-teens and had a dog chain around his neck and one hanging down the side of his pants. He said something to Billy, then began walking toward Jack. Jack caught a glimpse of Billy's bemused smile before he turned his attention to the boy. He took a drink of his coffee and lowered the mug.

He'd always hired boys over the summer to sweep up or run for parts. But if this kid wanted a job, he was out of luck. Not so much because of the way he looked, but because he didn't have the sense to dress better and leave the chains on his dog when he went job hunting.

He had hair like a hedgehog, dark with white spikes on the ends. His bottom lip was pierced near one corner and his black T-shirt said anarchy in blood-red letters. He held a skateboard beneath one arm, and his jeans fit so loose, if he stood up straight, they'd fall down around his ankles.

'Can I help you?' Jack asked as the kid came to stand in front of him.

'Yeah. My mom told me you knew my dad?'

Jack knew a lot of dads. 'Who's your mother?' he asked and took another drink of his coffee.

'Daisy Monroe.'

The coffee scalded the back of his throat and he lowered it. Daisy hadn't left town.

'I don't know if she ever mentioned me. I'm . . .' his voice cracked and he swallowed hard. 'I'm Nathan.'

Whatever he'd expected Daisy and Steven's kid to look like, this was not it. First off, he'd thought their child was much younger. 'She mentioned she had a son, but I thought you were about five.'

A frown pulled his dark brows, and he stared at Jack through clear blue eyes. He looked a little confused like he didn't know how someone could mistake him with a five-year-old. 'No. I'm fifteen.'

The kid must have been conceived shortly after Steven and Daisy got married. The thought of Steven and Daisy together conjured up a long-buried animosity and bothered him more than it should have. More than it had a few days ago, before he'd made love to her on the trunk of the car just a few feet from where her son stood. Before he knew how good it was to be with her again. 'I take it your mom is still in town?'

'Yeah.' He stared at Jack as if he expected him to say something more. When he didn't, the boy added, 'We're staying with my grandma until my aunt Lily gets better. My mom thinks that might take a week or so.'

He'd wondered what had taken place to make Daisy run from his kitchen Saturday. 'What happened to your aunt?'

'She drove her car into Ronnie's living room.'

Damn, he guessed fighting in front of the Minute Mart

hadn't been enough revenge for Lily. 'Is she going to be okay?'

'I guess.'

The grinder started once more and Jack showed Nathan into his office and shut the door against the noise. Even if Nathan had come dressed properly for a job interview, having Daisy's kid work in his shop would be a nightmare. Seeing him would remind Jack of Daisy. And no matter how sweet that particular memory, it was over and best forgotten.

'Your dad and I were good friends at one time. I was sorry to hear about his death.'

Nathan set the tip of his skateboard by his black sneaker and leaned it against his leg. On closer inspection the underside of the board had a scantily dressed nurse painted on it. 'Yeah. He was a good dad. I miss him a lot.'

Jack had lost his father when he hadn't been much older than Nathan. He knew what it was like. Giving the kid an application to take with him wouldn't hurt. 'Did he ever tell you about all the trouble he and I used to get into?'

Nathan nodded and the fluorescent lighting shined on his lip ring. 'He told me about you guys stealing rotten tomatoes and throwing them at cars.'

Steven had been blond, like a California surfer. Maybe it was the hair, but this kid didn't look like Steven had growing up. Not even a little bit. Didn't look a whole lot like his mother either. Maybe around the mouth. Well, except for the lip ring. 'We made a tree fort in his backyard. Did he tell you about that?'

Nathan shook his head.

'It took us one whole summer. We made it out of wood we scrounged and old cardboard boxes.' He smiled at the memory of them dragging home junk from miles away. 'Your mom helped us, too. Then just when we finished, an F2 twister blew it all to hell.'

Nathan laughed and motioned toward the door with his head. 'Is that a 'Cuda 440–6 out there?'

'Yeah, it's got the original 426 Hemi.'

'Sweet. When I get a job, I'm gonna buy a Dodge Charger Daytona with a 426 Hemi.'

Now it was Jack's turn to laugh. He sat on the edge of his desk next to his Buick Riviera clock. He didn't want to rain on the kid's parade, but only about seventy Daytonas with a 426 Hemi had ever been produced. If he did manage to find one, it was going to run him about sixty grand. 'Four-speed, right?'

'Yeah.'

He took a drink. Naturally. The kid had just narrowed his odds even further considering Dodge had only put out about twenty four-speeds.

'I saw one once at a car show in Seattle.' Nathan swallowed and his voice cracked with excitement. 'The Daytona held the closed-course-track speed record for thirteen years. Ford and Chevy couldn't touch it'

Lord, he was just like Billy – and like Jack's father, Ray, had been. Blinded by speed. Jack loved fast cars too, but not like those two. How had Steven and Daisy managed to produce a gear head?

'Do you watch "Monster Garage"?'

'Occasionally.' Billy was the 'Monster Garage' fanatic.

'Did you see the episode where they turned a NASCAR into a street sweeper?'

'No, I missed that one.' But he'd heard all about it from Billy.

'It was tight.'

Tight? Jack supposed that meant good.

Billy stuck his head in the door as Jack crossed his feet. 'We've got a problem with the right-front rotor on that Plymouth.'

There was always a problem with something, and Jack had learned not to sweat it long ago. 'Billy come on in here and meet Steven and Daisy Monroe's boy, Nathan.'

Billy came farther into the office wearing his dark blue shirt that buttoned up the front and had a Parrish American Classic's patch on the left breast pocket. Jack introduced them and they shook hands. Billy spoke first, 'I was real sorry to hear about your dad. He was a good guy.'

Nathan looked down at his shoes. 'Yeah.'

'Billy here loves "Monster Garage," ' Jack said and the two of them jumped into a discussion about which episodes were the best and which ones weren't.

'Turning that PT Cruiser into a wood chipper was lame,' Nathan said.

'Jesse James wasn't into that one until they started feedin' stuffed animals through the chipper.'

'Yeah, heh-heh-heh,' Nathan laughed, tilting his head back a bit. 'They blew stuffing all over the place.'

'Did you see the Barbie get stuck in there?' Billy's eyes shined with humor and he laughed too, a rapid heh-heh-heh.

Christ, Jack thought, Billy had finally found someone who loved to watch 'Monster Garage' as much as he did.

'Did you catch the episode with the Grim Reaper?' his brother asked.

'Yeah, that would have been tight if it'd worked.'

Billy shook his head. 'They smoked the first belt and

the pump got too hot before they even got any of the cylinders to move those hydraulic arms.'

'I heard a theory that the hearse was haunted and that's why the mission failed.'

'The mission failed because the hydraulics failed.'

'Did you see Jesse when the ambulance caught on fire?' Nathan asked, so excited his eyes shined with it. 'That was cool.'

'That's my favorite episode.'

'Did you see his wife screaming at him?'

They both started to laugh at the same time. Billy's voice was lower, but Jack couldn't help but notice that their laughter was real similar. The same heh-heh-heh sound, and they both tipped their heads back at the same angle. The longer he looked at the two of them standing side by side swapping 'Monster Garage' moments, the clearer he saw beyond Nathan's bizarre hair and the lip ring.

Then within the span of a second, the world around Jack shifted and changed. The hair on the back of his neck rose and his scalp got tight. Time ground to a halt, cracked down the middle, and fell in halves.

A half-second ago, everything had been okay in Jack's life, and in the next it wasn't. One half he'd been noticing his brother and Nathan laughing and sounding alike, and in the next he was looking at a fifteen-year-old version of his father, Ray Parrish. For half a second he'd been sitting on the edge of his desk and in the next he was standing with coffee down the front of his shirt, scalding his chest. 'Christ!'

'What's the matter?' Billy asked.

He didn't take his gaze from Nathan. He looked at the shape of his face and nose, and there was no turning back the clock to a few seconds ago. He was definitely looking at a young version of his father. It was so obvious, he didn't know why it had taken him so long to see it. 'You didn't come here for a job, did you?'

Nathan's smile fell and he picked up his skateboard. 'No.'

Suddenly, it all made perfect sense. Daisy's insistence that they talk. That she had something to tell him. Something she couldn't talk about on the phone or in a letter or at Showtime Pizza. Something important like a son. He felt like someone had kicked him in the stomach. 'When is your birthday?'

'I've got to go now.'

He reached out and grabbed Nathan's arm. 'Tell me.'

Nathan's eyes got wide and he dropped his skateboard. He tried to back up, but Jack didn't let go. He couldn't.

'December,' he finally answered.

Jack pulled him even closer. 'And you're fifteen aren't you?'

He could see Nathan's throat work as he tried to swallow. 'Yes,' he said just above a whisper.

On some level Jack knew he frightened Nathan and that he should let go. He should calm down, but he couldn't. Thoughts raced through his head until it felt like something was squeezing his brain. 'Son of a bitch.'

Billy grabbed a hold of Jack's shoulder and stepped between him and Nathan. 'What's the matter with you? Have you lost your mind?'

Yes. He'd lost his mind. He let go and Nathan took off so fast, it was like he'd never been there. Except that his skateboard was still on the floor. Nurse-side up.

Jack stared after him. 'Didn't you see it, Billy?'

'All I see is you acting crazy.'

He shook his head and turned to his brother. 'He looks like dad.'

'Who?'

'Nathan. Daisy's son.'

'Daisy and *Steven*'s son.'

Jack pointed to the empty doorway. 'Did he look like Steven to you?'

'I don't really remember what Steven looked like, to tell you the truth.'

'Not like our dad.' He set the mug on his desk. He had a son. No. Impossible. He'd always used contraceptives. But not always with Daisy. They'd been young and stupid and still believed nothing bad would ever affect them. 'She was pregnant when she left and she didn't tell me.'

Billy put his hands up. 'Wait, I never even knew the two of you were involved back then. And even if you were, how do you know he's your kid?'

'You're not listening to me.' He scrubbed his face with his hands. 'There's a picture. A picture of dad when he graduated high school. He looks just like that kid.' He dropped his hands to his sides. 'That's why she's here,' he spoke his thoughts out loud as if they made better sense that way, when in reality, they made no sense at all. 'To tell me about him.'

'This is crazy. He's fifteen.'

Yes. It was crazy. Crazy as hell to think he had a fifteen-year-old son. A son he'd never known about because he'd never been told. 'I'm right, Billy.'

Billy stepped in front of him and looked him in the eye. 'You better make damn sure you're right before you go grabbing that kid and scaring him again. You don't know for sure he's yours, but even if he is, he might not know it.'

Billy was right. 'I didn't mean to scare him.'

Movement beyond Billy caught Jack's attention and he looked through the open doorway at Penny. He pushed by his brother and said on his way past the secretary, 'I'm going out for a while.'

He walked out the back of the garage, across the driveway, to his house. He went straight to a spare room that used to belong to Billy and he opened the closet crammed with boxes. He pulled out one after the other and dumped them on the floor. Old trophies and magazines, keepsakes from his and Billy's childhood that their mother had carefully packed away, fell everywhere.

'What are we looking for?' Billy asked as he picked up a box.

Jack hadn't even realized Billy had followed. 'Mom and Dad's old wedding album. The picture is in their wedding album.'

They found the album in the fifth box they opened. The outside was covered in lace and silk flowers, the girly stuff his mother had favored. The lace had yellowed, the flowers flattened; Jack flipped it open. Inside, the pages had lost their stickiness and the photographs behind the loose cellophane slid together. The picture Jack searched for fell at his feet, and he knelt to pick up the black-and-white photo of his father at the age of seventeen. In one corner of the picture, his father had written in faded black ink, *To my favorite girl Carolee, Love Ray.*

Jack stood and stared at the photo. He hadn't imagined it. Give his father hedgehog hair and a lip ring, and he'd look a hell of a lot like Nathan Monroe. Only he wasn't Nathan Monroe. He was a Parrish.

Billy came to stand behind Jack and he looked over his shoulder. His low whistle sounded louder than usual in the empty room. 'Do you think Steven knew?'

Jack shrugged. She'd been three months pregnant; at some point Steven had to have known. He walked out of the bedroom and down the hall into the kitchen. He opened a cabinet and pulled Steven's letter from where he'd place it Saturday. With the photograph of his father still in one hand, he tore open the envelope and read:

Jack,

Please excuse my handwriting and misspellings. As my illness progresses it gets more difficult for me to concentrate. It is my hope that you never see this letter. That I will beat this disease and tell you these things in person once I am well again. If not, I want to write down my thoughts before I am unable.

Let me begin by saying simply that I have missed you, Jack. I don't know if you have missed me or forgiven me, but I have missed my buddy. There have been many times in the past fifteen years when I have wanted to call and talk to you. Many times I have laughed by myself thinking of the things we used to do. The other day I saw two boys riding their bikes in the rain and I remembered the many times we used to ride our bikes in real toad-stranglers. Riding around Lovett, finding the deepest puddles to ride through. Or the times sitting on my mother's sofa, watching the old Andy Griffith shows, and laughing our asses off when Barney locked himself in jail. I think that is when I miss you the most, when I laugh alone. And I know it is my fault. There have been many times I have felt the loneliness of losing you, my friend.

I have never forgotten the last time we saw each other and the horrible things we said. I married Daisy, and you loved her. But I loved her too, Jack. I still do. After all these years I love her as much as the day I married her. I know she loves me. I know she has always loved me, and yet some times she gets a very far away look in her eyes, and I wonder if she is thinking about you. I wonder if she is thinking that she is sorry she chose to come with me to Seattle. I wonder if she thinks what her life might have been like with you, and I wonder if she still loves you like she did. If it is any consolation, then know that I have suffered a bit of hell, because I know how much she loved you once and perhaps still does.

The night we left Lovett, Daisy was three months pregnant with your child. She's no doubt told you all of this by now. When she came to me and told me she was carrying your baby, she was very afraid and believed that you didn't love her any longer. I let her believe it even though I knew it probably wasn't true. She believed not telling you about the baby was for the best. She didn't think you could handle the pressure of having a child at that time in your life. I let her believe that too. I told her she was right, that you couldn't, but I knew it wasn't true. I knew you could do anything you set your mind to doing. So I married her and took her away from you. I know that I should regret what I did, but I can't. I don t regret one day that I have spent with her and Nathan. But I do regret the way in which things were done and not telling you about Nathan sooner.

Nathan is a good boy. He is a lot like you. Fearless and impatient and buries everything deep. I know that Daisy *will do her absolute best to raise him, but I believe he needs you. It has been my pleasure to raise him, and of all my regrets in this life, and there are many, I regret that I will not get to see him grow into a man. I would have liked to have seen that.*

In closing, I ask that you forgive me, Jack. I know that is perhaps asking too much of you, but I'm asking anyway. I am asking so you can let go of the bitterness and go on with your life. On a purely selfish level, I am asking with the hope that you will forgive me so that I can die with a clearer conscience. And so that when I see you on the other side, we can embrace as friends once more. If you can't forgive me, I understand. I don't know that I could ever forgive you if I were in your place. I took a lot from you, Jack. But maybe you can occasionally look back and laugh at the good times we had together.

Steven

The letter and photograph of his father fell to the counter as Jack struggled to catch his breath. His insides felt sliced up, just like they had fifteen years ago.

'Is he yours?'

Jack nodded.

'That's goddamn evil,' Billy said. 'She's a damn evil bitch.'

For years he'd felt betrayal because his best buddy had married his girlfriend. He hadn't even known the half of it. It had never even occurred to him that when they'd left, they'd taken his child. It had not occurred to him that their betrayal ran so deep.

'What are you going to do?'

He unbuttoned his shirt and pulled it from the waistband of his pants. 'Talk to Daisy.'

'Well, don't start yelling at her first thing.'

'I thought you just said she was an evil bitch.'

'She is. I'm not even going to ask you if you want to be a part of Nathan's life, because I know you. I know how you are. I know that you're hurt and angry, and you have every damn right to feel that way. But she's his mama and she could just pack him up and take him away.'

For years he'd pushed it back and locked it away. He'd walled up all the pain and anger. Since Daisy had been back, it had seeped out a little. But nothing like this morning. This morning the walls he'd built were blown all to hell.

'Jack, promise you won't go medieval?'

He wasn't promising a damn thing.

12

Daisy laid Pippen on her mother's bed and partially closed the door behind her. His little world was chaotic and he'd been so tired and cranky for the past few days. Daisy had taken him to the hospital to see Lily this morning, and he hadn't wanted to leave. He was scared and upset and had cried all the way home, finally falling asleep as they pulled into the driveway. Her mother was still at the hospital with Lily, waiting for news from the doctors as to when Lily might come home.

Daisy changed into her dark green tank top and khaki shorts. She swept her hair up off the back of her neck and secured it with a big black claw. She was exhausted and in serious need of caffeine. She might have curled up beside Pippen, but Nathan wasn't home and she didn't want to be asleep when he returned.

She moved down the stairs to the kitchen and grabbed a Coke out of the refrigerator. Nathan had stuck a note to the refrigerator door with a little magnet in the shape of

Texas. He wrote that he was out riding his skateboard. The note didn't say when he'd be back, though. She had wanted to remind him that he needed to estimate when he'd be back, so she wouldn't worry so much.

This was Lovett, she reminded herself. There really wasn't that much to worry about. There weren't that many places he could get into trouble, but if there was one thing she'd learned from having a boy, it was that if there wasn't trouble, they'd invent it. If there was a puddle, they'd jump in the middle of it. A rock, they'd throw it. A Coke can, they'd smash it. A bird, they'd pretend to shoot it. A handrail on a set of five or more cement steps, they'd ride it on a skateboard, fall and need stitches.

The doorbell rang as Daisy popped the top to her Coke. She took a long drink as she moved through the living room. A bowl of glass fruit sat on a wooden end table and she placed the can next to it. She opened the door and half expected to see Nathan playing a silly joke by making her answer the door. He was like that sometimes. Wanting to be treated as an adult, yet at times acting like her little boy. But it wasn't her son.

Jack stood on her mother's porch, sunlight overhead. The shadow of his straw cowboy hat concealed the top half of his face. A little flutter tickled her chest and before she could think better of it, the corners of her lips turned up. 'Hey there.'

'Are you alone?' he asked, and her smile fell at the flat tone in his voice and grim line of his mouth.

He knows, was her first thought, but just as quickly she dismissed the thought. He couldn't know. 'Pippen's here but he's asleep.'

'Where is Nathan?'

Oh, God. The fluttering in her chest picked up a notch or two. 'He's riding his skateboard.'

He didn't wait for her to invite him in. 'No. He's not,' he said as he walked into the house, bringing with him the scent of a warm Texas morning on his skin. He handed her Nathan's board as he passed.

She took it from him and held it against her breasts. A ribbed T-shirt hugged the muscles of Jack's arms and chest and made him appear bigger and badder than usual. 'Where is he?'

He turned and looked at her for several nerve-racking moments before he said, 'I don't know.'

'How did you get this?'

'He came to see me this morning.'

'He did?' Nathan's going to the garage wasn't a coincidence. It was a surprise, but not a real shock. Nathan was the kind of kid who jumped into things first and thought later. A lot like Jack had been.

'He left the board on his way out.'

She didn't think that he'd said anything to Jack about being his biological child. Of course, it hadn't occurred to her that he'd ever show up at the garage on his own either. 'What did he say?'

'He talked about Steven and about "Monster Garage." '

Maybe he doesn't know. Maybe he was being a hardass for a totally different reason. This was Jack, after all. The king of hard-asses. 'That's it?'

'I think he really came by to get a good look at me.' He pushed up the brim of his straw hat and she got a good look at *him*. If the glittering rage in his green eyes hadn't removed all doubt about what he knew or suspected, the next words out of his mouth did. 'I read Steven's letter.'

Now she was shocked. 'How did you get Steven's letter?'

'You left it Saturday.'

Had she? She didn't remember. A lot had happened Saturday. 'You just read it today?'

'I didn't want to read it at all.' His voice was deadly calm when he said, 'Tell me, Daisy. I want to hear you say it. After all these years.'

His veneer of calm did not fool her for a second. His anger rolled off him like heat waves rolling across asphalt. Her speeding heart fell right to the pit of her stomach. She'd waited fifteen years for this moment. Knew it had to happen at some point, and there was no other way to say it but, 'He's your son, Jack.'

His expression didn't change. 'Does he know?'

'Yes. He's known most of his life.'

'So, I'm the only one who wasn't told.'

'Yes.'

'Do you have any idea,' he said in that same *awful* calm tone, 'what I'd like to do to you?'

Yes, she had a pretty good idea. She didn't think Jack would hurt her, but she took a step back. 'I was going to tell you.'

'Is that so?' One brow lifted up his forehead. 'When?'

'The first night I saw you. I came to your house to tell you, but Gina was there. I told you I needed to speak with you about something important. I told you that night and the night of Shay's wedding, and at the pizza place, and at Slims.' Her face felt hot, and she took another step back and tossed the skateboard on her mother's blue floral couch. 'I came to the garage to tell you Saturday, but then . . . Lily ran her car into Ronnie's living room. Which is why I guess I forgot all about leaving Steven's letter.' She pulled the claw from the back of her hair and took a deep breath. He had a right to his anger. She should have told him years ago. She was a coward. 'That's why I'm in town. I'm here to tell you that you have a son.'

His gaze locked with her. 'He's fifteen.'

She swept her hair back up, twisted it, and secured it once more. 'Yes, he is.'

'You're telling me fifteen years too goddamn late. You should have told me when you missed your first period.' He thought a moment then added, 'Unless you didn't know whose it was back then.'

'I knew.' Now he was just being mean. 'You were the first person I was ever with. How could you think such a horrible thing?'

'Maybe because up until a few days before you married my best friend, you were having sex with me. How do I know that you weren't doing us both at the same time?'

'You know I wasn't. You're just being ugly now.'

'You don't know ugly,' he said and his temper finally rose to the surface. He took a step toward her and stared down into her face. His eyes narrowed and the line of his jaw hardened. 'You did the lowest thing a woman can do to a man. You had my child and kept him from me. I should have been there when he was born. I should have been there to see him. To see him take his first steps and ride his first bike. I should have been there to hear his first words, but I wasn't. Steven was, though. Steven got to hear him say Daddy, not me.' He was dead serious when he added, 'It's a good thing you're not a man, because I'd beat the hell out of you. I'd enjoy it, too.'

One of the hardest things she'd ever done was stand

there toe-to-toe with Jack and not take another step back or look away from his angry eyes. 'You have to understand that we never meant to hurt you. We both loved you.'

'Bullshit.'

'It's the truth.'

'If that's what you do to people you love, I can't imagine what you have in store for people you hate.'

Her head began to pound and she put a hand to her brow, but she didn't remove her gaze from his. 'You have to remember what it was like between you and me back then. We were fighting and making up all the time. That first month, I was so scared, and I told myself I was just late. Then the second month I told myself not to think about it, but by the third month, I had to face it.' She dropped her hand. 'Your parents had just died and you were going through such a bad time. The night I came to tell you I was pregnant, you said you needed a break from me. I didn't think you loved me anymore. I didn't know what to do.' The backs of her eyes stung but she refused to give in to tears. 'I didn't have anyone to talk to about it but Steven. I went to him and he asked me to marry him. He said he'd take care of me and my baby.'

'You keep forgetting that the baby was mine. That I should have been told about it before the two of you ran off to Seattle.'

'We talked about telling you, but we thought that if you knew, you'd want to marry me out of obligation, but Jack, you were in no position to take care of me and a baby. You were only eighteen and already dealing with so much. It seemed like the only solution.'

'No, it was the easy way out for you. Steven had money and I had nothing.'

'That's not why I married him. You know that I always loved Steven. If you weren't so angry, you'd remember that you loved him too.' She placed her hands on his bare arms. Jack might never forgive her, but she had to make him understand. 'I married him because I was scared. You didn't love me anymore, and I didn't know what to do.'

'How did it feel, Daisy?' His voice lowered, got rough and smooth at the same time. 'How did it feel to get back at me for not loving you? Did taking my child make you feel good? Did it satisfy your revenge?'

'It wasn't about revenge.'

He grabbed her wrists and removed her hands from his arms. 'Did lying with Steven Monroe get me out of your head. Your heart? When you were with him, were you thinking of me?'

'No!'

'Remembering how it used to be between us?' His voice lowered even further and he pinned her wrists behind her back. 'How good it was.' He pulled her up against his body and said against her temple, 'How good it still is.'

The brim of his hat touched the top of her head. 'Stop it, Jack.'

'All those years, were the two of you laughing it up over what you'd done to me?'

'No, Jack. It wasn't like that. No one was laughing.' Her heart knocked in her chest and she swallowed hard. 'Believe me. I know I should have told you sooner.'

His voice got real quiet next to her ear when he asked, 'Who's listed as daddy on that boy's birth certificate?'

'Steven.'

He pulled back far enough to look into her face. 'Goddamn you, Daisy.'

'We thought it would be easier for him in school. I'm sorry.'

'I don't give a flying fuck how sorry you are. Because it's not half as sorry as you're going to be.'

'What do you mean?'

He set her back on her heels and slid his hands to her shoulders. 'All those years ago when you chose Steven over me because I was just a poor kid with grease on my hands, working in my daddy's garage – that's not how things are now. I'm not poor anymore, Daisy. I can afford a real good lawyer, and if I have to, I'll fight you.'

'There won't be a fight.'

'I want to know my son.'

'You can get to know him. I want you to. And when we leave—'

'When *you* leave,' he interrupted. 'He stays.'

'That's ridiculous. He's not staying here with you. His home is with me. In Seattle.'

'We'll see about that.'

'I know you're angry. I don't blame you.'

'Nice to know you don't blame *me*.' He released her and turned to the door.

'I should have told you about Nathan years ago, but don't punish him because you're mad at me.' She followed close behind him to the front porch. 'He's been through so much. He lost his dad and now this.'

Jack turned around so fast she almost ran into his chest. 'He didn't lose his dad. Steven Monroe wasn't his father.'

Daisy wisely didn't point out that Nathan thought of Steven as his dad and had loved him. 'Nathan's been through a lot in the past few years. He needs a little peace. Some calm in his life.' She didn't add that she needed it too. 'I'll talk to him. See what he wants to do, and I'll call you.'

'I'm not going to wait around for you to call me, Daisy Lee.' He moved down the steps toward his Mustang parked at the curb. 'After I talk to Nathan, I'll tell you how it's going to be,' he said as he walked away, the morning sun shining down on his straw hat and his wide shoulders.

'Wait.' She ran down the steps after him. 'You can't talk to him alone. I'm his mother. He doesn't know you.'

He walked around the front of the car then stuck his key in the driver's side door. 'Whose fault is that?'

She looked at him from across the top of the car. 'I should be there.'

He looked back at her and laughed. 'Like I should have been there for the past fifteen years?'

She grabbed the door handle to jump in his car but the door was locked. Then she remembered Pippen and realized she couldn't go even if she forced her way into his car. 'Nathan is my son. You can't exclude me.'

'Get used to it.'

'We can work this out. I know we can.' She didn't know anything of the sort, but she was determined to keep things from getting too ugly. 'I should have told you. I know that, and except for handing over my son, I'll try and make it up to you.'

'How? On the trunk of a car?' He unlocked the Mustang's door. 'Not interested.'

So much for keeping things from getting too ugly.

*

Nathan sat with his back against the basketball pole at Lovett High. The backboard and hoop cast an oblong shadow on the court to the free-throw line.

He gazed across the football field to the tennis courts. He didn't like it here. He didn't know what he expected Texas to look like, maybe like Montana. He and his dad had been to Montana once, but Texas wasn't like that. Texas was flat. And hot. And brown.

Texas was nothing at all like Seattle.

He pushed with his feet and slid up the pole until he stood. He adjusted the chain around his neck and glanced at the high school behind him. 'High school,' he scoffed. It wasn't even as big as the grade school he'd gone too. They probably all wore cowboy boots and rode horses to school. Probably all listened to crappy country and western music and chewed tobacco. Probably nobody rode skateboards or listened to Korn or Weezer or played Sniper Fantasy for XBOX.

Nathan pulled up his pants and hardly noticed when they slipped back down his hips. Problems bigger than his baggy pants occupied his thoughts. He'd dropped his skateboard at Jack Parrish's garage, and then he'd run away like a big scared baby.

He *really* wished he hadn't done that, but the way Jack had grabbed his arm had freaked him out. And the way he'd looked and swore at him, too. One second they'd all been laughing, and in the next, Jack had grabbed him and stared at him so intensely, he'd about crapped his pants. Nathan didn't know if Jack had figured it out in that moment, but by the look on his face, he thought maybe he had. Then before Nathan had even realized what he was doing, he ran away like a little kid.

Jack probably thought he was a dork.

With a shrug of his shoulders he told himself he didn't care. His dad had told him lots of stories about Jack. He made him sound real cool, like someone Nathan would really like. But he didn't think he liked Jack. He liked Billy, though. Billy watched 'Monster Garage.' Billy was cool.

He picked up a rock and threw it hard against the backboard. It made a satisfying thwack, rebounded and almost hit him in the head. Obviously, his mom hadn't told Jack yet. Nathan had just assumed that she'd told him already or he never would have walked into that garage today. After all, that's why she was here. To tell Jack about him. At least, that's why she'd *said* she was coming here.

He moved back across the field toward the opening in the chain link fence. He was pretty mad at his mom, and feeling really stupid. Plus, he had to figure out a way to retrieve his board. Maybe he'd just let Jack keep it because he really didn't want to go into the garage again and ask for it back. Not now.

The grass beneath his black skater shoes squished and he figured the sprinklers had been on that morning. Water droplets collected on the leather toes of his shoes and he watched them roll off. His mom should be back from the hospital by now. He had to tell her where he'd been. She'd probably get mad at him, but he didn't really care. The more he thought about it, the madder he got at *her*. If his mother had told Jack, or at least told Nathan that she hadn't, he wouldn't have gone to the garage and made such a dick weed out of himself.

When he looked up, he noticed a girl walking toward him a few feet away on the other side of the fence. Through the links he could see that she had shiny dark hair and smooth tan skin like she spent time sunbathing. They met at the opening at the same time, and he stepped aside to let her go through first. Instead, she stopped and stared at him.

'You're not from around here. I know most everyone, but I've never seen you,' she said with a definite Texas twang, drawing out her words. She had big brown eyes, and beneath one arm she held poster board and construction paper.

'I live in Washington,' he told her.

'Washington, DC?' She said it like his mother and grandmother did. Like there was an *r* in the word 'wash.' She wore a blue T-shirt with the words Ambercrombie and Fitch in silver glittery letters. She was a prep, and he didn't like preppie girls. Girls who shopped at Ambercrombie and Fitch and The Gap. Goodie-two-shoe girls.

'No. State.'

'Are you here visitin' someone?'

No, he had no use for preppie girls . . . but she had the kind of lips that made him think of kissing. Which he'd been thinking about a lot lately. 'Yeah, my grandma, Louella Brooks, and my aunt Lily.' He'd kissed one girl in the sixth grade, but he didn't think that counted.

A frown pulled at her brows. 'Lily Darlington?'

'Yep.'

'Ronnie's cousin Bull is married to my aunt Jessica.' She laughed. 'We're practically related.'

He doubted that made them related at all. And what the heck kind of name was Bull? 'What's your name?'

'Brandy Jo. What's yours?'

Despite being a prep and having a drawl, Brandy Jo was hot. The kind of hot that made his stomach feel fuzzy and his chest feel heavy and made him think about how complicated girls were. And it was at these times, when he was thinking about girls, that he missed his dad the most. 'Nathan,' he answered. A guy just couldn't ask his mother about certain stuff.

She studied him a moment and her gaze lowered to his lip. 'Did that hurt?'

He didn't have to ask her what she was talking about. 'No,' he answered and hoped his voice didn't crack. He *hated* when that happened. 'I'm getting a tattoo next.'

Her big brown eyes rounded and he could tell she was impressed. 'Your parents will let you?'

No. He'd have to get it without his mother knowing somehow. A few months ago they'd made a deal, he could keep his lip ring if he promised to never get a tattoo as long as he lived. He'd promised, but he figured he only had to keep his word until he was eighteen and old enough to get one himself. Tattoos were cool. 'Sure.'

'Where?'

He pointed to his shoulder. 'Right there. I don't know what I want yet, but when I do, I'm definitely getting a tat.'

'If I could get one, I think I'd get a little red heart on my hip.'

Which Nathan thought was pretty lame and really girly. 'That'd be cool.' He dropped his gaze to the poster boards beneath her arm. 'What are you doing with that stuff?'

'I'm gonna teach city-rec art classes to little kids this summer. It's gonna be a lot of fun, and I'll get paid five-seventy-five an hour.'

Teaching art to little kids didn't sound like a lot of fun to Nathan, but getting paid five-seventy-five an hour was sweet. He quickly did the math in his head and figured that if a kid worked five hours a day, five days a week, he could make around five hundred and seventy dollars in one month. He could buy a lot of CDs or new board trucks with that kind of money.

A black Mustang pulled alongside the curb on the other side of the fence, and Nathan watched Jack Parrish get out. He pushed his cowboy hat up his forehead and gazed at Nathan over the top of the car. 'You forgot your board at the garage.'

Jack didn't look so scary this time, but the fuzzy feeling in Nathan's stomach got worse. Like when he rode the Zipper too many times at the Puyallup fair. 'Yeah.'

Brandy Jo looked from Nathan to Jack then back again. 'See ya around.'

Nathan glanced at her. 'Okay, see ya.' As she walked away, he returned his attention to the man both his mom and dad said was his biological father. As far as Nathan could see, he didn't look much like Jack.

'I took your skateboard to your grandmother's.'

Nathan stepped through the opening in the fence and stood next to the passenger door. If the feeling didn't go away, he was afraid he'd get sick. And he *really* didn't want to do that. 'Was my mom home?'

'Yes. She and I talked.' He rested a forearm on the top of the car. 'She said you've always known that I'm your father.'

'Yeah.' He swallowed past the lump forming in his throat. He didn't know why he felt so weird. It wasn't like he cared what Jack thought. He'd gone to the garage earlier out of mild curiosity. That was it. He didn't care what anyone thought. 'I've known.'

'Well, I'm glad that at least she didn't lie to you.' Jack

looked at the watch strapped around his wrist and tapped his fingers three times on the top of the car. 'Do you want a ride home?'

'Okay.' Nathan waited for Jack to unlock the door, then he climbed inside. He sat in the soft beige leather seat and his stomach churned a little bit more. He didn't know what this car was worth, but a lot more than his mom's stupid minivan back in Seattle. That's for sure. 'Is this a Shelby?'

'Yep. It's a nineteen-sixty-seven GT 500.'

Nathan didn't know that much about Mustangs except that if you were going to have one, this was the one. 'What's the engine?' he asked as he shut the door.

'The original 428 Police Interceptor.'

'Tight.'

'I like it.' Jack shifted, glanced behind him, then pulled back out onto the street.

'How fast will it go?'

'A hundred and thirty-two. Of course that's nothing compared to the Daytona. How fast did you say it was clocked on the closed course?'

'Two hundred on the closed course. One-eighty right out of the showroom in nineteen sixty-nine.'

Jack laughed and moved his hand from the steering wheel to shift again. 'You know, Billy could use some help with that Barracuda that's in the shop. Since you're here for a while and going to own a Daytona someday, you might want to give him a hand with that Hemi.'

Was he kidding? Nathan would crap all over himself just to *touch* a Hemi. 'That could be cool, I guess. But I don't know how long I'm gonna be in town.'

Jack looked over at him, the shadow of his hat fell

across his nose. 'We'll talk to your mom and see how long you're going to be here.' He turned his attention back to the road and shifted the big engine into third. 'Of course, just 'cause you're family doesn't mean we can pay you more than the other guys.'

Pay? As in earn money working on a Hemi? He'd crap all over himself *twice*. Nathan looked down at the chain hanging from one loop of his pants. He cleared his throat and bobbed his head a few times. 'Sweet.'

'We'll start you out at seven-fifty an hour.'

He tried to do the math in his head, but something that usually came pretty easy to him was impossible at the moment. 'Okay.'

'Nathan?'

He looked back across the car at Jack. 'Yeah?'

'I should have known about you before today,' he said, but he kept his gaze on the road.

Nathan agreed, but he didn't say so.

'If I had known, I would have been in your life. No one could have kept me out.'

He didn't know what to say to that, so he kept quiet.

'Maybe while you're here, we could get to know each other.'

'Cool.'

'And if we don't get on each other's nerves too much, you could think about staying the summer.'

The whole summer? In Loserville? No way.

'When the 'Cuda's done, I'm going to need someone to test-drive it for me. You think you could do that?'

He bit the inside of his lip ring to keep from smiling. *Oh man!* 'I could do that.'

'You got your driver's license, right?'

His excitement plummeted. 'No, I'm only fifteen. You gotta be sixteen.'

'Not in Texas. You can get it when you're fifteen.'

'Really?'

'Yep. You have to have your license to test-drive the 'Cuda for me. It's company policy for insurance purposes. That means you'd have to sign up for driver's education. That might take half the summer.'

Since before Nathan could remember, he'd dreamed of the day he'd get his driver's license.

'You don't have to give me your answer today. Think it over and let me know.'

If he stayed in Texas for the summer, he could get it early. Plus work on a Hemi and make serious bank. He adjusted the chain around his neck. 'I'll have to ask my mom.' And she wasn't going to like it one bit. She was always telling him no. She didn't want him to have fun or grow up. She wanted him to be bored and stay a little kid forever.

'I'll talk to her for you.'

'You would?'

'Oh yeah.' His smile showed his white teeth. 'It will be my pleasure.'

'You remember Azelea Lingo, don't you?'

'No.' Daisy answered absentmindedly as she stared out her mother's front-room window.

'Sure you do, she's the one who bought Lily half a vacuum when she got married,' Louella continued as if Daisy had been at Lily's wedding, which she hadn't.

'How does a person buy half a vacuum for a wedding present?' Daisy asked, although she really didn't give a damn at the moment. It had been over an hour since Jack had come and gone. Over an hour and she hadn't seen hide nor hair of him or Nathan.

'She put it on layaway and Lily had to pay to get it off. Cost her fifty bucks for a ninety-dollar vacuum. And you know, Azelea isn't poor. She's so big she has to sit down in shifts, so it isn't like she can't afford a whole vacuum.'

Daisy had started to leave a dozen times only to decide that staying put was the best course.

'Anyway, Azelea's husband, Bud, left her a few years

back and married a gal from Amarillo. Only the gal in Amarillo doesn't know that Bud's been sneaking back to Lovett the whole time for a little lovin' on the side with Azelea.'

Daisy massaged the deep crease that had formed between her brows. Her head was going to explode.

'What is it, darlin'?' Louella paused in her story to ask Pippen. 'Oh, you want your hat? Daisy, honey, where's Pip's hat?'

Daisy was so tense it felt like she had to unlock her jaw to speak. 'Probably in your bedroom.'

'Go check grandma's bed.'

'You go,' Pippen demanded in his tiny voice.

'We'll go together.'

Daisy kept her gaze out the window as they left the room. She grabbed a handful of her mother's dark blue velvet drapes and pressed her forehead to the glass. Since Nathan hadn't returned, she figured Jack had found him, and all sorts of scenarios ran through her head. Ranging from the two of them sitting somewhere talking to Jack kidnapping Nathan and heading some place where she'd never find them. The last scenario she didn't really think was likely, but with Jack she never knew.

She opened the front door, and stuck her head out to look up and down the street. There was no sign of either of them.

'You're letting all the bought air out. Shut that,' her mother said as she entered the room. Daisy glanced behind her, at her mother dressed in a pink blouse with fake pearls sown on it and a denim prairie skirt. Pippen stood beside her, wearing his coonskin cap and a pair of Big Bird pull-ups.

'This afternoon as I was leaving the hospital, they brought in Bud Lingo,' her mother continued where she'd left off. 'Appears he had heart failure while he was with Azelea. I couldn't stay at the hospital, but I am powerful curious to know what's gonna happen when Bud's wife gets her tail up here from Amarillo.' Louella walked to the cabinet where she kept her VHS tapes and opened it up. 'And their youngest girl, Bonnie, was there too. She's the one who had that real ugly baby last Valentine's Day. Lord, when I picked the blanket off the baby's face in church, I 'bout had heart failure myself. It was all bald and pink and skinny like a newborn rat, bless her heart. Of course, I lied and told her it was precious. You remember Bonnie, don't you. Short. Dark hair . . .'

Her mother was determined to make Daisy's head explode. Daisy stepped out onto the porch and shut the door behind her. She sat on the first step and rested her temple against the white post that supported the roof. Her nerves were frazzled. Her head pounded, and her patience had deserted her awhile ago. It was barely one o'clock in the afternoon, and she knew the day was bound to get worse. Jack hated her now, and he was going to make her life a misery, just as he'd promised the first night she'd seen him. While she understood his anger at her, she couldn't let things get ugly. If they did, the one person who was totally innocent would be the one to suffer the most. Nathan.

She glanced downward at her bare feet and red toenails. For the first time, she noticed the perfect fingertip bruises on her thighs. She didn't have to wonder how they'd gotten there. Jack. He'd left his mark on her long after he'd made love to her.

It was apropos, she supposed. Jack had left his mark on

her years ago too, and she didn't mean Nathan. He'd marked her where no one could see. He'd left an indelible mark on her heart and her soul. One that no matter how far away she traveled, how long she stayed away, or how long she hid from it, had not faded nearly as much as she'd thought.

Despite his feeling toward her, she was very much afraid that she was falling in love with Jack again. She knew the signs just as surely as she knew better than to let it happen.

The sooner she grabbed Nathan and got out of town, the better. Jack knew he had a son now. He could call or write or visit Seattle sometime in the future. Lily was recovering and would be home soon, but she was still a basket case. Yet, Daisy had problems of her own, and she had to get away before her life fell completely apart.

From half a block away, she heard the unmistakable rumble of Jack's Mustang. She looked up and turned her attention to the black car moving toward her. As she stood, the car rolled to a stop at the curb in front of her mother's house. Jack shut the car off then turned to look at her. From across the distance, their gazes met: His angry; hers resigned to his anger. Daisy leaned her head to one side and looked beyond Jack to Nathan. Her son sat in the passenger seat and kept his attention pinned to his lap. He said something, then the two of them exited the Mustang. Both doors shut at the same time, and Jack waited for Nathan at the front of the car. The hot Texas sun baked Daisy's shoulders, and it took every ounce of her self-control to keep her feet planted at the bottom of the steps and not running toward her son.

The two moved up the walk, their strides keeping

perfect time with the other. Nathan's hands swung at his sides; his walk, an I'm-fifteen-and-trying-so-desperately-to-be-cool amble. Yet his blue eyes were guarded; he was wondering if he was in trouble or not.

Jack had one hand buried to his knuckles in the front pocket of his Levi's, the other hung loose at his side. As always, he moved as if he were in no hurry to get anywhere in particular.

'Where have you been, Nathan?' she asked when he stopped in front of her. She had to fight the urge to throw her arms around him and tell him everything would be okay. 'I've been very worried about you. You know I hate it when you leave and don't tell me when you'll be back.'

'We went for a little drive,' Jack told her.

A furrow appeared between Nathan's brows and she asked him, 'Are you okay?'

'Yeah.'

But he didn't look okay. He looked tired and upset, and his cheeks were pink from the heat. 'Are you hungry?'

'A little.'

'Why don't you go inside and have your grandma fix you something to eat.'

He turned to Jack. 'I guess I'll see you later.'

'Count on it,' he said. 'I'll call you after I talk to Billy.'

'Cool.' With his pants riding low on his hips, and his dog chains jingling, Nathan moved up the steps.

'Where did you find him?' Daisy wanted to know as she watched her son shut the door.

'At the high school. He was talking to some girl.'

'Where did you take him after that?' She turned to face him. The blazing sun penetrated the thick weave of his hat and shot pinholes of light across his nose and mouth.

'Around.'

'Around where?'

He smiled. 'Just around.'

She placed her hand across her brows and shielded her eyes from the sun. He was really enjoying this. 'What did you talk about?'

'Cars.'

'And?'

'Him working for me this summer.'

'Impossible,' she said and waved the notion away with her hand. 'We have plans.'

'Change them. Nathan says he wants to work for me this summer.'

She looked up into his green eyes, surrounded by those long dark lashes of his. 'Are you going to tell me that he came up with that all on his own?'

He shook his head and white pinholes of light slid along his top lip. 'Doesn't matter who came up with it. It's what we both want.'

'We can't stay here all summer.' She felt a bead of perspiration slip between her breasts. 'I've already been here longer than I intended.'

'There's no reason for you to stay. In fact, it might be better if you left.'

'I'm not leaving my son here with you. You've known him an hour and you've already manipulated him into staying.'

'I simply offered Nathan a job helping Billy tear down a Hemi 426. He jumped at it.'

She lifted her hands upward. 'Of course he did. The child has slept on NASCAR sheets most of his life and had his first car picked out at the age of three. A Porsche 911.'

'Jesus!' he swore. 'You let my son pick a European piece of shit?'

Under any other circumstance, she might have laughed. 'What the heck does it matter?'

'He's a Parrish.' He grabbed his hat from his head and rubbed his forehead against his short sleeve. 'It matters to us.' He ran his fingers through one side of his hair then jammed the hat back on. 'If he'd been raised right, he'd know better,' he said in a low grumble.

How dare he criticize the way she'd raised Nathan. She may not have always been the best mother, but she'd always tried her best. She'd kill anyone who tried to hurt him.

'If he'd been raised right,' Jack continued, 'he wouldn't have a ring through his lip and dog chains hanging off him.'

Her nerves snapped, and in an instant she forgot all about trying to get along with Jack for Nathan's sake. She no longer cared whether Jack had a right to his anger, he'd just crossed the line and insulted her son. 'He's a great kid,' she said and poked her finger in Jack's chest. 'What's on the outside isn't as important as what's on the inside.'

Jack glanced down at her finger then back up into her eyes. 'He looks like a hedgehog.'

'A lot of boys where we live look like that.' She poked him twice more. 'Goat-roper!'

His eyes widened then narrowed. He wrapped his hand around hers and removed her finger. 'You've turned into a Yankee woman with no manners and a bad accent.'

Daisy gasped, and this time she went for the kill. She stood on the balls of her feet and said, 'I'll take that as a compliment coming from a second-rate grease monkey.'

'You conceited bitch.' He grabbed hold of her shoulders

like when they were ten years old and fighting over who had the best bike. They cut into each other with words, going at it tooth and nail, and all the while never raising their voices above a low rumble.

'You always did think the sun rose and set on your scrawny butt,' he said.

'And you always thought you were God's gift to a pair of jeans.' She put her hands on his chest and shoved, but he didn't move at all. 'But I'm here to tell you on behalf of all women, what you've got in your jeans isn't that extraordinary.'

'You thought so Saturday on the trunk of the Custom Lancer. In fact, you burst into tears because you enjoyed what I've got in my jeans.'

'Don't flatter yourself. It'd been a long time. It could have happened with anyone.' She smiled, too angry to be embarrassed. 'You could have been Tucker Gooch,' she added, knowing full well that Jack had always disliked Tucker.

He laughed. 'Tucker doesn't have what it takes to make you bawl like you just had a religious conversion.'

The front door opened and Louella stuck her head out. 'You're putting on quite a show for the neighbors.'

Jack let go of Daisy's shoulders and had the grace to look embarrassed. 'Good afternoon, Miz Brooks.'

'Hello, Jackson. Hot enough for ya?'

'Hotter than a stolen tamale,' he said, taking off his hat and exchanging pleasantries as if to show *he'd* been raised right.

'I haven't seen you in a long time.'

'No, ma'am.'

'How's your brother?'

'He's fine. Thanks for askin'.'

'Well, tell him I said hello.'

'I'll do that. How've you been, Miz Brooks?'

Daisy sat on the second to the last concrete step. She rested her forehead in her hand and waited for her mother to break into a long-winded story about her near heart failure at having seen Bonnie Lingo's ugly baby. And for once, Daisy was grateful because it would give her time to compose herself.

Instead Louella said, 'Well aren't you kind to ask. I'm feeling just fine.'

'Glad to hear it, ma'am.'

Daisy could almost feel her mother staring a hole in the back of her head. Since she already felt like an idiot for fighting with Jack on the front lawn, she refused to turn around and receive her mother's meaningful glare. 'Did Nathan hear us?' she asked.

'No. We couldn't hear you inside, but we did see you two going at it.'

'Great,' Daisy whispered.

She heard the front door shut behind her mother, and she dropped her hand and looked up at Jack. 'We have to get along.'

He shook his head. Even with bad-hat hair, he managed to look good. 'Not going to happen.'

'Then we're going to have to fake it. For Nathan's sake.'

'Well, I'll tell you something, buttercup,' he said as he stuck his hat back on his head. 'I just don't think I'm that good at lying.'

His recent lie about a trip to Tallahassee came to mind. 'Right.'

A frown wrinkled his brows. 'Not as good as you, anyway.'

She stood on the bottom step and looked into his face. 'Do you think Nathan will want to stay here with you knowing that you hate me?' She didn't wait for him to answer. 'He likes to act all grown up. He likes to think that I baby him, but the fact is, he still needs me.'

The furrow in his forehead smoothed. 'Are you saying you're going to let him stay for the summer?'

She didn't think she had a choice. She'd talk to Nathan, and if he really wanted to work in Jack's garage and get to know him, Daisy wouldn't stand in his way. 'If that's what he wants – but I won't leave him here alone with you. I left him with relatives in Seattle for less than two weeks, and he couldn't handle it.'

She let out a deep breath and thought out loud. 'He only brought a backpack full of clothes. I have the one suitcase. Neither one of us would last the summer on what we brought.' She was going to have to make a trip home to Seattle to get some of their things.

Jack folded his arms over his wide chest and smiled. He'd won this round and he knew it.

'You have to promise, no more fighting.'

'Agreed.'

'We have to get along.'

'In front of Nathan.'

But Daisy wasn't through with him. 'You have to pretend to like me.'

He tilted his head back and the shadow from his hat slid from his nose, over his lips, to his chin. 'Don't push your luck.'

Daisy added water to the vase of fresh-cut lilies and returned it to the spot on the stand next to her sister's hospital bed. Daisy disliked the cloying scent of lilies. They reminded her of death. 'I'm not going to be here when you go home tomorrow,' she said and reached for the vase filled with peach tulips and white roses.

'Are you and Nathan going home?' Lily asked as she reached for the lime Jell-O on her dinner tray.

'Just me, and just for a few days.' Daisy moved to the sink and added water to the vase. 'It seems we're going to stay the summer.' Lily didn't say anything and Daisy looked over her shoulder at her sister. She had a white bandage covering the stitches on her forehead. One eye was black and blue, the other green and yellow. Her top lip was still a little swollen, her left forearm was bandaged and her right ankle and foot were in some sort of traction cast.

'What happened?' Lily finally asked. 'Did you tell Jack about Nathan?'

'Not exactly.' She set the vase next to the other and sat in a chair beside Lily's bed. 'Nathan kind of told him,' she answered, then filled her sister in on the rest. 'I tried to tell Jack how sorry I am, but he isn't ready to hear it.'

Lily turned her head on the pillow and her blue eyes gazed out from all the color on her face. 'I'm sorry is just two words, Daisy. They don't mean anything unless you really mean them. Ronnie used to tell me he was sorry every time he cheated, but what he really meant was that he was sorry he got caught again. Sometimes sorry isn't enough.'

From outside the room, Dr Williams was paged to star-line four; inside, Daisy got a real good glimpse into suffering on the other side, from the person feeling the most pain.

'Yes, I know.' She wrapped her hands around the wooden arms of the chair. 'That's mostly why I've agreed to stay for the summer. I owe Jack. I may have done things for what I thought were the right reasons, but I shouldn't have waited fifteen years to tell Jack about Nathan. I have a lot of guilt about that.'

'Don't let guilt make you crazy.' Lily set her Jell-O back on the tray. 'Remember the night we went to Slim Clem's?'

'Of course.'

'I slept with Buddy Calhoun that night.'

Daisy was too stunned to speak.

'He came over after I got home and we hooked up. He was real sweet and the sex was great. But after he left, I started to feel guilty, like I was cheating on my marriage. Ronnie had cheated on me for years, left Pippen and me for another woman, and *I* was feeling guilty.' She scratched her forehead next to the bandage. 'It was crazy, and I got so mad I drove over to his house. He wasn't home, but I drove up and down his street waiting for him, getting madder and madder. I don't remember much after that, but I guess I got so mad, I drove my car into his front room.'

'Lily.' She stood and walked to the bed. 'What are you saying? Not to let guilt make me that insane, or I should probably expect Jack's Mustang to plow through mother's front room?'

'Neither. I don't know. I just know that I want to feel normal again.' She pushed the tray away. 'Can you scratch my big toe?'

Daisy moved to the end of the bed scratched her sister's toe. Lily's ankle was huge.

'What did you tell the police about the accident?'

'That I was going to see Ronnie about child support and I must have gotten one of my bad migraines and accidentally hit the gas instead of the brake.'

"They bought it?"

She shrugged. 'I went to school with Neal Flegel. He never did like Ronnie very much. He gave me a ticket for failure to control speed. My insurance is paying for the damage to the house, but I'm sure the premiums will go so high I won't be able to drive for a while.'

Which Daisy figured was probably a blessing. 'Have you given any more thought about counseling?'

'Yeah, I've thought about it. Might not be a bad thing.' Lily reached for the controls and lowered the bed. 'But I think running my car into Ronnie's put things into perspective for me.'

That sounded healthy.

'No man is worth making me feel so bad about myself. When I'm not being crazy, I'm a pretty nice person.'

Daisy smiled. 'Darn right.'

'Ronnie isn't worth spit, let alone worth me.'

'Nope.'

'I'm going to concentrate on getting better and raising Pippen. I'm over feeling bad about Ronnie. I don't need a man in my life to make me feel important.'

'That's true.' Lily really did sound as if she were on the road to complete mental health.

'Why should I base my self-worth on a man who counts his hard-ons as personal growth?'

Daisy laughed. 'You shouldn't.'

Lily pulled off a piece of tape holding a cotton ball to the inside of her elbow. 'Men are the scum of the earth and should be killed.'

Well, maybe not *complete* mental health.

14

Jack watched his son as Billy showed him how to remove the crankshaft from the Hemi 426. Since he'd picked Nathan up at the high school that first day, he'd been trying not to stare. He didn't want to scare the kid again, but after three days of him working in the garage, he was finding it more difficult not to study him. Even with his hedgehog hair and lip ring, Nathan resembled the Parrish side of the family even more than Jack did himself.

Jack rolled up his sleeves, grabbed a socket, and removed the few remaining bolts. He didn't work on actual restoration as much as he used to. Mostly he spent his time making deals or chasing parts all over the country. Running the business side while Billy was in charge of the labor side, but for the last three days, he'd been spending a lot more time in the garage with the mechanics.

'The lobes are retarded,' Billy said as he inspected the camshaft. 'Just like we thought.'

'What does that mean?' Nathan asked.

'It means they're warped,' he answered.

'And it means that the valves stay open too long or not long enough and the engine loses power,' Jack added.

Nathan looked up at him from across the big V8, and there was a hesitance in his eyes that Jack hated to see there. He kept his gaze on his son as he spoke, 'The replacement should be here by the time you and Billy are ready to rebuild.'

My son.

Billy handed the shaft to Nathan, and he held it up to study the lobes. 'What do we do with this old one?'

'Toss it in the scrap-metal Dumpster I showed you outside,' Billy told him.

As Jack watched Nathan move from the garage, his blue coveralls baggy in the butt, he thought he should feel more than he did for the boy. Something more than a lump in his throat and an avid curiosity. He should feel a connection to Nathan. A connection like he'd had with his own father, but he didn't.

Nathan was connecting with Billy, though. He'd watched them work side by side all week. Nathan seemed to feel comfortable with the other mechanics who worked in the garage, too. But around Jack, he was more quiet and reserved.

That night over a bottle of Lone Star in Billy's backyard, he talked to Billy about it.

'I don't think Nathan likes me much,' he said as he watched Lacy and Amy Lynn play on the big jungle gym Billy had built for them last summer. It was around seven o'clock and shade from two oaks crept halfway across the lawn to the patio where he and Billy sat. 'He seems to like you a lot more than me.'

'I think he's just more nervous around you.'

The two brothers sat on Adirondack chairs, legs stretched out in front of them, their cowboy boots crossed at the ankles. Jack wore a jean shirt with the arms cut off while Billy had on a wife-beater. Rhonda had taken the baby with her to some sort of makeup party and had left Billy in charge of the older girls.

'I don't know what I can do to make him more comfortable,' Jack said as he raised the bottle to his lips and took a drink.

'For starters, you can stop staring daggers at his mother when she comes and picks him up, like you did today.'

That afternoon was the first time he'd seen Daisy since they'd had it out in her momma's front yard. She'd been in Seattle for a few days and he hadn't known she was back until she showed up. Just as he hadn't known he looked at her any certain way.

'And when he brings up his dad,' Billy continued, 'you can quit getting so pissed off.'

'Steven isn't his dad.' Jack looked at his brother and said, 'I never say anything bad about him.'

'You don't have to. Whenever Nathan brings him up and you're around, your eyes get hard and you make that sound through your teeth like you're an air hose.' Billy sat forward and yelled across the yard. 'Lacy, don't walk in front of your sister like that when she's swingin'. She's likely to kick you in the head again.'

Jack set his bottle on the arm of the chair. 'Does Nathan talk about Steven when I'm not around?'

'Yeah.' Billy sat back. 'It sounds like before Steven got sick, they used to do a lot together.'

Jack caught himself making that air-hose noise Billy

was talking about. He was jealous. Jealous of a dead man and jealous of his own brother. He didn't like the feeling one bit.

'I know you're angry, and you have every right, but you need to remember that Nathan loved Steven. Right or wrong, sounds like Steven was a good daddy to him.'

'Steven didn't have the right to be good, bad or indifferent. He and Daisy took off together. They got married and kept my son from me for fifteen years.'

'Which are you more pissed off about? That Daisy didn't tell you about Nathan, or that she chose Steven and not you all those years ago?'

'That she took Nathan.' Of course that was worse, but the two were so connected, he couldn't separate them.

'You look at her like you hate her now, but I saw the way you were looking at her at Lacy's birthday party. You were eye-eatin' her the second you sat down.'

Had he? Probably. 'I used to have a real thing for her, growing up,' he confessed as he watched Amy Lynn jump from the swing and land on her feet.

'I read Steven's letter, and it sounds to me like you *both* had a "thing" for Daisy Brooks. Sounds like you both loved her.'

There was no use denying it. 'Since about the eighth grade, I guess. Maybe even before that.' As he watched Amy Lynn get back in her swing, he thought back to before the night Steven and Daisy had married. 'Being with her was like ... racing down the old highway pushing a hundred and fifty. You know that feeling you get when you're balls-to-the-wall? Your heart's up in your throat and adrenaline is crawling across your skin and making your hair stand up?'

'Yeah, I know.'

'It was like that.' Jack shook his head, then reached for his beer. He'd never talked to anyone about Daisy before. 'I was crazy about her, but we used to fight a lot. She was so jealous, and I would throw a fit if any other boy even looked at her.'

Billy leaned forward in his chair again. 'Amy Lynn, don't swing so high.' He sat back and said, 'Well, you must have made up a time or two or else she wouldn't have ended up pregnant.'

Jack recalled with perfect clarity the many times he'd made love to her in the backseat of his car, standing up somewhere with her legs around his waist, or in her bedroom while her mom worked late. 'I think we used to fight just so we could make up in the backseat of my Camaro.'

'Sounds like teenage hormones,' Billy said, looking over at Jack through his clear blue eyes as if things had been that simple.

'It was more than just hormones.' He'd been with girls before Daisy, but with her, it had been more than just getting off. Last Saturday on the back of the Custom Lancer proved that she could still make him feel that way. After all these years. Of course, that had been before he'd found out about Nathan. Now all he felt for her was a biting anger. He took a drink, and rested the bottle on the top of his right thigh. 'I thought she was it for me. She's all I used to think about.'

'If you were in love with her, why did you break up with her?'

'How do you know that I broke up with her?'

'It was in Steven's letter.'

'It was?' He recalled little about the letter other than the mention of Nathan. 'Mom and dad had just died and I was dealing, or trying to deal, with all of that.' He lifted a finger off the bottle and pointed at his brother. 'You remember what pure hell that was.'

'Sure.'

'About that same time Daisy got even more possessive and emotional than usual. It seemed like she was always hanging on my neck, and the more I tried to get her to loosen her grasp, the more she choked me. I just couldn't handle it, so I told her we needed time apart. The next thing I knew, she'd married my best friend.'

'Pregnant women get really weird. Believe me, I've been through it three times now.'

'I didn't know she was pregnant.'

'True. She told Steven and not you because you'd dumped her.'

'I didn't dump her.' Christ, Billy was starting to piss him off. 'I just needed some time to think. If I'd known, I would have done the right thing.'

'I know you would have.'

Finally, a little support from his family.

'But she felt dumped all the same, and she went to Steven and he helped her out instead of you.'

'What the hell? You're my brother. You're supposed to be on my side.'

'I am. Always. But you're so angry, I just don't think you can see things clearly, is all. I understand how you feel, but someone needs to point out to you that you had a hand in Daisy marrying Steven.'

'Maybe,' he conceded for the sake of argument, but he wasn't sure he believed it. 'But that doesn't excuse either of them from not telling me about my son. I'll never forgive Daisy for that.'

'Well, you know what Tim McGraw says about never?'

He didn't give a shit what Tim McGraw had to say about anything. Tim was married to Faith Hill, and Faith hadn't run off with his babies and kept them a secret for fifteen years.

Billy took a long pull off his beer and told him anyway. 'Old Tim says something about the trouble with never is never never works. I think there's some wisdom in that.'

And Jack thought Billy needed to slow down on the Lone Star. 'I was thinking that maybe I'd grab the boat and take Nathan to Lake Meredith fishing,' he said purposely directing the conversation away from Daisy. 'Maybe camp out for a night.'

'Rhonda and I took the girls and camped out at the lake last summer. We stayed at that Stanford-Yake campsite right there by the marina. It had a real nice comfort station for the girls.'

'I don't care how nice the toilets are.' Billy cared because he had to live with four females who'd bitch about it.

'I thought you might want to ask Nathan's momma to come along.'

Jack stood and walked across the patio. 'What's gotten into you?' He wanted to get to know his son without anyone else around. Now that he knew about his reaction whenever Nathan brought up Daisy or Steven, he could control it. 'Are you being contrary just to piss me off?'

Billy laughed and stood also. 'No, I just thought Nathan might be more comfortable with her there. He might open up more.'

Maybe, but sleeping with Daisy in the same tent was not going to happen. It wasn't even an option. And it had nothing to do with sex and everything to do with him maybe putting a pillow over her head while she slept. He moved to the Rubbermaid garbage can by the side of the house, opened the lid, and tossed the bottle inside. 'We'll be okay alone.' He secured the lid down tight. 'We'll catch some walleye and maybe a few largemouth bass.'

'Sounds good.'

'Hey, you two,' Jack called across the yard. 'Get over here and give me some sugar so I can leave.'

Lacy slid down the yellow plastic slide, and a few seconds later Amy Lynn jumped off the swing. They both ran across the lawn. Lacy with her head down as usual – Jack knelt on one knee, safely removing his nuts from head-butting level.

Billy moved across the patio and threw away his bottle. 'Maybe next week sometime, we should have Nathan over so he can meet his cousins.'

'To meet your two yard babies?' Jack asked as he grabbed Lacy and set her on his knee.

'I'm not a yard baby,' Amy Lynn protested, but she wrapped her arms around his neck and kissed his cheek.

'What are you, then? A yard bird?'

'What's that?'

'A chicken.'

'Nuh-uh.'

'Swear to God. That's what your grandma Parrish called chickens. 'Course, she was raised on a farm in Tennessee and they really did have chickens in their yard.' He gave Lacy a kiss, then set her back on her feet. He stood with Amy Lynn's arms still around his neck.

'Don't go,' she protested.

'Got to.' He tickled her armpits and she giggled and

dropped to her feet. 'I have to make some big fishing plans.'

'You'll have fun,' Billy predicted as he scooped up Lacy and followed Jack to the gate at the side of the house. 'Nathan's a good kid. You can tell he's being raised right.'

Jack glanced over his shoulder at Billy. 'You saw the way he looks. That ring through his lip and that hair. Those dog chains and his pants down around the crack of his ass.'

'That's the way some kids look today. Doesn't mean he wasn't raised right.'

True, but Jack wasn't in the mood to give Daisy credit for anything, especially since Billy seemed determined to play devil's advocate. 'When he was three, he wanted a Porsche 911.'

Billy stopped dead in his tracks. 'He's a Parrish.'

Finally, he'd made his point.

Jack raised his hand and knocked twice on Louella Brooks's front door. The sun was beginning to set, washing the porch in dull gray light.

The door swung open and he came face-to-face with Daisy. Her hair was down around her shoulders, kind of messy as if she'd just got out of bed. She wore a pink dress that tied behind her neck and laced up between her breasts. Her feet were bare and she was sexy as hell. A contrary mix of anger and desire pulled low in his abdomen.

'Hi, Jack.'

'Hey. Is Nathan around?'

'Nathan left with my mother, but . . .' Her brows lowered and she licked her lips. 'What time is it?'

He looked at his watch. 'A little after eight.'

'Oh. Well, Mom and Nathan went over to Lily's to help her with dinner.'

'How's your sister?'

She brushed her fingertips beneath her eyes. 'Better. She went home from the hospital two days ago.'

'Did I wake you up?'

'I guess I nodded off during "Frasier" reruns.' She gave him a warm, sleepy smile. 'Nathan should be back anytime.'

'Do you mind if I wait for him?'

'Are you going to be nice?' She drew out the word *niiiiiice*. Daisy Lee had found her accent.

'Reasonably.'

She thought about if for a moment, then stepped back. 'Come on in.'

He followed her through the darkened living room. The technicolor light from the televison flashed white and blue patches across her bare shoulders and back. She led him into the kitchen and flipped the switch.

It had been a long time since he'd been in Louella Brooks's kitchen.

'Would you like something to drink? Tea, Coke, water?' She smiled back over her shoulder at him. 'Bourbon?'

'No thanks.'

She raked her fingers through the top of her hair as she opened the refrigerator and pulled out a blue bottle of water with her free hand. Her fingers combed through her hair to the ends, then she twisted the top off the bottle and knocked the door shut with her hip.

'How was your trip?' he asked.

'It was real sad.' The silk strands of her hair slid back in place, and she leaned a shoulder into the refrigerator and looked up at him. 'I finally packed up most of Steven's things. Junie came over and got what she wanted. Good Will came and got the rest.'

Jack saw the sadness in her brown eyes and told himself he didn't care. She lifted the bottle to her lips and took a long drink. When she lowered it again, a clear drop of water rested on her top lip. 'I have some photos for you.' The droplet rested there for several long moments before it slid down and disappeared into the seam.

'What photos?' If they were pictures of her and Steven and Nathan living it up in Seattle, then she could keep them.

'The photo taken in the nursery when Nathan was born, of him riding his trike, blowing out birthday candles, playing football. Stuff like that.' She held up a finger. 'I'll be right back.'

He didn't want her to be reasonable. Giving him photos went beyond pretending to be nice in public. He didn't want her to be nice at all. He didn't want to watch crystal drops of water slide between her pink lips. He didn't want to watch her leave, his gaze slipping down her back to her behind and the bottom of the dress where it touched the backs of her thighs.

When she returned, she had a shoe box under one arm. 'I have tons of pictures of Nathan; these are just a few that I thought you might like.' She carried them to the breakfast nook and took a seat. Jack slid into the seat across from her as she took off the lid to the shoe box. She pulled out a few photos and handed them to him. 'This is his hospital picture. He was kind of bruised up because they had to use forceps on him.'

Jack gazed down at the photo in his hand of a tiny baby

with a bruise on his cheek. His eyes were kind of puffy and his mouth was pursed as if he where about to kiss someone. The next picture was of Daisy as he remembered her looking in high school. Like the day she'd left him. Her hair was big, and she sat in a hospital bed holding a baby wrapped up tight in a striped blanket. His baby boy. His girl. Only by then she hadn't been his anymore.

'I didn't know if you'd want that one because I'm in it,' she said, 'but I'm in all the pictures taken in the hospital.' She dug out a few more. 'Any of these you don't want, just leave them with me.' This time when she handed the photos over, she leaned across the table. 'This was taken on Nathan's first birthday.' She pointed to a baby standing on a kitchen chair. He had chocolate cake smeared on his face, clear up into his hair, and he wore a huge grin. The remains of a smashed cake sat on the table in front of him.

'I'd just made his cake and turned my back to wash the dishes,' Daisy explained. 'When I turned back, he was standing on that chair and had grabbed big hunks of cake. By the time I got my camera, he'd stuffed a bunch in his mouth and rubbed it on the top of his head.' Jack laughed and she looked up from the photo and smiled. 'He was such a pistol,' she said and returned her attention to the picture. His gaze slid to the side of her neck. Her breasts were pressed against the table, pushing her cleavage over the top of her dress. If he leaned forward, he could smell her hair. 'That was about the time we had to start locking him in our bedroom,' she said.

Jack leaned way back. 'Why?'

She straightened. 'Because that boy started crawling out of his crib when he was seven months old. We had to get him a little bed that was really low to the ground because we were afraid he'd hurt himself. Then one day, a little after his first birthday, I was making his bed, and under his satin baby pillow, I found three screwdrivers.' She shook her head. 'The only thing I could figure out was that he was roaming around the house after Steven and I fell asleep. So that's when we had to lock him in our bedroom with us.'

The three of them all in bed together. One big happy family. It should have been him. It should have been him with her and with Nathan. But she'd chosen Steven.

She should have chosen him. It should have been him in that bed, but the harsh truth was that he couldn't blame her for her choice.

Not anymore. Not when she'd chosen Steven because she'd been eighteen and scared. But being eighteen and scared didn't excuse her from keeping his son from him. He didn't think he'd ever forgive her for that.

She spread some more photos out on the table. 'I have a lot of photographs of Nathan through the years. He's my favorite subject. I have some really nice black-and-whites of him that I took a few years ago when we went climbing around the rocks at the bottom of Snoqualmie Falls. Black and white just balanced everything around him beautifully.' Her lips turned up at the corners. 'Color would have been too overwhelming, and he would have been lost in the shot.'

'You sound like you know a lot about taking pictures.' He had one of those auto-everything cameras, and still forgot to bring it to the girls' parties.

'I'm a photographer. It's what I used to do for a living.'

He hadn't known that about her. Didn't know very much about her life in Seattle, as a matter of fact.

'It's what I plan to do again. I'm going to open my own studio. I've been checking into small business loans, and I talked to a realtor about leasing a space in Belltown, which is in the downtown area.' She dug through the box and handed him more photos. 'It's going to be a little scary at first, but with the money I get from selling our house, and the money I received from Steven's life insurance policies, we'll be okay.'

She was moving on with her life. Moving forward while he felt as if he were firmly stuck in the past. Unable to move.

Louella walked into the kitchen with Nathan trailing behind, wearing even more chains than usual and a black T-shirt with a skateboarder on the front.

Daisy slid from behind the table and moved to meet them. 'Nathan, Jack came over to talk to you.'

Nathan's gaze met his over the top of Daisy's head. Jack set the photo on the table and stood. He turned his attention to Daisy's mother. She had blue smudges beneath her eyes and her hair listed left. 'Good evening, Miz Brooks.'

'Evening, Jackson.'

'How are you?'

'I've felt better,' she said. 'Lily insists that she stay at her own home when it would be better if she stayed here.' She set her big black purse on the counter and moved to stand a few feet in front of him. 'Last year Tiny Barnett's youngest girl, Tammy, had woman trouble and had to have surgery. Did you hear what happened to her?'

Jack wasn't sure Louella was speaking to him. She was looking at him, but he didn't know anyone named Tiny Barnett or her daughter Tammy.

Evidently a reply wasn't necessary, though. 'She died because she went home from the hospital early.'

'Mom,' Daisy said on a sigh, 'Lily isn't going to die.'

'That's what Tammy thought too. Left behind a little boy about Pippen's age. Left a husband too. He was a Yankee fella from one of those eastern states, and when Tammy made her heavenly journey, he packed up that baby and left. Tiny hasn't seen hide nor hair of him since. And Tiny is a good woman. She's stuck with Horace Barnett all these years. And everyone knows that man was born tired and raised lazy. I don't think he ever did work a job for more than a month straight.'

She paused and it all came back to Jack in a flash. The reason he and Steven usually waited on the porch for Daisy. Fifteen years, and she hadn't changed. Louella Brooks could still talk water uphill.

'And he had that mentally retarded sister, bless her heart. She used to come by the diner and order gizzards, every now and again. I used to think that . . .'

Jack felt a pressure in the back of his skull and looked behind Louella to Daisy and Nathan. They stood in profile, Nathan a few inches taller than his mother. He stared down at Daisy, his narrowed gaze communicating something. Daisy shrugged as if to say, 'What do you want me to do?' While Louella rambled on about gizzards and chicken fried steak, Daisy and Nathan carried on a whole conversation without saying a word. Mother and son.

Nathan rocked back on his heels and slashed his finger across his throat. Daisy covered her mouth with her hand and started shaking her head. They were a family. Just the two of them. Comfortable with each other. Relaxed. He wasn't a part of it.

As if she felt his gaze on her, Daisy looked at Jack, then she burst into laughter.

'Goodness, Daisy. What's gotten into you?' Louella asked as she turned to look at her daughter.

'Just thought of something that happened today.' She brushed her hair behind her ears and said, 'Jack came over to talk to Nathan, so maybe we should leave them to it.'

'Actually, I was hoping that you and Nathan could walk me out to my car.'

'Cool.'

'Sure.'

He turned his attention to Louella. 'Good evening, ma'am. Give Lily my best the next time you see her.'

'I will.'

The three of them walked through the living room and out the front door, with Jack bringing up the rear.

'Why didn't you stop her?' Nathan asked as soon as the door was shut behind them.

They moved from the porch and down the sidewalk. The setting sun filled the night sky with blazing reds and oranges, fading in the distance to pink and purple. It seemed to catch in strands of Daisy's hair, turning it gold.

'No one can stop your grandmother once she gets started,' Daisy answered.

'All the way home from Lily's she would *not* stop talking about someone named Cyrus.'

'Cyrus is your great uncle who died when he was fourteen, bless his heart.'

'And I give a crap because why?'

'Nathan!'

Jack chuckled.

'Don't encourage his bad behavior, Jack,' she said as they came to the end of the sidewalk.

'Wouldn't dream of it.' He turned to his son. 'How do you feel about fishing?'

He shrugged. 'My dad and I used to fish all the time.'

Jack forced a smile. 'I'm going bass fishing this weekend, and I wanted you to come along. I thought we'd leave Saturday morning and come back sometime Sunday.'

Nathan looked at Jack then turned to his mother.

'We don't have plans this weekend. Go ahead. You'll have fun.'

Nathan didn't say anything and Jack spoke to cover the silence. He opened his mouth and heard himself say, 'Daisy, why don't you come along too?' And he couldn't believe it. The pressure in the back of his skull moved up and squeezed his brain. He'd just done the one thing that he'd gotten mad at Billy for even suggesting.

All he could do now was hope like hell she refused.

A slight breeze rippled across the surface of Lake Meredith while sunlight reflected off the water like bits of tinfoil. Birds circled overhead, fish jumped, and the heavy bass guitar and hard drum beats of Godsmack pounded the air like a fist.

Daisy sat cross-legged in the front of Jack's boat and gazed at Nathan through the lens of the Fuji digital camera she'd brought with her when she'd returned from Seattle. She wore her white one-piece swimsuit beneath a red tank top and jean shorts. A big straw hat shielded her face from the sun.

Nathan brought his pole back to cast and she snapped his picture. He wore a ball cap, the bill curved low on his forehead and just above his silver and black Oakley sunglasses. His khaki shorts rode low on his behind and showed his red and white striped boxers. He wore skater shoes without socks. His cheeks were very pink, and he'd taken off his T-shirt although she'd warned him against it.

'You treat me like a baby,' he'd complained like a baby. But he gave in and allowed her to rub him down with sun screen.

She turned her camera on Jack, who stood across the stern from Nathan fishing from the opposite side of the boat. He'd pushed his straw cowboy hat low on his forehead and wore a pair of sunglasses with mirrored blue lenses. His old green T-shirt was worn around the neck and the short sleeves fit loose around the hard mounds of his biceps. Earlier he'd caught her staring at the little hole in the shoulder, and he'd told her it was his lucky fishing shirt. A pair of faded Levi's hugged his hips and thighs. The edge of the waistband was slightly frayed, and the five-button fly cupped his package in soft faded denim. She wondered how much luck those pants brought him. Probably a lot. On his feet he wore cowboy boots. What else?

He glanced across his shoulder at her and she snapped his picture. Irritation wrinkled his brow before he turned his attention back to his line. She didn't know if he was irritated because she was taking his picture or because Godsmack had just said the F-word again. Although, she'd certainly heard him throw that word around. *I'm going to fuck you till you faint* came to mind.

He'd picked her and Nathan up that morning driving a white Dodge Ram truck. To her surprise, it wasn't 'vintage.' It was fairly new and pulling a twenty-one-foot bass boat. When he'd asked her and Nathan the other day if they wanted to go fishing, she'd envisioned an aluminum boat with a little putt-putt motor. She should have known better. Jack wasn't the kind of guy to have a putt-putt anything.

The gray-and-red boat had dual consoles with seats that looked better suited for a race car. A third fishing chair was perched in the back by the huge outboard engine. Below the clock on the wood-grain console was the CD player. Earlier as they'd set up camp, Nathan and Jack made a deal. They would alternate music. Jack went first and then Nathan. The problem was that Jack had a human-sized CD case, while Nathan had a case about the size of the New York phone book. They were in for a ground-thumping few days.

Nathan caught the first fish. A twelve-inch Walleye that brought the first real joy she'd seen on his face in a long time. Jack netted it for him and helped him remove the hook. With their head bent over the fish, Daisy snapped a few pictures. She was too far away and the music was too loud for her to hear what they said to each other, but when Nathan tipped back his head and laughed, Daisy felt it in her chest. The pang in her heart wasn't solely due to the pleasure of her son's laughter, though. It was Jack too. He was reaching out to Nathan. Trying to make a connection with his son, and for some reason that Daisy didn't understand, she felt herself fall a little more in love with him. Not the fast wham-bam love of adolescence. Not the flash of heat and fire like a lightning bolt, which she'd once tried and failed to grasp in the palm of her hand. This was easier. A gentle beat against her heart, a soothing *ahh* in her chest, which scared her more than the first time she'd fallen for him. This love was more mature. She was more mature, and she knew exactly what to do about it.

Absolutely nothing.

Matt Flegel had called her the other night and asked her to dinner. It had been so long since a man had asked her out; she'd been shocked. She'd sputtered something about contacting him once she returned from her camping trip. At the time, she hadn't really wanted to go. Now she wondered if it wasn't a good idea. Something to take her mind off Jack and her feelings for him.

She snapped another picture and watched Jack through her lens as he returned to his fishing pole and picked it up. The sun glinted off the silver reel as the spool spun around and around. The movement of his hands and arms was smooth and precise, and his boots were planted a shoulder's width apart. The CD player shut off and she could hear the soft *tick-tick-tick* of his reel. Her heart picked up its soothing pace and she clicked his photo.

White sunlight poured over one side of him while the shade of his hat slashed across his nose and mouth. He brought in the line and reached up to pull a weed from the hook. Then in one fluid motion, he flipped the bale with his thumb, flung the tip of the pole straight out to his side, then whipped it forward again. His lure sailed across the water as a breeze bowed the line, catching it on a current like a spider web, suspending it in air for a few short moments before the lure hit the water with a *kerplunk* and pulled the line down with it.

She lowered her camera and looked away. She couldn't hide behind her lens from either her feelings or his. Jack hated her, and he'd never forgive her. He'd made that perfectly clear. Around her, he was very guarded, and she didn't even know why he'd asked her to come along on this fishing trip. He acted like she was a necessary evil, like bug spray. She was leaving at the end of the summer, and she probably wouldn't see him again until next year. There was no future for her and Jack, except that at some point she hoped it would be possible for them to be friends again.

She wasn't going to hold her breath, though.

She was making a future for herself and Nathan a thousand or so miles away in Washington. She'd talked to Nathan about selling their house, and he was okay with it. He'd been sad, like she was. The house held as many good memories as bad, but he liked the idea of moving into a loft in Belltown even if it meant a change in schools. She'd already called a realtor, a friend of Junie's, and put the house on the market. Junie had always had an extra key, so she arranged to give a copy to the realtor.

Daisy was definitely getting on with her life now. She'd never been on her own before. Never solely responsible for all decisions. She was scared. And if she thought about it too much, she got little anxiety attacks, but she knew things would be okay.

It was well past noon and everyone was hungry by the time they made it back to camp. While the boys cleaned the fish they'd caught, Daisy set the picnic table with a red-and-white checkered cloth and red plastic plates and utensils.

When she spoke with Jack the night before, she insisted that they split the meals. He was in charge of dinner. She wondered if he'd pull out a package of hotdogs and a bag of chips and call it good.

She set a roasted chicken, salad, and a loaf of rye bread on the table. By the time she'd sliced the chicken and added dried pieces of fruit and raspberry dressing to the salad, Nathan and Jack were walking from the shore toward her. Nathan had put on his shirt and he carried his ball cap. His hair was sweaty and smashed to his head. She couldn't help but notice that when Nathan forgot to act cool, he moved a lot like Jack did. More easy and relaxed. Jack took off his sunglasses and brushed the side of his face against the shoulder of his lucky T-shirt – which had proved to be lucky once again, since he'd caught two smallmouth bass and a crappie.

'I'm going to change and be right back,' he said as he tossed his hat and glasses on the table. He moved toward the four-man tent they'd pitched beneath a cottonwood tree. 'Watch out for faaar ants,' he warned, drawing out the vowels. 'I saw a nest of 'em over by the toilets.' He grabbed a fistful of his shirt and pulled it over his head as he threw the tent flap back.

'Mom,' Nathan called to her.

Daisy pulled her gaze from the tent and the fleeting glimpse of Jack's bare back, the smooth planes and indent of his spine, the sliver of the white elastic just above the bluer waistband of his jeans . . . 'Hmm?'

'What's a faaar ant?' he asked just above a whisper.

'Fire.' She chuckled and shook her head. 'Fire ant. They have a nasty bite that burns.'

Nathan smiled. 'Well, why didn't he just say fire?'

'He thinks he did.' She placed some chicken and salad on a plate and handed it to Nathan. She'd brought a Thermos of ice tea, and she put ice in three red Dixie Cups and poured. 'Are you having a good time?' she asked her son.

Nathan sat and shrugged in that way of his that could have meant anything. 'I guess.' Then he grinned and drawled like a Texan, 'I'm gonna catch my limit if it harelips the governor.'

'Just don't get bit by faaar ants,' she warned him.

Nathan tipped back his head and laughed a steady *heh-heh-heh*.

'What are y'all laughing about?' Jack asked as he

walked toward them, closing the snaps on his shirt. It was beige, cowboy cut, with the arms hacked off.

'Nathan says he's going to catch his limit if it harelips the governor.'

Jack looked up and his green gaze touched Daisy's face from across the table. 'Damn straight.' He grabbed a plate and placed a few pieces of chicken on it. 'What is that?' he asked as he looked into the salad bowl.

'Salad.'

He scowled. 'It looks like chick food. Like flower petals, weeds, and leathery fruit chunks.'

Nathan laughed and Daisy frowned at him. 'It's very good.'

'I'm going to take your word on that.' He put three pieces of bread on his plate and then looked across the table at her. 'Butter?'

'You still eat butter?' She hadn't used butter in so long, it hadn't occurred to her to pack any. 'I have cream cheese.'

He shook his head and walked away. He moved to the back of his truck, lowered the tailgate and rummaged around in his cooler. When he returned, he had a stick of butter. He unwrapped the stick then set it on the table. 'You've been living up North too long, Daisy Lee.' He pulled a pocket knife out of his front pocket and made wafer-thin pats. 'Do you want some of this?' he asked Nathan.

Nathan nodded and Jack stabbed a few thin pats with the knife, then handed it over to him. Nathan laid them out on his rye bread and paused a moment to eye the knife before he handed it back.

'How about you, Daisy?'

'When was the last time you cleaned that knife?'

'Hmm.' He finally sat down and pretended to think a

moment. 'Last . . . no, the year before last. It was right after I used it to gut an armadillo.'

Nathan laughed as he took a big bite of his bread.

She was sure he was lying. Well, almost sure. 'No thanks,' Daisy answered.

'Pansy-ass,' he said right before he sank his teeth into his bread covered in little squares of yellow butter.

She took a big bite of her salad. 'Scardy-cat. Afraid of a little arugula and raspberry dressing.'

'Hell, yeah,' he said as thin creases appeared in the corners of his green eyes. 'If a man eats stuff like that, the next thing he knows, he's wearing pink and tying a sweater around his neck.'

Nathan held up his hand and Jack gave him five.

'I thought you liked my raspberry salad.'

'No,' Nathan said. 'I'm hungry.'

Daisy didn't believe him. Jack was turning him into a traitor. A guy just like him.

'So what did you bring for dinner?' she asked.

Jack used his armadillo-gutting knife to cut his chicken. 'Wild rice.'

'That's it?'

'No, I brought some real lettuce and some bleu cheese dressing.'

'We're having wild rice and salad?'

He stared across the table at her as if she couldn't possibly be so dense. 'And the fish.'

'You were that sure you'd catch our dinner, that you didn't bring anything else?'

'Hell, yeah. I wore my lucky shirt.'

Daisy turned her attention to Nathan, who was highly amused.

Jack took a long drink of tea then set the glass on the table. 'I coat the fish in flour, then fry 'em up.'

'Sounds good,' Nathan said.

Jack lifted a finger off his red plastic glass and pointed at his son. 'It's the kind of meal that'll put hair on a guy's tea bag.'

Her confusion must have shown on her face because Nathan cleared things up for her. 'Gonads.'

Gee, she probably could have gone all weekend without knowing that. 'But,' Daisy said weakly, 'I'm not a guy.'

'And you don't have a tea bag,' her son pointed out needlessly.

She shook her head and placed a hand on her chest. 'And I sincerely don't want a tea bag. Ever.'

'That's what they all say before they try it,' Jack said through a grin, then he and Nathan busted up laughing as if they got some secret joke that she didn't.

As she looked across the table at her son laughing, she felt left out. Left out of the guy club, but this was what she wanted, wasn't it? Since she'd flown down here weeks ago? Jack and Nathan to get to know each other? For Nathan to know his real father? Tea bag and gutting knife and all?

Yes, but not at her expense. She didn't want to be excluded. She wanted to be a part of the tea bag club, too. It wasn't fair to be excluded because she didn't have the right equipment. Growing up, Jack had used the same tactic to exclude her from a lot of things.

'I know what you're doing, Jack,' she said.

He looked at her.

'You're trying to exclude me like you and Steven used to when you didn't want me around.'

His brows lowered but his smile stayed in place. 'What are you talking about, buttercup?'

'Remember when you excluded me from your television club. You made a rule that in order to be a member, I had to pee on a tree while standing.'

'I remember that, but I don't remember anything about a television.'

She thought a moment. 'It was the CBS club or something like that.'

He thought a moment, then said, 'Ahh. You mean the NBBC. I forgot about that.' He grinned. 'You thought that was a televison club?'

'Of course.'

He shook his head and chuckled. 'Honey, that was the Nekkid Boobs and Butts Club. It's where we got together and looked at porn.'

'Sweet.'

'You guys had porn? You were in the sixth grade, for cryin' out loud.' She was appalled. 'You were little pervs and I didn't even know it.'

His grin told her that she didn't even know *the half* of it.

16

After lunch, Daisy dragged a chaise longue to the shore and dropped her shorts. She wore sunglasses and her white one-piece swimming suit, cut high on the hips. It had a built-in bra top and thin straps. The boys had gone fishing again, and she'd opted to stay behind. She pulled out the latest issue of *Studio Photography & Design* and stretched out on the chaise. She read an article on the Hasselblad V-System and dreamed about the spectacular photographs she could take with it. Then she must have fallen asleep for real, because she dreamed she'd won first place in a Kodak photography contest and she hadn't even entered. She dreamed she was up on stage, bluffing her way through a speech about a photograph she didn't remember taking, and Steven was in the front row watching.

She dreamed about him often, and in her dreams, he always appeared as he had before his illness. Healthy and happy and she was always glad to see him. He never spoke, he just gave her a smile that let her know that he was okay, and that she was okay too.

The sound of an outboard engine woke her up and she opened her eyes. Her sunglasses where still on her face, but the trade magazine had slipped to the ground. She sat up and wondered how long she'd been asleep. She swung her feet to the side and took off her sunglasses. The sun was definitely lower, although it would be a long time before it set. Her tan skin had a twinge of red; she would pay for falling asleep in the Texas sunlight.

She tossed her glasses and the magazine on the chair, then stood. She moved toward the shore as Jack's boat came nearer, parting the water with its pointed nose. Daisy raised a hand to her forehead and shielded her eyes from the sun. Jack stood at the bbw; his cowboy shirt unsnapped, the edges fluttering against his bare chest and stomach. Nathan sat in the driver's seat, his intent gaze on Jack.

'Turn it off and raise the motor,' Jack called out.

Nathan looked down and the sound of the engine got louder as it rose out of the water, then it stopped. The boat drifted closer and gently bumped into the shoreline.

Jack looked over his shoulder as he spoke to Nathan, telling him what a great job he'd done. He turned back and went down on one knee to grab a rope tied to the front of the boat.

'You got sunburned while we were gone,' Jack said as he slowly raised his gaze to hers.

Daisy looked down at herself. She pressed her fingers to her chest above her suit. Her fingertips left white prints on her pink skin. 'I fell asleep.'

He dropped the anchor over the side of the boat into

shallow water, then he jumped down from the bow and stood in front of her, blocking the sun. 'You burned your love bite.'

Again she glanced down at herself. Visible just above the top of her swimsuit, her birthmark was a little darker than the rest of her skin. 'What are you doing staring at my birthmark?'

The corners of his mouth slid upward into a slow, sexy grin. 'Just making casual conversation, buttercup,' he drawled.

Asking about her love bite wasn't casual. The last time he'd commented on it, they'd both been naked. The heated look in his eyes told her he was remembering that time too.

Daisy swallowed past the sudden lump in her throat. She lowered her gaze from his mouth, along the thin line of hair that ran down his chest and flat stomach to his navel. She recalled perfectly what his skin felt like beneath her palms.

'Mom, guess what?'

Daisy returned her gaze to Jack's, to the desire he tried but failed to hide. 'What?'

'I caught a bigmouth bass.' Nathan jumped from the boat and landed next to Jack.

'It's a beauty,' Jack confirmed and his gazed dropped to her mouth.

She turned her attention to her son. Whatever was between her and Jack was best left alone. 'Show me.'

Nathan jumped back up on the bow of the boat, then moved to the stern. Daisy walked past Jack and waded into the water up to her hips. She held on to the outside of the boat as Nathan opened the live well and pulled out a stringer.

Jack watched his son as he held up the bass for his mother. It swung close to Daisy's face and she jumped back.

'You're such a girl,' Nathan said through a teasing laugh.

Jack turned and moved up the shore toward camp. He and Nathan had had a good time fishing. He felt closer to his son than he had before they'd come to the lake. While they fished, Nathan had talked about his life, and Steven had been a big part of that life.

'Before I quit, I was quarterback on my Optimist football team,' he'd told Jack. 'My dad told me you guys played football growing up.'

His dad. Jack had been very careful not to show the slightest emotion. 'We did,' he'd said past the bitter taste in his mouth. 'I played quarterback until I quit my junior year.'

Nathan had nodded. 'That's what dad said. He said you had to quit to work for your dad, and that's how he got to be quarterback his last two years of school and get all the good lookin' girls.'

'Your dad was a pretty smooth guy. He never had any problems with the girls.' The longer they talked about Steven, the easier it got. The easier it was to swallow the bitterness. Jack remembered what it was like to lose a father – the confusion and the loneliness. For a few hours, he was able to forget about anger and betrayal and talk to Nathan about what it had been like to grow up with Steven Monroe.

In the end, he was surprised to discover the more he talked about Steven, the more he got to know Nathan. And the more he got to know his son, the more he wanted to know. He still didn't feel like a father, although he wasn't even sure what a father was supposed to feel like.

Jack poured some water into a basin and washed his fishy hands with liquid soap. He glanced up as Nathan tore off his shoes and shirt and jumped into the lake next to Daisy. She hollered his name as he splashed her.

It was very clear to Jack how Nathan felt about his mother. He might bitch that she babied him, but he loved her. He might have hedgehog hair and a ring through his lip, but Billy was right. Daisy and Steven had done a good job raising Nathan. He was a good kid.

And Jack had nothing to do with it. He grabbed a towel and dried his hands. He tried not to let the bitterness he'd hidden from Nathan rise up and eat a hole in him. He succeeded in keeping it tapped down, right next to the burning ache in his gut that wanted Daisy Lee so bad it was driving him half crazy.

How could he still want her? Want to touch her as he sealed his mouth to hers? To feel the golden strands of her hair tangled around his fingers and the warmth of her skin against his palms? To smell her neck and to look into her brown eyes as he made love to her? How could he want that and at the same time want to shake her and hurt her as much as she'd hurt him? It didn't make a bit of sense to him.

Jack hung the towel on one shoulder and watched Nathan dive at Daisy. She screamed and he pulled her under. Jack smiled despite himself. Daisy had a way of making him laugh when he didn't want to. Of making him remember things that brought a smile to his lips before he even realized what she was doing. Of reminding him that they'd had a lot of good times together in the past, before things had gotten so fucked up.

If he closed his eyes, he could remember back to what

she felt like in his arms. The weight of her body as she leaned into him. The texture of her hair as he rested his chin on the top of her head. The sound of her voice saying his name in anger or in ecstasy. The tastes and textures of Daisy Lee. He remembered it all and wished like hell he didn't.

Jack started charcoal burning in the fire pit and got out a cookstove. He put some Jimmy Buffet on the portable CD player and mixed flour, salt and pepper for the fish. While Jimmy sang about fins circling around, Jack couldn't seem to keep his eyes off a certain white swimsuit jumping around and diving into the lake. Coming back up and looking almost transparent, but not quite.

When he and Nathan had returned this last time, Jack had stood on the bow of the boat and watched her walk toward the water. Toward him, looking like she was an underwear model wearing one of those one-piece teddies that was cut up real high on her hips. Sexy as hell. Like a living, breathing wet dream. And for a few seconds he'd wondered what it would be like if this was really his life. To return from a day out with his son and have Daisy waiting for them. To grab her up and hold her against him. To touch her all he wanted. Anytime he wanted. Anywhere he wanted. For a few brief seconds, the thought of that life nearly sent him to his knees.

But that was not his life. Not reality, and he had no business even thinking about it.

Jack rolled the fish in the flour, then started the rice on the cookstove. Daisy and Nathan returned from the lake and took turns changing in the tent. When Daisy emerged, she wore a soft blue pullover sweat shirt with GAP on the front, matching sweat pants, and white Nikes with a blue swoosh. Her hair was pulled back in one of those claw things. She set the picnic table while Jack cooked the fish in a skillet over the coals. They ate dinner together like a family. Talking and laughing. Jack had to remind himself that it wasn't real.

After dinner they played poker with wooden matchsticks. When it got dark, Jack got out the lanterns and they played until Nathan yawned and announced that he was going to bed.

'It's early,' Jack pointed out and tossed in his cards.

'I'm a tired camper,' he said as he headed toward the tent.

'He does this sometimes. A few days ago, he went to bed right after dinner and slept clear through till breakfast,' Daisy informed Jack as she gathered the cards and stuck them in the box. 'I think he's growing so fast, he just gets worn from the inside out.'

Jack rose and moved out of the pool of light to his truck. He grabbed his jean jacket out of the cab, then walked to the fire pit. Stars crammed the big Texas sky as he stirred the coals. He threw a few logs in the pit and took a seat in one of the folding chairs he'd placed around the pit. He stretched his legs out in front of him and watched the wood catch fire. He thought about their sleeping arrangements and wondered if he should have borrowed another tent from Billy. Sleeping in the same tent wasn't going to be easy. Jack had never slept in such close proximity to a woman when they both weren't naked. This would be a first, and thank God Nathan would be between him and Daisy. Because lately his thoughts were definitely carnal where she was concerned, and he'd hate to fall asleep and wake up face-first in her cleavage.

'It's been a long time since Nathan and I got to get away and just relax,' Daisy said and sat in a chair next to him. 'Thanks, Jack.'

'You're welcome.' He threaded his fingers together over his stomach, crossed his booted ankles, and pushed all thoughts of Daisy's cleavage from his brain. The fire cracked and popped. In between comfortable silences, Daisy told him more about her plans to sell the house she'd shared with Steven, and more about opening her own photography studio. She was ready to get on with her life and eager to start.

They talked about Billy and his family, and she filled him in on the latest with Lily. Lily's divorce was to be final in a few days. According to Daisy, Lily was getting herself together at last. Jack had his doubts, but he didn't mention them.

'Being back here in Texas brings back a lot of memories for me,' Daisy said. 'Most of them good.' He could feel her gaze on him and he looked across his shoulder at her. Firelight danced in her hair and across her face. It touched her mouth and drew his gaze to her lips. 'Remember when you and I and Steven made that time capsule out of a coffee can and buried it in your backyard?' she asked.

Yeah, he remembered that, but he shook his head and glanced up at the sky crammed with stars in the inky black night. He hoped she'd let it drop. He should have known better.

'We put our most valuable treasures in a coffee can, and we were supposed to dig it up in fifty years.'

She laughed and Jack returned his gaze to her profile.

'I can't remember what I put in there.' She thought a moment then snapped her fingers. 'Oh, yeah. A fake diamond ring you'd won for me at the fair. A pink fuzzy barrette Steven had found someplace and given me. You put some Matchbox cars in there, and Steven put some of those green army men.' She looked over at him and a frown creased her brow. 'There had to be more.'

'Your diary,' he said.

'That's right.' She started to laugh, but it died on her lips. 'How did you remember that?'

He just shrugged and rose to stir the logs on the fire. 'Good memory, I guess.'

'Did you dig it up?' He didn't answer and she moved to stand next to him. 'Jack?'

He pushed a log with the toe of his boot. It snapped and shot red embers up into the darkness. 'Me and Steve.'

'When?' she asked.

'About a week after we buried it. We had to know what was in your diary. It was killing us.'

She gasped. 'You guys invaded my privacy. Abused my trust. You were horrible!'

'Yep, and as I recall, your diary was boring as hell. Steven and I thought we were going to read all kinds of juicy stuff. Like who you had a crush on or if you'd kissed a boy. Or what really goes on at those girly slumber parties you were always going to.' He shoved his hands in the front pockets of his Levi's and shifted his weight to one foot. 'As I recall, it was mostly filled with stuff about your damn cat.'

'Mr Skittles?' Her mouth fell open and she grasped his arm through his jacket and turned him to face her. 'You read my private thoughts about Mr Skittles?'

'I hated that cat. Every time I walked into your house, he hissed at me.'

'That's because he could tell you were up to no good.'

Jack laughed and looked down into her face as the firelight danced across her cheeks and nose. Where Daisy Lee was concerned, he'd always been up to no good. He grabbed her hand to remove it from his jacket, but he held it instead. 'You don't even know the half of it.'

'Sylvia told me she showed you her bottom in the fifth grade.'

He had seen quite a few bottoms by the fifth grade. 'It wasn't as good as yours.' He brought her hand to his mouth and pressed a kiss to her knuckles. He looked into her eyes. 'Your bottom was always the best.'

She blinked once and her lids lowered to half-mast. Her lips parted. She wanted him every bit as much as he wanted her. It would have been so easy to slide his other hand behind her head and bring her mouth to his. Desire twisted in his groin and urged him to grab her up and hold her against him. He dropped her hand.

'I've missed you, Jack,' she said. 'I didn't even realize how much until I came back.' She took a step forward and raised onto the balls of her feet. She ran her palms up his jacket to the sides of his neck. 'Did you ever miss me?' She placed her soft lips against his, then asked, 'Even a little?'

He stood completely still, staring into her dark eyes. His chest burned as he breathed in her exhaled breath.

'Even when you didn't want to miss me?'

The dull throb of desire settled heavy in his groin, and he grabbed her shoulders and pushed her away. 'Don't do this, Daisy.'

She looked up at him. 'Matt Flegel asked me out.'

Shit 'Bug?'

'He never liked when you called him that.'

'Are you going to go out with him?'

'Do you care?'

He looked right into her eyes and answered as if he didn't want to punch Flea in the face. 'No. I don't care what you do.'

'Then I'll probably go out with him.' She turned on her heels and bid him goodnight over her shoulder as if she hadn't just tried to kiss him and get something going. He watched her disappear into the tent and he turned back to the fire.

She could do whatever she wanted, he told himself as he took a seat. So could he. He hadn't had sex since he'd had it with her on the back of the Lancer. Maybe that was his problem. Maybe he needed to get laid to get her out of his head.

He waited until the coals burned to ash before he entered the tent. When his eyes adjusted to the darkness, he discovered that Nathan had taken the sleeping bag on the far side, which left Daisy asleep in the middle. What she thought of sleeping so close to Jack, he didn't know. She seemed okay with it because she was out.

Jack took off his boots and jacket and crawled into his sleeping bag. He put his hands behind his head and stared up at the ceiling of the tent. He could almost hear her breathing. Almost hear a soft hush of breath pass her lips.

He turned his head and looked at her through the darkness. Her back was to him and her blond hair spilled across her pillow. He'd made love to her. He'd made a child with her, but he'd never spent the night with her. Never seen her sleep.

His last thoughts as he fell asleep were of her, wondering what she'd do if he hooked his arm around her waist and pulled her into his chest.

When he woke, the ceiling of the tent was awash in predawn light. He figured he'd gotten about five hours as he grabbed his jean jacket, shoved his feet in his boots, and headed out of the tent. Early morning shadows clung to the campground and the buttes surrounding the lake. He built a fire and put coffee on to percolate. The sun rose over the water as he poured his first cup. Nathan was the first to join him. His son's hair stuck straight up in back, and he wore a big blue sweat shirt, jeans and his sneakers. Nathan grabbed a bottle of juice and a bag of Chips Ahoy and the two of them walked to the shore.

'Today before we leave,' Jack said as he blew into his coffee, 'we'll go after some channel cats.'

'My dad and I went deep-sea fishing once.' Nathan ripped open the bag and held it toward Jack, offering him a cookie. 'Have you ever done that?'

'Thanks.' Jack took one chocolate-chip cookie and bit into it. 'I try to fish in the Gulf at least once a year. Next time I go, maybe you can come along.'

'Tight.' Nathan stuck the bag under one arm and polished off two cookies before he spoke again. 'My dad and I used to talk about stuff.'

Jack took a drink and looked out over the lake, at the morning sun lighting up the surface like glass. He wondered if Daisy had told him that she had a hot date with Flea. It wasn't his place to ask. 'What kind of stuff?'

'Stuff a guy can't talk to his mom about.'

'Like?' he asked and ate his cookie.

'Girls.'

Ah. 'Do you have something on your mind?'

Nathan nodded and took a drink of his juice.

'Maybe I can help you out. I've known a girl or two.'

He looked at his toes and his cheeks turned pink. 'Girls are complicated. Boys aren't that complicated.'

'That's true. Girls are contrary as hell. They tell you one thing and expect you to get the meaning to something else.'

He turned and looked up at Jack. 'You said you and dad used to look at porn. So, what I want to know is . . .' He blinked a few times then asked, 'Where do you touch girls? I saw a diagram in health class, but it was confusing. Boys aren't confusing. Everything we have is just hanging out there.'

Whoa. 'We're not talking about a girl's emotions are we?'

He shook his head. 'My friend stole his mom's book about sex. It sounds like you have to touch a girl everywhere at once.'

Nathan looked so serious. And he'd come to Jack. Not Daisy. 'Any girl in particular you're thinking about touching?'

'No. I'd just like to have it all figured out before my first time.'

'You want to be an expert right out of the chute?' Jack thought Nathan was a little young to be worrying about sex. Then he thought back to the NBBC and he realized Nathan wasn't too young at all.

'Well, yeah. It's going to be scary enough the first time without worrying about sucking at it.'

Jack rocked back on his heels and weighed his words. He really didn't want to screw this up. Warmth spread through him and tightened his chest like a fist around his heart. Suddenly, for the first time in his life, he felt like a dad. His son had come to him with questions about sex, just like countless other sons had gone to their fathers. Just like he had. 'The first thing you have to know is that any fool can have sex, but it takes a real man to make love. If you don't feel something for a girl, then you have no business unzipping your pants.'

'Yeah.'

'You have to wear a condom. Always. If you're not mature enough to protect yourself and the female, then you're not mature enough to have sex.' As he spoke, he wondered if Nathan got the irony of this conversation. He waited for him to point out that Jack hadn't always practiced what he was preaching, and he took a drink of his coffee as he figured out a good response. He'd obviously have to admit that he hadn't always been responsible, but that—

'I know about safe sex,' Nathan said, interrupting Jack's thoughts.

Jack swallowed. 'That's good.' He smiled at his son, vastly relieved that there would be no hard questions about his own sex life.

'What I want to know is . . .' Nathan stole a look back at the tent. 'Where is the clitoris exactly?'

Jack's smile fell and he opened his mouth. No words came out so he closed it.

Nathan had no problem forming his words, though. 'And what the heck is a G-spot?'

17

Driving wasn't as easy as Nathan thought it would be. On his second day of driver's education, he got to drive a Saturn. Not exactly his idea of a hot car, but the other class had to drive a station wagon. By the third week, he'd mastered the Saturn and figured he was ready to take his new dream car for a spin. Jack's Shelby Mustang. Jack didn't know it yet, but Nathan wanted to drive that car. *Bad.*

After the first week, he'd made a few friends with some of the other boys in his class. They didn't ride horses or listen to crap-ola music. Some of them did chew tobacco, though, which was cool with Nathan.

On the day of classes, his mom dropped him off in front of the high school. He usually walked to Jack's afterward because it was only a few blocks away. He'd been in Lovett for a month now, and he guessed it wasn't as bad as he thought it was the first few days he'd been here. He liked working in Jack's garage. He liked shooting the bull with the other mechanics, he thought as he walked to the back of the school.

Jack had shown him the business side of running Parrish American Classics, and it looked pretty cool. Maybe he could come here and work next summer too; and when he graduated from high school, he could work with Jack and Billy full-time.

That'd be tight, but his mom would have a fit. She wanted him to go to college like his dad. She talked about it as if he had no say in it at all. She was trying to run his life like he was a little kid.

Nathan picked up a rock from the blacktop and threw it at the basketball backboard like he had that day he'd first met Jack. The rock fell to the ground and he kicked it.

He didn't know what to call Jack anymore. Calling him Jack felt weird, but he couldn't call him dad. His dad was Steven Monroe, but Jack was starting to feel like his dad too. They got along pretty good now. Sometimes after work, they just hung out and talked about cars and stuff. He'd gone over to Billy's and met the rest of the family, too. Billy's little girls screamed and giggled a lot, and the middle one ran with her head down and you had to watch out for her.

Jack usually invited his mom to come along, and it was kind of like they were a family, but not. Sometimes Nathan caught Jack looking at his mom like he loved her. Then he'd blink or look away or say something and Nathan would think he was imagining things. If Jack was in love with his mom, Nathan really didn't know how he felt about that. Maybe it was okay since Jack was his dad. Sort of.

Jack had only made him mad one time. Nathan had gotten angry at his mom on the Fourth of July, and he'd yelled at her because she wanted to know where he was going and what he was doing. Jack had given him a really hard look and said, 'You don't talk to your mother like that. Now apologize.'

He would have apologized anyway. His mom bugged him sometimes, but he loved her. He hated to see how sad it made her when he yelled. It made him feel like his chest was caving in, but he never realized he was doing it until it was too late.

Nathan started across the field to the opening in the fence. It was Saturday and he didn't have work. Maybe he'd go take a nap for a while or play the XBOX that his mom had brought back with her when she'd gone to Seattle.

His footsteps slowed as he watched Brandy Jo move through the opening and walk toward him. She wore a red dress with tiny straps and big chunky flip-flops on her feet.

'Hi, Nathan. I haven't seen you in awhile. What are you up too?'

'Taking driver's ed.' He stood up a little straighter, then slouched to put his hands in his pockets. Brandy Jo was about the prettiest girl he'd ever seen. Even wearing those big shoes, the top of her head barely reached his chin. He got that caving-chest feeling, only this time it had nothing to do with his mom. 'What are you doing here on Saturday?'

'I forgot my sweater in the school.'

The sun shone in her dark hair, and when she licked her pink lips, his stomach twisted. 'Need help?' he asked and almost groaned out loud. *Of course she didn't need help.*

'No, but I'd like your company.'

He swallowed and tried not to smile. He nodded and said, 'Cool.'

'When are you going to get your driver's license?' she asked as they walked around the side of the school.

'I have to take the test pretty soon.' Her bare arm bumped him right beneath the sleeve of his T-shirt and his shoulder kind of tingled.

'I got my license last month,' she said.

'Do you have a car?'

She shook her head and her hair brushed the tops of her shoulders. 'Do you?'

'Jack is going to let me drive his.' He bumped his arm into hers to see what would happen, and the tingle traveled across his chest.

'Who's Jack?'

'He's . . . like my dad.'

She looked up at him through her big brown eyes. 'What do you mean? "Like your dad"? Is he your step-dad?'

'No. He's my real dad, but I just met him about a month ago.'

She stopped on her big flip-flops. 'You just met him?' she asked, in the drawl of hers that he was starting to think was real cute.

'Yeah. I've always known about him, but when my dad died . . . When my first dad . . . other dad . . .' He sighed. 'It's confusing.'

'My mom's been married three times,' Brandy Jo told him as they started toward the front again. 'My daddy died, but my baby brother's daddy lives in Fort Worth. I have another step-daddy right now, but it's not looking too good. Everybody's family is confusing for one reason or another.'

They walked side by side into the building, bumping arms and pretending it was an accident. Brandy Jo found her sweater in the art room and somehow by the time they walked back outside, Nathan held her hand in his. His throat kinda closed, and then she smiled up at him and he thought his heart stopped. It squeezed tight and he was afraid he'd pass out right there next to the stupid boulder with the words 'Lovett Stallions' chiseled in it. Right there beneath the hot Texas sun. Right in front of the prettiest girl he'd ever seen. He *really* didn't want to do that.

Nathan looked down at Brandy Jo as she talked about her family. He squeezed her hand, and she moved closer until their arms touched. His heart swelled like a balloon in his chest and it felt good and horrible and overwhelming. He'd never been in love before. Well, except with Nicole Kidman, but that didn't count. But on that day, beneath the endless blue sky over his head, Nathan Monroe fell in love for the first time in his life.

Daisy stuck her thumb in the end of the garden hose and sprayed down the hood of her mother's Cadillac with water. Then she plunged a soft sponge into a bucket of soapy water and washed dirt from the car. The hot afternoon sun beat down on her, and she could feel it toast her shoulders, chest and her back above the scoop of her red tank top.

She'd spent most of her day over at Lily's, cleaning house and doing laundry while Lily sat on the couch with her cast resting on pillows. Lily's divorce was final now, and her lawyer had come through for her! He'd showed the judge bank statements prior to Ronnie draining the account, and the judge had ordered Ronnie to pay Lily ten thousand dollars, monthly child support, and he had to pay Pippen's medical insurance, too.

Her mother was still over at Lily's fetching and toting. Daisy knew that her sister was having a hard time doing simple tasks since she'd come home from the hospital. She didn't mind helping out, but Lily's messed up life had put Daisy in a bad mood.

Actually, it was more than just a bad mood. She felt unsettled, but Lily had very little part in that. Lately, Daisy's mood had more to do with the sum total of her life rather than just one piece. She was anxious to get on with her life, yet scared and uncertain. Her house in Washington hadn't sold yet, but it had only been on the market for about a month. She was moving forward with her plans to open a photography studio, yet she felt a stitch of anxiety when she thought of leaving Texas. It seemed to her that one moment she was crystal clear about what she wanted, and in the next she was confused as hell.

She'd gone out twice with Matt and she'd had a good time. But when he'd kissed her, she'd known there wouldn't be a third time. She was in love with someone else, and it wasn't fair to Matt.

Daisy leaned as far as possible over the Caddy's hood and washed a spot she'd missed. She glanced up as one of the biggest reasons for her confusion pulled his Mustang beside the curb in front of her mother's house.

Jack got out of his car and walked across the yard toward her. A lock of dark hair hung over his forehead, and for once he wasn't wearing a hat. Sunlight refracted little blue pinwheels off the lenses of his sunglasses. His green shirt buttoned up the front and he wore faded Levi's. It was Saturday and he hadn't shaved. Dark stubble shadowed his face and drew attention to the sensual lines of his mouth. Every time she saw him, her heart squeezed a little while her head told her to run screaming in the opposite direction.

'Hey there,' she said as she straightened and rinsed soap from the hood. 'What are you up to, besides no good?'

'I'm looking for Nathan. I thought he might stop by my house after his driver's ed class, but he didn't.'

'He's not here yet,' she said and could feel his gaze on her from behind his glasses. 'I'm sure he'll be here soon if you want to wait.'

'I'll wait a few,' he said as he glanced down the street. He'd been doing that a lot since they'd returned from the lake about a month ago. Undressing her with his eyes then turning away. Of course it was entirely possible that he wasn't even looking at her with any more interest than a bug. It was very possible that she was imagining it all. Kind of like wishful thinking. Which made her not only sad and pathetic and extremely delusional, but as crazy as the rest of her family. Scary thought.

She picked up the bucket and hose and moved to the opposite side of the car from Jack.

'Tomorrow night, Billy and some of the guys are getting together to play football over at Horizon View Park.' He rested his weight on one foot and returned his gaze to her. 'I talked to Nathan about it the other day, and he was going to get back to me about whether he could make it.'

'We don't have anything planned, so I don't have a problem with him going.' Daisy set the bucket on the ground and raised the hose to the roof of the car. 'Tackle or flag?'

'Flag football is for sissy men,' he scoffed as he moved to stand directly across from her. 'And girls.'

She decided to let that one pass. 'I don't want Nathan to play without a helmet and pads.'

'We'll make sure he has all the right equipment.' He

tilted his head to the side as if he where sizing her up too. 'Why don't you come on down in one of your old cheerleader outfits? You can do cartwheels and backflips like you used to.' The corners of his mouth slid upward into a purely carnal smile. 'Or those toe-touch jumps. You used to give a beauty of a crotch-shot.'

Daisy's thumb found the end of the hose again and water sprayed across the roof of the car, hit Jack's chest and shoulders, and splattered his sunglasses.

'Oops,' she said and removed her thumb.

His brows lowered and disappeared behind the lenses. 'You did that on purpose.'

She gasped. Scandalized. 'No. I didn't.'

'Yes,' he said very slowly, 'you did.'

'Wrooong.' She shook her head, stuck her thumb in the end of the hose again and hit him dead center in his chest between his shoulders. Water sprayed up to his chin and down to the front of his shirt. 'Now that,' she said when she pulled her thumb out, 'was on purpose.'

'Do you have any idea,' he spoke as he removed his sunglasses and stuffed them in the pocket of his soggy shirt, 'what I'm going to do to you?'

'Nothing.'

His green gaze promised retribution as he walked around the hood of the car. 'Wrooong,' he mimicked her.

She took a step back. 'Stay where you are.'

'Scared?'

'No.' She took another step back.

'You should be, baby girl.'

'What are you going to do?'

'Quit movin' and you'll find out.'

She stood her ground, raised the hose and shot him in

the head with a stream of water. He ducked, and before she could even think to run he was on her, pinning her against the back passenger door and wresting the hose from her hands.

'Jack, no!' She started to laugh. 'I'll never do it again. I swear.'

He looked down into her face and water ran from a lock of hair hanging above his forehead and dripped on his cheek. His long eyelashes were wet and tangled on the ends. 'I know you won't,' he said as he pulled out the front of her tank top and shoved the hose inside.

'That's cold – *auggg*!' She grabbed his hand and attempted to wrestle the hose from her shirt.

'Laugh it up, funny girl.' He pinned her with his body and was getting just as wet as she was.

'Stop!' Water shot between her cleavage and ran down her stomach. Her nipples puckered from the cold. 'That's freezing.'

With his face just above hers he said, 'Tell me how sorry you are.'

She was laughing so hard she could barely talk. 'Sooooo sorry,' she managed as she tried to squirm her way out from beneath him. His hips held her exactly where he wanted her.

'That's not good enough.' He pulled the hose from her shirt and dropped it on the ground. 'Show me,' he said, his voice rough.

Daisy's laughter died on her lips and she looked into his face. Really looked at the desire shining through his green eyes. He stood with his feet on the outsides of hers. His thighs, hips and lower abdomen pressed into her, and she was suddenly aware that at least eight inches of him was very happy to see her. A ribbon of warm sensation uncurled in her stomach. Her heart told her to stay while her head screamed at her to run. 'How?'

'You know how.' He lowered his gaze to her mouth. 'And make it good.'

She ran her cold hands up his wet chest and shoulders and through the side of his hair. She lifted her face and slid one hand to the back of his head. She touched her mouth to his and she felt her heart expand. It filled her chest and made breathing difficult and there was no denying it for exactly what it was. She'd felt it before. Only this time it was stronger. Less confused. Like turning the camera's focus ring until it was very clear.

She was in love with Jack Parrish. Again. Her heart had won this round.

The thinnest slice of sunlight separated their mouths. They both held their breaths; their gazes locked. Waiting for the other to make the first move.

Daisy gave him a sweet little peck. 'Is that good?'

His lips brushed across hers as he shook his head. 'Try again.'

'How about this?' Her lips parted and she touched the seam of his mouth with the tip of her tongue.

He sucked in a breath and his voice was rough when he asked, 'Is that the best you can do?'

She raised a hand to the side of his face and brushed her fingers against the stubble of his jaw. 'No, but I don't think you can handle the best I can do.'

'Try me.'

Daisy's eyes drifted shut and she melted into him just a little. The tips of her breasts brushed the front of his shirt and her nipples puckered from more than the cold.

Warmth spread across her flesh and settled between her legs. She pressed her open mouth to his and kissed him. At first she gave him soft teasing kisses that had Jack chasing her tongue for more. A frustrated groan rose from his chest, and he tilted his head to one side and turned up the heat. He forced her mouth open wider and took over.

With their lips locked together, he wrapped his arms around her and took a step back. He grabbed her behind in his big hands and pulled her onto the tips of her toes.

He drew back and looked into her face. 'You feel good.' Very slowly he let her body slide down his, then he pulled her back up. 'No one has ever felt as good as you.' His mouth covered hers again. Cold water from the hose ran across her toes as the kiss turned hot.

Behind her, Daisy heard someone clear his throat, a split second before Nathan's voice penetrated her lust-filled haze. 'Ah, Mom?'

Jack raised his face, and she dropped onto her heels and spun around. 'Nathan!' It took a few dazed moments for her to realize that he wasn't alone. A teenaged girl stood next to him. Nathan looked from her face to Jack's and his cheeks turned deep red,

'How long have you been standing there?' Jack asked, his voice calm and collected for a man who'd just had his hands on Daisy's behind, sliding her up and down his body.

'We saw you from down the street.' Nathan returned his gaze to Daisy. He didn't say anything more and she couldn't tell what he was thinking.

Daisy forced a smile on her face and said, 'Are you going to introduce your friend?'

'This is Brandy Jo.' He pointed toward Daisy. 'That's my mom and Jack.'

'It's a pleasure to meet y'all.'

Daisy moved to take a step forward but Jack's hand on the waistband of her shorts kept her in front of him. She looked up over her shoulder at him, he raised a brow, and the light dawned. Jack was using her for cover. She felt heat creep up her neck to her cheek. Just like Nathan. The only person who didn't seem embarrassed was Jack.

She turned her attention to Nathan and Brandy Jo. 'Do you live close by?' she asked, to cover the awkward silence.

'Over on Taft.' Brandy Jo glanced up at Nathan. 'The first day Nathan and I met, I told him that we're kind of related. My aunt Jessica is married to Ronnie Darlington's cousin Bull.'

Well, at least she wasn't a blood relative to Ronnie. 'Lily and Ronnie's divorce was final a few weeks ago.'

'Oh. I didn't know that.' She smiled and said just above a whisper, 'Ronnie's a dog and no one could figure out what Lily ever saw in him.'

Brandy Jo was obviously a smart girl.

'I came by to talk to you about that football game tomorrow night,' Jack said.

'And you couldn't find anything to do until I got here, so you decided to make out with my mom in the front yard?'

Daisy's mouth fell open.

Jack laughed. 'It seemed like a good way to pass the time.'

Daisy turned around and looked at him.

'*What?*' he said through an evil grin. 'You thought so too.'

18

Daisy had lived in the Northwest for fifteen years, but she'd never forgotten how seriously Texans took their football. Be it the Texas Stadium in Dallas, a high school field in Houston, or a small park in Lovett, football was considered a second religion and was worshipped accordingly.

Amen.

What Daisy hadn't known was that this particular game was an annual event. A yearly meeting where grown men gathered to sweat, ram into each other, and compare battle wounds. There were no yardline markers. No referees. No goalposts. Just two sidelines and end zones marked off with DayGlo orange spray paint, and someone with a stopwatch. Jack's team wore red practice jerseys, the other team wore blue.

Each team brought grit and spit and a desire to tear each other's heads off all in the name of fun. This was football in its rawest, purest form, and Nathan Monroe was going to be the only player who wore pads and a helmet. A fact that angered him to no end.

Daisy tried to talk him out of his anger by pointing out that he was fifteen and he was playing against men who were all a lot older and bigger. He didn't seem to care that he'd get hurt, only that he'd looked like a wuss.

'Nathan, I paid over five thousand dollars for your straight teeth,' she'd told him. 'You're not going to get them knocked out.'

It wasn't until some time later, when Brandy Jo showed up at the park and told him she liked the way he looked in pads and helmet, that his mood seemed to brighten a bit.

She and Nathan caught a ride with Jack to the park, and as the three of them moved closer to the playing field, Jack took a closer look at her dress. 'That doesn't look like your cheerleader outfit,' he said when Nathan walked over to Billy to get his red-mesh jersey.

Daisy had ignored Jack's suggestion that she wear her cheerleader skirt and sweater, and had chosen instead a peach apron dress that crisscrossed down the back. She looked down at the hem of the dress just above her knees. 'Too long?'

'And it doesn't have a back.'

'I guess I won't be doing any of those toe-touch jumps that you were apparently so fond of in high school.'

His gaze scanned the members of his team assembled in the center of the field. 'In the dress you got on, you'd probably hurt your pom-poms. And that would be a true shame.'

'You don't need to worry about my pom-poms.' She stopped at the red sideline. 'They're fine.'

'They certainly are,' he said over his shoulder as he continued toward his team.

Daisy stared after him and smiled. He wasn't wearing anything beneath his mesh jersey, and his tan skin showed through the tiny holes. Her gaze slid down his back to his tight, butt-hugging football pants. Jack Parrish was mighty fine himself. His pants encased his legs to just below his knees, and he wore black football socks and cleats. He moved as if he hadn't a care in the world. As if he wasn't about to spend the next hour or so getting run over and the stuffing knocked out of him.

Tucker Gooch called her name and waved to her from the middle of the blue team. She waved back to him and noticed a lot of faces she'd gone to school with. Cal Turner and Marvin Ferrell. Lester Crandall and Leon Kribs. Eddy Dean Jones and several of the Calhoun boys, Jimmy and Buddy included. She wondered if Buddy knew that after he'd had sex with Lily, she'd gone crazy and driven her car into Ronnie's front room.

Probably not.

She recognized a lot of other faces too. The people she'd grown up with in Lovett. Penny Kribs and little Shay Calhoun. Marvin's wife, Mary Alice, and Gina Brown.

Jealousy knotted Daisy's stomach. She wondered if Gina and Jack had been together in the past month. They probably had. Jealousy moved up from her stomach to twist her heart. She knew the feeling and was familiar with it. She'd felt it fifteen years ago when just the thought of Jack with someone else used to torment her, sending her emotions bubbling up over the top.

But Jack wasn't hers and she wasn't a kid anymore. She knew what to do with jealousy now. She didn't fight it or pretend it didn't exist. She felt every prickly thorn of it. Then she let it go as best she could.

Her head won this round over her heart, and she sat in a folding chair next to Rhonda and the girls on the sidelines. All three little girls wore red cheerleader outfits and jumped about like their legs were made of springs.

'Last year Billy tore a groin muscle,' Rhonda told her as she pulled off Tanya's socks so the baby could wiggle her toes. 'He whined about it for three weeks.'

'Marvin broke his thumb last year,' Mary Alice added as she leaned forward in her chair.

Groins and thumbs weren't covered by padding and helmets. Daisy stood, ready to drag Nathan away from the team huddle, then she sat back down. He would never forgive her if she did that. So she crossed her fingers instead.

The game kicked off at seven-thirty. It was ninety degrees in the shade and sweat poured off the players. Jack was the quarterback for the red team, and Daisy had forgotten how much she liked to watch him play. Every time he drew his arm back to drill that ball down the field, his jersey pulled up and Daisy was treated to a view of his fiat stomach and navel just above the waistband of his pants. When he got knocked flat, she got a glimpse of his chest.

Horizon View Park was soon filled with the shouts of men calling out to each other, cleats pounding down the field and muscle hitting muscle. Of bodies hitting the ground with an audible thud followed by a whoosh, and the cheers and jeers of spectators on the sides.

In the first quarter, Jack threw a short pass to Nathan, who caught it and ran with it for about ten yards before he got tackled. Daisy held her breath until her son got back up and brushed a chunk of grass from his helmet. In the second quarter, Jimmy Calhoun made a touchdown for the red team. Unfortunately he was tackled in the end zone and went down hard. When he was finally able to get back up, he limped to the car and Shay took him to the hospital. Everyone predicted a knee injury. Buddy hoped it wasn't something more permanent.

'Shay's got her heart set on a big family,' he said as he watched his brother being whisked away. 'Hope he didn't rupture any *thang* vital.'

During half-time, Daisy helped Rhonda and Gina pass bottles of water out to both teams. Each man looked somewhat worse for the wear, and they had half the game left. On the blue team, Leon Kribs's left eye was swelling, and Marvin Ferrell had a busted lip. While Tucker Gooch wrapped his ankle, he asked for her phone number.

She didn't give it to him.

She excused herself and talked to Nathan to make sure he was all right. Billy grabbed him around the neck and rubbed his knuckles in Nathan's hair. Instead of getting angry like Daisy half expected, Nathan laughed and socked Billy in the gut.

'Billy really wants a little boy,' Rhonda told her. 'But he's going to have to settle for playing with Nathan.'

Billy only had about three weeks before she and Nathan were returning to Seattle. Daisy wondered how Nathan felt about leaving. If he was still excited to get back home.

Was she? Her little tug of anxiety turned into a hard yank at the thought, and she was very much afraid the answer was no. Just yesterday she and Nathan had been driving through the small downtown area of Lovett and she'd noticed a vacant space right next to Donna's Gifts on

Fifth. Before she even realized what she was doing, she'd visualized herself there. A sign hanging beneath the striped awning, DAISY MONROE PHOTOGRAPHY painted on it. Or maybe she'd name her business Buttercup or . . .

Her heart and head were at war, and she'd better figure things out quick before she signed a lease in Seattle.

She handed water to Eddy Dean who had bloody knuckles and to Cal Turner who was already limping. But the limp didn't keep Cal from asking her to meet him at Slim's later that night. She glanced at Jack, standing a few feet away, deep in conversation with Gina. He stood with his hands on his hips, a white towel hanging off one shoulder. Gina gestured to the left, but Jack's gaze was on Daisy as she approached him.

'I'll talk to you later,' Gina said and moved to the sidelines.

'Okay, thanks.' Jack grabbed two bottles of water and twisted the cap off one. He had a bloody raspberry on his left elbow and his white pants were covered in green. He drank half of one bottle and poured the rest over his head.

'Are you going to go out tonight with Cal?' he asked as he wiped his face with the towel.

She'd wondered if he'd heard Cal. 'Would that bother you?'

He looked at her over the top of the white cotton, then hung the towel around his neck. 'Would it matter to you if it does?'

She turned her attention to the sidelines and Gina. 'Yes.'

Jack placed his fingers on her cheek and brought her gaze back to his. 'Yes, it would bother me. Don't go out with Cal or Flea or anyone else.'

'I'm not going out with Cal or anyone else.' She looked down at her feet then raised her gaze back up the lacing of his football pants, his red jersey, then into his green eyes. 'Are you still going out with Gina?'

He moved to stand so close they almost touched, and he tucked her hair behind one ear. 'I haven't been with anyone,' he said just above a whisper. 'Not since I put you on the Custom Lancer.'

She wondered if he was talking about the car. Knowing Jack, she doubted it. 'Really?'

'Yeah.' His fingertips slipped to the side of her neck. 'How about you?'

She smiled because she couldn't help it. 'Of course not.'

He smiled too. 'That's good.' He pressed a quick kiss to her mouth then walked around her toward the rest of his team. As kisses went, it shouldn't have counted. It was hardly a kiss at all, but it had been just wet enough to leave the taste of him on her lips. Just warm enough to slide inside and light a fire next to her heart.

During the third quarter, the blue team scored a touchdown, but Daisy wasn't paying close attention to the game. She had bigger worries on her mind. She was in love with Jack. She could no longer ignore it. She'd come to Lovett to tell Jack about Nathan. She hadn't meant to fall in love with him again, but it had happened, and now she had to decide what she was going to do about it. Fifteen years ago, she'd run away from the pain of Jack not loving her in return. She wasn't going to run this time. When and if she left, she would know how Jack felt about her.

Three minutes into the fourth quarter, Jack got creamed by Marvin Ferrell, who had to outweigh Jack by a good hundred pounds. He went down with a *umph,* and

Daisy's heart dropped a few inches. He lay on his back for several long moments until Marvin helped him to his feet. Jack moved his head from side to side as if getting out the kinks, then he slowly walked back to the huddle. His next pass was a fifty-foot bomb to Nathan, who ran it all the way for a touchdown. Nathan tore off his helmet and spiked it into the ground. He jumped around, giving high-fives, and smashing knuckles with his teammates. Jack hooked his arm around Nathan's shoulders. Father and son, their heads close as they talked and walked to the sidelines, both of them smiling as if they'd just won the million-dollar lotto.

After the game, Nathan was still so excited he forgot himself and gave Daisy a hug that picked her up off her feet.

'Did you see that touchdown?' he asked and released her.

'Of course. It was a beauty.'

Nathan pulled the shoulder pads over his head as Brandy Jo and a group of teenagers approached. They all seemed quite impressed that a fifteen-year-old had been invited to play football with the men.

'I got to play because Jack and Billy play on the red team,' he said.

A boy wearing a Weezer T-shirt asked, 'Who're Jack and Billy?'

'Billy's my uncle.' Nathan paused and looked over the top of Daisy's head. 'And Jack's my dad.'

She felt Jack behind her a split second before he squeezed her shoulders. She looked up into his unfathomable eyes and his pleased smile, she then turned her attention back to Nathan. The two men in her life stared at each other and seemed to reach an unspoken understanding. No weeping or crying or falling on each other's necks. Just an acknowledgment like the slapping of hands and smashing of knuckles.

Instead of coming home and celebrating his touchdown with her and Jack, Nathan asked if he could go hang out with his new friends. By the way her son looked at Brandy Jo, Daisy knew she'd just been usurped in her son's life by a fifteen-year-old girl with long brown hair and a Texas twang. She felt an unexpected pang of jealousy. Nathan was growing up much too quickly, and she missed the little boy who used to hold her hand and look up at her as if she were the most important thing in his world.

'Are you ready to go now?' Jack lowered his face to the top of her head. 'I want to get you out of here before Cal comes over and hits on you again.'

He wasn't really fooling her. She could hear the pain in his voice. 'What hurts?'

'My shoulder,' he answered as they moved toward the parking lot, 'like a son of a bitch.'

'I don't understand why you guys don't wear pads.' She held up a hand. 'Don't say it. I know. Pads are for sissies.'

Jack opened the passenger-side door for her. She moved to get inside but looked back across the field one last time at Nathan. 'He's growing up too fast,' she said as she watched him walk in the other direction with Brandy Jo on his arm. 'He was always so rowdy and independent. I couldn't take him anywhere cause he'd just run off. So I got one of those leashes you put on little kids so you don't lose 'em. I always felt so much better knowing he was on the other end of the leash. I'd give a hard tug, and he'd come rolling out from wherever he was hiding from me.'

She grasped the top of the car door that separated her body from Jack's. 'I wish I could just give him a tug now and make sure he stays out of trouble.'

Jack put his hands on the outside of hers. 'He's a good boy, Daisy. He'll be fine.'

She looked up into his eyes and he leaned forward and gently pressed his mouth to hers, easing into a kiss so slow and sweet, it just seemed to melt her heart. He smelled of sweat and grass and Jack. His thumbs brushed over the backs of her hands as the tip of his slick tongue touched hers. Jack took his time, and the kiss turned more deeply intimate. It touched places deep in her soul that recognized him. This was more than a mating of mouths. More than the hot rush of sex that demanded to be satisfied.

When he pulled back, he looked at her the way he used to all those years ago. His guard down. His wants and needs and desires unmistakably clear in his green eyes.

'Come home with me,' he said as his hands moved to cover hers in his warm palms.

She swallowed and the corners of her mouth turned up. She didn't have to ask what he had planned. 'I thought your shoulder hurt?'

'Not that bad.'

'I could massage it for you.'

He shook his head. 'You need to save your energy to massage other things.'

19

Daisy ran her hands across Jack's smooth shoulders and pushed her fingers into his knotted muscles. She massaged his back and ran her thumbs up and down the indent of his spine. A bead of water dropped from his wet hair, slid down his back and was absorbed in the thick blue towel hung low on his hips.

The drive from the park to Jack's had taken less than ten minutes. Usually it took fifteen, but Jack had run several stop signs and blown through a traffic light.

At present, he sat on a ladder-back kitchen chair next to the dining room table. His legs straddled the seat while his arms rested across the top rung. He'd insisted on taking a quick shower to get rid of the grime before he'd let her touch him, and when he'd come out wearing nothing but a towel, she'd about jumped him then and there.

'How's this feel?' she asked as her palms slid down his hard muscles, then up again.

'Like something I could get used to.' The heat from his

skin warmed her hands, and she felt the contours and textures as she learned the definition of him all over again.

'Daisy?'

She looked down at the back of his head. The dining room light shone through his dark hair, picking out strands the color of coffee. 'Hmm?'

'When we were at Lake Meredith, you said you've missed me.' He reached up and grasped her by the wrist. 'Is that true?' He looked over his shoulder at her. His intense gaze told her the answer was very important to him.

'Yes, Jack. It's true.'

He pulled her arm down around his chest and said, next to her right cheek, 'I missed you too, Daisy Lee. All these years I've missed you more than I knew.' He placed his free hand on the left side of her face. 'More than I ever wanted you to know.'

Her chest got tight and achy, and she lowered her mouth and said against his lips. 'I love you, Jack.'

He closed his eyes and let out his breath. He was quiet for several long moments then he said, 'I have always loved you. Even when I didn't want to.'

'Turn around,' she whispered.

His eyes opened. 'What?'

'Stand up.'

As soon as he stood and turned toward her, she put her hand on his shoulders and pushed him back down again. 'I don't know what happens next for us,' she said as she pulled up her dress and sat in his lap facing him. He spread his thighs and her bottom hit the seat of the chair. Her bare feet hung over the sides. 'Whatever it is, I will always love you. I can't help it.'

His hands slid up and down her thighs as his green eyes looked at her through his lashes. 'I'll show you what happens next.' His palms moved to her waist and his fingers searched the tie on the side of her dress.

She settled more firmly between his legs and asked, 'Is that a tent pole or are you happy to see me?'

A blatantly sexual smile pushed the corners of his mouth upward. 'Both. Wanna see?'

'Oh yeah.' She moved her hands from his shoulders and down his chest. Her palms covered his nipples and she leaned forward and kissed the side of his throat. The thick towel and the thin layer of her panties separated them.

Jack tugged and the top of her dress loosened. 'Raise your arms,' he told Daisy. She did as he asked, and he slid the dress above her waist and pulled it over her head. Her hair fell free about her bare shoulders, and Jack looked into her brown eyes, at the passion staring back at him. He tossed the dress on the floor, then covered her naked breasts with his hands. Her puckered nipples poked the centers of his palms and he brushed them with his thumbs. Her lids lowered a fraction and she licked her lips. He knew her. He knew the weight of her against him and the beat of her heart in his palms. He knew the sigh of pleasure on her lips and the scent of her skin.

This was Daisy. His Daisy.

'Are you sure your shoulder doesn't hurt?'

Shoulder? He didn't give a shit about his shoulder. The only pain he felt was in his groin. 'Nothing hurts as bad as wanting you.' Every fantasy he'd ever had had begun and ended with Daisy Lee. Now here she was. Except for a strap of silk panties, naked in his lap. If he had his way, she would never leave.

Her soft hand slid down his belly and she pulled at the towel around his waist. She unwrapped him like a Christmas present, then reached inside and closed her fist around his erection. He was so hard he throbbed. He sucked in his breath. He looked at Daisy, past the rose-colored tips of her breasts, down her tan abdomen and belly button to her tiny white panties. Within her small hand, she held his thick shaft. She brushed her thumb over the head. Lust pulled his gut into a hard knot and he had a difficult time drawing air into his lungs. He wrapped his hand over hers and moved it up and down, sliding within the soft velvet of her palm. She leaned forward and kissed his throat. Her warm moist tongue leaving a trail of fire.

He raised her face to his, and his hungry mouth slanted across her lips. He gave her hot, feeding kisses; there was nothing tender or soft in what he gave this time. The moment his mouth touched hers, it was greedy, a maddening chase and follow. A slick advance and retreat of hot tongues and mouths. She arched into him, crushing her hard nipples into his chest and shoving her crotch against his erection.

He wanted this. He wanted it every damn day of his life. He wanted the drive of her tongue in his mouth, the weight of her in his arms, the catch in his chest when he looked into her eyes or buried his nose in her neck.

He wanted her. All of her. Forever. He loved her. He'd always loved her.

Jack stood and the towel fell to the floor. He set Daisy on the kitchen table in front of him and looked down into her dazed eyes.

'Lie down, buttercup.' She rested back on her elbows and watched as he kissed her breasts and sucked her puckered nipple into his mouth. He worked her over until her breath was choppy, then he worked his way south. He sucked a patch of skin next to her belly button and reached for the chair behind him. He pulled off her panties then sat between her thighs.

'Jack,' she said, her voice a dry whisper. 'What are you doing?'

He put her bare feet on his shoulders and kissed each ankle – 'I'm going down.' He bit the inside of her thigh as he brushed his thumb across her slick clitoris and pushed a finger deep inside where she was very hot and very wet. He parted her slick flesh and placed a hand beneath her bottom. He raised her as he brought his mouth down on her.

She tasted like Daisy. Good. Like sex and desire and everything he'd ever wanted.

She moaned his name as her head fell back. He kissed her between her legs. In the same spot he'd kissed her fifteen years ago – only he was better at it now. Better at knowing how to use his tongue and how hard to draw her into his mouth. He teased and sucked until she used her feet to push him back.

She rose from the table and stood in front of him, a little unsteady on her feet as she looked down at him. 'I want you, Jack.'

He picked up the towel from the floor and wiped his mouth. 'I need to get a condom.'

She stared at him as if she didn't know what he was talking about. Then she said, her voice heavy with passion, 'How long has it been since you've had sex without a condom?'

So long he couldn't remember. 'Probably the last time I was with you fifteen years ago.'

She smiled as she grabbed the towel from him and tossed it aside. She grasped his shoulders, then she put her feet on the low rung at the bottom of the chair and stood. He wrapped his arms around her and kissed her stomach. 'I had my period last week,' she said as she lowered herself over his lap. 'I won't get pregnant this time.'

He might have protested. He might have questioned her more, but the head of his penis touched her slick crotch, and he slid inside her hot wet body. There was no thought of protesting anything after that.

A groan tore into Jack's chest. Her hot flesh surrounded him and a shudder worked its way up his spine. Her lips were parted. Her breathing shallow, and her cheeks were flushed pink. The hunger in her brown eyes was focused on him as if he were the only man who could give her exactly what she needed.

She squeezed her muscles around him and he felt every ripple of her tight passage. He had to fight to keep from coming right then and there. Every cell in his body was focused on her. On the way she felt inside. On the warmth of her contracting muscles. On the sharp pain and dull ache twisting his groin.

'Goddamn,' he swore and he moved his hands to her hips. 'You feel so good.' He lifted her and brought her back down. It was like white-hot liquid enveloped him, and he didn't think he'd felt anything as good as the inside of Daisy.

She raised her hands to the sides of his head and brought his mouth to hers. 'I love you, Jack,' she said as they moved together, building a slow and steady rhythm that turned into a fever. He grabbed her behind and brought her down hard, again and again. Driving up as she pushed down, and everything got a whole lot hotter and wilder. Their breathing became ragged with the punctuating thrust of his hips. She grasped his bare shoulders and clung to him as the walls of her body pulsed around him. It went on and on faster, harder, pumping into her again and again until the air whooshed from his lungs.

Daisy moaned and squeezed him tight, pulsing and constricting around him. The strong contractions of her orgasm wrung a release from him that he felt up into his chest. He came deep inside where she was hot and slick, and even as he pumped into her one last time, he knew he wanted more.

He wanted it forever.

Daisy didn't burst into tears this time. She almost did the next time, though. Jack took her hand and led her to his bed where he made love to her again. He was so sweet and loving and drew out the torture until she'd had a multiple orgasm. The first of her life, and that had her feeling kind of weepy.

She lay on her stomach on blue sheets. The rest of the bedding was in a tangled heap by her feet. Jack lay half on top of her; his arm around her waist, one leg between hers. His groin pressed into her behind and hip. A lamp flooded the bed with warm yellow light, and the only sound in the room was of heavy, spent breathing. Their skin was glued together and a warm fluttery afterglow settled on her flesh. She hadn't felt this happy and content in a very long time. Jack loved her. She loved him. Things were going to work out for them this time.

She thought Jack had fallen asleep until he moaned. 'My God, it just keeps getting better. I didn't think anything could top the chair.'

Daisy smiled.

'Damn, did you just come twice?'

'Yes. Thank you.'

'You're welcome.'

His hand stirred at her waist, as if he tried to lift it but didn't have the energy. Carefully, she turned onto her back and looked at him. His hair was stuck to his forehead and his eyes were closed.

'What time is it?' she asked.

His lids fluttered open and he lifted his arm from across her stomach. He looked at his watch and said, 'Early.'

She grabbed his wrist and looked at the digital face. 'I have to get going before Nathan gets home.'

Jack rolled on his side and spread his fingers wide on her stomach just below her breasts. 'Don't leave,' he murmured as he kissed her shoulder.

'I have to.' She sat up and pushed the hair from her face. 'But I'll come back for breakfast.'

'Don't leave Lovett.' He lay on his side and raised onto his elbow. 'You and Nathan should move here.'

She'd been thinking along those lines too. She just hadn't known he had also. 'When did you decide this?' she asked and looked down into his green eyes.

'Probably when we were fishing, but I got serious about it yesterday when we were swapping spit in your momma's front yard and I didn't care who was watching.' He sat up and took her hand in his. 'I wanted people to watch. I wanted people to see us together. I wanted people to see us kissing today. I want everyone to know that you're mine.' He kissed her fingertips. 'I want a life with you and our son.'

It was exactly what she wanted too. Hearing him say it made it less scary.

'I love you, Daisy Lee. I've loved you all of my life.'

She looked into the pain and passion in his gaze. 'I love you too, Jack.' *But*, a little voice in her head wondered, *was it enough this time?* It hadn't been last time.

She excused herself to go to the bathroom, and when she returned, Jack had pulled on a pair of jeans. While she'd been in the bathroom, he retrieved her dress and panties and they lay on his rumpled bed. She stepped into her panties and he helped her with her dress.

'So, what are you going to feed me for breakfast?' he asked as he adjusted a strap on her back.

'I'll think of something good.'

'Something with whipped cream?'

She tied the strap at her side. 'And a cherry.'

He placed his arms around her and pulled her back against his chest. 'I love cherries,' he said against the side of her neck.

His bare chest warmed her skin and she had to fight the urge not to turn and kiss his neck. If she did that, she wouldn't make it home before Nathan. 'Jack, I want this to work between us this time.'

He squeezed her tight. 'It will.'

He sounded so confident she almost believed him. 'Let's talk to Nathan about it together.'

'Whatever you want.'

'I don't know how he'll feel about moving to Lovett, and I don't want him to think we're moving too fast.' She stepped out of his embrace and smoothed her hands over the wrinkles on her dress. 'It hasn't been a year since Steven's death, and I don't want him to be uncomfortable with you and me together.' She looked about the floor to see if he'd remembered her shoes. 'I don't care what other people think, but I don't want Nathan to think we're together just to replace his dad.' Her shoes must still be in the kitchen, and she returned her attention to Jack.

The loving man who'd just held her and assured her everything would work out this time turned to stone right before her eyes. His shoulders straightened. His jaws clenched and his gaze hardened.

'What's wrong?'

He walked across the room, passed the yellow light that spilled into the gray shadows. 'How long do we have to call Steven "Nathan's dad"?'

Daisy watched his bare back and said, 'I thought you might be getting over that.'

'I thought so too.' He yanked open a dresser drawer and pulled out a T-shirt. 'But I don't think I'll ever get over what that bastard took from me.'

She closed her eyes for several painful heartbeats. 'Don't talk about Steven like that.'

He laughed without humor. 'That's rich.' He shoved his arms through the short sleeves. 'You defending Steven Monroe to me.'

'I'm not defending Steven.'

He pulled the shirt over his head and down his stomach. 'Then what are you doing?'

'I loved Steven for most of my life. He was not only my husband; he was my best friend. We laughed and cried together. I could talk to him about anything.'

'Could you talk to him about how you felt about me?'

She'd almost had it this time. Almost, but it was slipping through her fingers like sand.

'Deep down in the pit of your stomach where it gets tight at just the thought of being with me.' He stalked back across the room and stopped just inches from her. 'Did you tell him that?'

'No, but he knew.' She looked up into his face, at the passion and bitterness in his green eyes. At the same passion and bitterness she'd seen the first night she'd seen him. 'Being with Steven wasn't *at all* like being with you. It was different. It was . . .'

'What?'

'Calm. It wasn't scary. It didn't hurt. I could breathe around him. I didn't feel like if I didn't touch him, I would die. Like a part of something inside of me belonged to someone else.'

'Isn't that the way it's supposed to feel? Isn't it supposed to feel like I want to smash you against my chest so hard I can still feel you after you leave?' He grabbed her shoulders and slid his hands to the sides of her face. 'Breathe the same breath. Feel the same heartbeat as you melt inside of me?'

Tears stung her eyes and she didn't even try to stop them. Her heart was breaking and her dreams had just slipped through her fingers. Again. 'It's not enough. It wasn't enough last time. And it isn't enough this time either.'

'What does it take, then? I love you. I've never loved any woman the way I love you.'

She believed him. 'Forgiveness,' she said as the first tears spilled from her eyes. 'You have to forgive me, Jack. You have to forgive me and you have to forgive Steven, too.'

He dropped his hands from her and took a step back. 'That's asking a lot, Daisy.'

'Too much?'

'Where Steven is concerned, yes.'

'And me?'

He looked at her and his silence was her answer.

'How can we be together if you can't forgive me of the past?'

'We won't think about it.' He grabbed his boots and shoved his feet inside.

'For how long? For how long won't we think about it before it comes up again? Tomorrow? A week from now? Next year? Do you really think we can live with that between us?'

'I love you, Daisy,' he said without looking at her. 'It's enough.'

'You also hate me.'

'No.' He shook his head and his gaze met hers. 'No, I hate what you did. How could I not hate that you kept my son from me?'

'What I did was wrong.' She wiped her tears from her face. 'I admit that. I should have told you about Nathan. I was scared and a coward. One day turned into one year. One year into two, and the longer I put it off, the harder it got. There is no excuse.' She held out her hand to him, then dropped it to her side. 'You have to understand. Steven—'

'Oh, I understand Steven,' he interrupted. 'I understood him the night y'all stood in my front yard and told me you were married. I understood that he loved you as much as I did and when he saw an opportunity to take you from me, he took it. He took my son too. And what you have to understand is, I can't just forget something like that.'

'I'm not asking you to forget, but if you and I are to have a future, you have to get past it.'

'You say it like it's easy.'

'It's the only way.'

'I don't know if I can. Especially where Steven is concerned.'

'Then we can't be together. It would never work.'

'Just like that? You get to decide?' He pointed a finger at her and slashed his hand through the air. 'You get to say "get over it" or get out of my life? You get to tell me how to feel?'

She shook her head and gazed at him through the blur of her tears. She breathed past the searing pain in her chest. She knew Jack felt it too. It was there in his raw gaze, and just like the last time, there was no way to stop it. 'No. I'm telling you that you have a right to your anger. You have a right to it for the rest of your life. But it seems to me very lonely company when you can have so much more if you could somehow let it go.'

On the drive to Daisy's, neither of them spoke. The deep purr of the Shelby's engine was the only sound within the dark interior of the Mustang. Jack pulled the car next to the curb, and Daisy looked at him through the inky darkness one last time. Giving him one last chance to change things that he could not change. To say the words that he could not say.

How could she ask him to forget and forgive? As if it were that easy. As if it hadn't eaten a permanent hole in his gut. As if it wasn't always there, right below the surface.

So he watched her walk away. Into her mother's house, and he slid the Shelby in gear and drove home. He hadn't tried to stop her this time. There would be no fight. No one to hit.

But the pain was just as bad as it had been fifteen years ago. No, he thought as he walked back into his house. It was worse now. Now that he knew what could have been. Now that he'd had a taste of that life.

The chair he'd sat in while he'd made love to Daisy was still pushed away from the table. The table where she'd lain while he'd taken her into his mouth. He stared at it as the hole in his gut burned hotter. Burned up into his chest and throat – he about choked on it.

He picked up the chair, carried it out the back door and tossed it into the pitch-black yard. Then he turned and stared at the heavy wooden table that had belonged to his mother. Where they'd eaten family meals.

Where he'd eaten Daisy.

In his present mood, he probably could have picked up the whole damn table and chucked it outside with the chair, but it wouldn't fit out the door. He went to the shed and grabbed his power tools. When he returned, he flipped the table with one hand. It hit the floor with a loud satisfying crash. He popped a beer, fired up his Black & Decker, and got busy.

By the time he was finished, the table was in pieces and lying about the yard along with the chair. He'd gone through a six pack and started on a bottle of Johnnie Walker. Jack had never been a big drinker. Never thought it solved a damn thing. Tonight he just wanted to dull the pain.

With glass in hand, he moved from the dining room, passed his open bedroom door. Passed the lamplight shining on his messed up sheets that he was sure still held the scent of her skin. He walked into the living room and drained his glass. He didn't bother turning on the light. He sat on his black leather sofa. In the dark. Alone.

Light from the kitchen spilled out into the hall and almost reached the toe of his boot. He was tired and beat up from the football game and from Daisy, but he knew he wouldn't sleep. He'd told her he loved her and she'd said it wasn't enough. She wanted more.

He closed his eyes and the room spun. He felt the pitch and roll of his stomach. He'd fucked up. He'd let her into his life. He'd known better. He'd known she'd carve him up again like he had a big X on his chest. He'd held his arms wide and given her a good shot, too.

I'm telling you that you have a right to your anger. You have a right to it for the rest of your life. She'd told him. *But it seems to me very lonely company when you can have so much more if you could somehow let it go.*

Jack was a man who was used to fixing things. Of working until it was as close to perfect as possible. But he knew his limitations. He knew the impossible when it faced him.

What Daisy asked of him was impossible.

Jack didn't even realize he'd fallen asleep on the couch until Billy's voice woke him up.

'What the hell?'

Jack's eyes opened and he squinted against the light. Billy stood before him wearing his work overalls. 'What—' His mouth felt like it was stuffed with cotton and he swallowed. 'What are you doing here?'

'It's almost ten. The shop's been open for an hour.'

Jack was sprawled out with his feet on the coffee table, and he'd slept with his boots on. He picked his head up from the back of the couch and felt like he'd been hit with a brick. 'Ah, Christ.'

'Have you been drinkin'?'

'Yeah.'

'By yourself?'

Jack stood and his stomach rolled. 'Sounded like a good

idea at the time.' He moved into the kitchen and grabbed a bottle of orange juice. He raised it to his mouth and drank until his throat wasn't so dry.

'Why are there only five chairs where the table used to be?' Billy asked as he looked across the hall into the dining room.

'I'm redecorating.'

Billy glanced at Jack, then returned his gaze to the five remaining chairs. 'Where's the table?'

'In the backyard with the missing chair.'

'Why?'

'I like it this way.'

He moved to the back door and looked out. He let out a low whistle and said, 'Having woman trouble?'

Jack reached into a cupboard and pulled out a bottle of aspirin. Woman trouble sounded as if it were fixable. Like a little fight or squabble.

'Daisy Lee?'

'Yep. She comes back into my life. Fucks it up and leaves it that way.'

'Are you sure it's fucked up?'

'Yeah. I'm sure.' He swallowed four aspirins and asked, 'Has Nathan shown up yet?'

'Yep. Right on time.'

'Give me a few minutes to shower and shave and get my shit together, and I'll be there.'

'Maybe you should take a day off.'

'Can't. Nathan will be leaving in a few weeks, and I want to spend as much time with him as possible.'

It took Jack a good forty-five minutes to pull himself together enough to show up at the garage. His body ached and head pounded.

Nathan looked at him and his brows lowered. 'Are you okay?'

'Yes.' Jack carefully nodded and sank into the chair behind his desk.

'Did you take too many bad hits in the game yesterday?'

'A few.' He'd taken the worst hit after the game. 'What are you doing tonight?'

'I'm going bowling with Brandy Jo.' He shifted his weight to one foot and pulled his lip ring into his mouth. 'I was thinking about kissing her. I think she wants me to, but I don't want to suck at it.' His gaze stared into Jack's and he asked, 'How did you learn to kiss a girl?'

Jack smiled and his headache subsided a bit. 'Lots of practice. And don't worry about not being good at it right out of the chute. If Brandy Jo really likes you, she'll want to practice with you.'

Nathan nodded as if that made sense. 'Did you practice with my mom?'

He pretended to give it some thought, but the truth was the memory of the first time he'd kissed Daisy on her porch was imbedded in his mind, eating at his brain like acid. 'No, I'd turned pro before I dated your mom.'

Nathan sat and they talked about girls and what girls liked to do besides put on makeup and shop. He was pleased to hear that Nathan was thinking about more than just how to make out with Brandy Jo. He wanted to buy her something nice and do nice things for her.

They talked about cars and Jack was surprised to hear that Nathan was over his obsession with the Dodge Daytona. He now wanted to buy a Mustang, like Jack's Shelby. Nathan was to get his driver's license next week.

Jack saw the snow job a mile away. He'd let Nathan drive the Shelby. Not a problem, as long as Jack was in the car.

Jack spent the rest of the day at his desk trying to tune out the irritating whine of sanders and power tools. Around two o'clock, his head quit pounding, but the pain and anger in his chest remained. A constant reminder of what he'd almost had, and what he'd lost.

When Nathan came to work that Thursday, it got a whole lot worse. He mentioned that Daisy was leaving Monday for Seattle. They'd sold their house.

That night as Jack finally dealt with the mess in his backyard, he couldn't help but think of Daisy and how she was getting on with her life. Moving forward, while he seemed forever stuck in the past.

He put all the pieces to his mother's table in a shed on the side of the house and he stuck the chair in there too. Maybe he should move. He'd thought of it a time or two. He'd thought of converting the house into more office space. That in turn would open up more space in the garage.

Jack sat on the back porch and looked out over the yard. He couldn't see tearing it down. The house held too many memories for him and Billy. It's where he and Steven had dug up the time capsule and read Daisy's diary. Right in the corner of the yard under the maple tree. It's where they'd reburied it too.

He stood, and before he could give himself time to think better of it, he walked to the shed and grabbed a shovel. The earth was packed solid. Sweat ran down the side of his face as he dug for over an hour. It was somewhere around seven-thirty and the sun was still blazing when the end of the shovel finally hit the old red can. He exhumed it from its twenty-one-year-old hiding place. The paint was faded and it showed signs of rust. The plastic lid had turned a dull yellow but was still intact.

Jack took the can to the back porch. He sat on the top step and dumped it out. Green army men, Hans Solo and Princess Leia Star Wars figures, and a switch comb fell out first. Next, Jack's 'Dukes of Hazzard' Matchbox car, a whistle and a pack of trick gum. Daisy's diary, a fuzzy pink barrette, and a cheap ring with about a three-carat hunk of glass fell on top of the pile. She'd said he'd given her the ring. He didn't remember it, though.

He picked up the ring and put it in his breast pocket. He reached for the little white book with a yellow rose on it, the lock busted from the last time he'd held it in his hands. The pages had yellowed and the ink had dulled. He leaned forward, rested his forearms on the tops of his knees, and read:

Mr Skittles bit Lily on the nose today. I think she was trying to kiss him, Daisy had written when they'd all been in about the sixth grade. *My mom put a stupid Snow White in our front yard. It's soooooo embarrassing.* Jack smiled and flipped past references of her cat and yard decoration. He stopped when he saw his name.

Jack got in big trouble for climbing on the roof at school. He had to stay after and I think he got a whooping. He said he didn't care, but he looked sad. It made me sad too. Steven and I walked home without him. Steven said Jack would be okay.

Jack remembered that. He hadn't gotten whooped, but he'd had to wash all the windows in the school. His gaze skimmed past more entries about her cat, what they'd all had for dinner, and about the weather.

Jack yelled at me today. He called me a stupid girl and told me to go home. I cried and Steven told me Jack didn't really mean it.

Jack didn't remember that one, but if he'd yelled at her it was probably because he had a little crush on her and didn't know what to do about it.

Steven gave me a sticker for my bike. It's a rainbow. He says it's too girly for his bike. Jack said it looked weird. Sometimes he hurts my feelings. Steven says he doesn't mean to. He doesn't have sisters.

He'd never known she was so sensitive. Well, yeah, he guessed he'd known that. But he'd never known she'd gotten upset over stuff like saying a sticker was weird.

Yesterday was Halloween. My mom made me be Annie Oakley again 'cause I haven't outgrown the stupid costume from last year. Jack was Darth Vader and Steven dressed up as Princess Leia. Steven had big cinnamon buns over his ears to look like her. I laughed so hard I about wet myself.

Jack chuckled. He remembered that costume, but he'd forgotten most of the other things Daisy had written about. He'd also forgotten that Steven loved to tell jokes. A lot of them Daisy had jotted down in her diary. He'd forgotten that Steven was a pretty funny kid and that they'd spent hours together laughing about Mrs Jansen walking her old dog, or their favorite episode of 'The Andy Griffith Show.'

I don't know why they talk about that show so much, Daisy had written. *It's stupid. 'The Love Boat' is sooooooo much better.*

Yeah, and Jack remembered he and Steven laughing about 'The Love Boat' behind Daisy's back.

The more Jack read, the more he laughed out loud at some of the things they all used to do. The more he laughed, the more he felt some of his anger subside – which surprised the hell out of him.

The more he read, the more he saw a pattern of Daisy turning to Steven when she was upset about something, or when Jack had unknowingly hurt her feelings. Last Sunday night, she'd told him that Steven was not only her husband, but her best friend. She'd said she could talk to him about anything. That she and Steven had laughed and cried together.

Jack wasn't the type of guy who cried. Instead he stuffed everything deep until it disappeared. Only it didn't. Daisy had been right. They couldn't be together if he couldn't get past his anger. Yes, he had a right to it, but being right *was* very lonely.

Jack shut the diary and looked out over his backyard. He had two choices. He could live the rest of his life with a chest full of anger and bitterness. Alone. Or he could move on. Like Daisy had said. At the time she'd said it, it hadn't seemed possible. Now he felt the glimmer of something in the pit of his soul.

Yeah, Daisy and Steven had kept his child a secret. Yeah, that sucked, but he couldn't let it eat at him any longer. He had to let it go or he was afraid he'd die a bitter and lonely old man. He hadn't known Nathan for the first fifteen years of his life, but Jack figured he had a good fifty or so ahead of him. And he had to decide how he wanted to spend those years.

He stood and shoved everything back into the old coffee can. He walked back into his house and took the letter Steven had written him from the drawer he'd tossed it in. This time when he read it, he read something he'd missed the first time. Steven wrote about the two of them and how much he'd missed Jack over the years. He talked about loving Daisy and Nathan. He ended by asking Jack's forgiveness. He asked Jack to let go of his bitterness and to get on with his life. And for the first time in fifteen years, Jack was going to try to do just that.

He didn't have a plan. He just thought of his life, and he didn't try to stop the memories. Good or bad. He didn't tap them down or shut them out.

He felt every damn one of them.

Friday after work, he asked Nathan to follow him into his office. They stood next to each other as he pulled out the coffee can and handed Nathan the switch comb. 'This was your dad's when he was in sixth grade,' he said without a trace of anger. 'I thought you might like to have it.'

Nathan pushed the button on the handle, and surprisingly it sprang open. He combed the side of his hair. 'Sweet.' Nathan took the *Star Wars* figures but decided against the green army men.

'You're getting your license Monday, right?'

'Yeah. Mom says I can drive her Caravan sometimes.' He frowned. 'I told her, no way.'

'It's hard to be cool in a Caravan.' Jack tried and failed not to smile. 'Hard to burn 'em off.'

Nathan shook his head. 'She just doesn't get it.'

Jack grabbed the coffee can and wrapped an arm around Nathan's shoulders. Together they walked from the office. 'And she won't either.'

' 'Cause she's a girl.'

'No, son. Because she's not a Parrish.' At least not yet.

'Mom! Guess what?' Nathan said the second he walked into the back of the house. 'Jack let me drive the Shelby. Sweet!'

Daisy was up to her elbows in cake frosting. She was throwing a party for Pippen, who'd gone three days without peeing in his pull-ups. 'What? You'll kill yourself.'

'He was very safe,' Jack said from the doorway. 'He even reminded *me* to put on my seat belt.'

At the sight of him standing there in a pair of khaki pants and a white dress shirt with the sleeves rolled up, her heart seemed to squeeze and swell all at the same time.

His gaze met hers and something hot and vital simmered in his eyes. When he spoke, it was low and sexy. 'Good evenin', Daisy Lee,' he said, and the velvet in his voice seemed to reach across the distance and touch her.

There was definitely something different about him tonight, but before she could respond, Lily hobbled into the kitchen on crutches. 'Hey, Jack. How's it goin'?'

He turned to Lily and whatever had been between Daisy and Jack evaporated like a heat mirage. 'Hey, Lily. Hot enough for ya?'

'Shoot. It's hotter than a honeymoon hotel.' She moved to the counter and looked in the mixing bowl. 'Did you drop by for Pippen's potty party?' Lily stuck her finger into the cake frosting, then licked it clean.

'Yes, Jackson, you have to stay,' Louella insisted as she walked from her bedroom into the kitchen. 'We bought coonskin hats for everyone, and we'll eat off Thomas the Tank Engine plates.'

Nathan moaned as if in severe pain and Jack looked at his son as if he sympathized. But he said, 'I'd love to stay, Miz Brooks. Thank you.' He moved to the counter next to Daisy, and the sleeve of his shirt brushed her arm as he tasted her frosting. He licked it off and looked down into her gaze. 'Mmm, that's good, buttercup.' Then he bent down and whispered into her ear, 'I wanna lick this off your thighs.'

'Jack!'

He chuckled and grabbed her hand. 'If y'all will excuse us for a few minutes, I need to talk to Daisy.' He pulled her behind him out the back door. As soon as the door shut behind them, he drew her against him and lowered his mouth to hers. The kiss was sweet and gentle and so heartbreaking she pulled away.

'I've missed you, Daisy,' he said.

'Jack, don't. This has been so difficult for me.'

He pressed his finger to her lips. 'Let me finish.' He dropped his hand to the side of her neck and looked into her eyes. 'I'm in love with you. It feels like I've been in love with you my whole life. You're it for me, Daisy. You always have been.' His thumb lightly brushed her jaw. 'Over the years, I've held on to a whole stomachful of anger and bitterness. I blamed you and Steven for everything, when the truth is, I had a hand in what happened to us. I still don't like that I wasn't around when Nathan was growing up, but I just have to believe things happened the way they did for a reason. I can't fight it or argue with it or hold on to it. I'm just letting it go. Like you said.'

'Are you sure you can do that?'

'I'm tired of being mad at you,' he said as if he meant it. 'And I'm tired of being mad at Steven too. I loved Steven when we were kids. We were buddies. In the letter he wrote to me, he asked if I ever missed him.' Jack took a deep breath, then cleared his throat. 'I've missed the Steven I grew up with every day. He's gone, and I can't hate a dead man.' He paused and his gaze skimmed her face. 'Remember the first night you came to my house and I told you I'd make your life a misery?'

She smiled. He'd broken her heart, and now he was fixing it. 'Yes.'

'I want you to forget I ever said that, because I want to spend the rest of your life trying to make you happy.' He fished around in his breast pocket and pulled out a cheap little ring. The gold was chipped off the band and the glass 'diamond' had dulled. He reached for her hand and placed it in her palm. 'I gave you this ring when we were in the sixth grade. If you'll have me, Daisy, I'll buy you a real one.'

Her mouth fell open. 'This is the ring I put in the time capsule.'

'Yeah. I dug it back up the other day. I have your diary too.' His fingers brushed the side of her throat. 'Marry me, Daisy Lee.'

She nodded. 'I love you with all my heart, Jack Parrish. I have always loved you, and I believe it is my fate to love you forever.'

He let out a pent-up breath like there had been a doubt. He pulled her into a hug that lifted her off her feet. 'Thank you,' he said and pressed his smile to her lips.

The back door opened and Nathan stepped out. 'Mom,

you have to come inside. Grandma—' He stopped when he realized what was going on.

Jack set Daisy on her feet and she turned to face her son. Jack wrapped his arms around her middle and pulled her back against his chest. Nathan looked from one to the other until his gaze stopped on Daisy.

'Your grandma is what?' Daisy asked.

'She's rambling on about people I don't know and don't give a crap about again,' he answered, distracted by the sight of the two of them. He raised his gaze to Jack. 'What's going on?'

'I asked your mother to marry me.'

Nathan stood perfectly still as he absorbed what that meant.

'I've loved your mother since the second grade when I looked across the playground and saw her standing there with a stupid red hair bow.' Jack's fingers brushed her stomach as he spoke. 'I let her get away once. I'm not going to make that mistake again.' He pulled her tighter against his chest. 'I want the two of you to move here and live with me.'

'To Lovett?'

'Yeah. What do you think?'

Daisy didn't remember him asking her what she thought.

Nathan looked at both of them as he mulled over his options. 'Do I get the Shelby?'

For several long moments Daisy feared Jack would say yes. 'No, but you can have your mom's Caravan.'

'That's not funny.'

'Maybe we can work something out.'

Nathan smiled and nodded as he walked back into the house. 'Sweet,' he said.

Jack leaned down and whispered into her ear, 'Can we skip the potty party?'

'No.' She turned and wrapped her arms around him. Breathing in the smell of his shirt and of him. 'But we don't have to stay long.'

She felt him press a smile on the top of her head. 'Sweet.'